PURSUIT OF JUSTICE

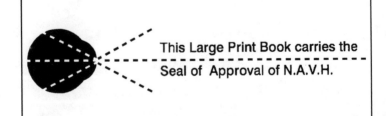

This Large Print Book carries the
Seal of Approval of N.A.V.H.

PURSUIT OF JUSTICE

PAMELA TRACY

THORNDIKE PRESS

An imprint of Thomson Gale, a part of The Thomson Corporation

Detroit • New York • San Francisco • New Haven, Conn. • Waterville, Maine • London

THOMSON

GALE

LIBRARY OF CONGRESS CATALOGING-IN-PUBLICATION DATA

Tracy, Pamela.
   Pursuit of justice / by Pamela Tracy.
      p. cm. — (Thorndike press large print Christian mystery)
      ISBN-13: 978-0-7862-9758-0 (hardcover : alk. paper)
      ISBN-10: 0-7862-9758-1 (hardcover : alk. paper)
      1. Large type books. I. Title.
   PS3620.R34P87 2007
   813'.6—dc22   2007015641

Published in 2007 by arrangement with Harlequin Books S.A.

Printed in the United States of America on permanent paper
10 9 8 7 6 5 4 3 2 1

Listen to my cry for help, my King and
my God, for to You I pray. In the morning,
O Lord, You hear my voice; in the
morning I lay my requests before You and
wait in expectation.

— *Psalms* 5:2–3

To my husband, Donald Osback,
who watched as I wrote during our
honeymoon, as I edited during
road trips, and who continuously models
what a "hero" really is.

ONE

Flashing lights, on a plain, brown sedan, blinked an unwanted command.

She momentarily closed her eyes, willing the image in the rearview mirror to disappear. When she opened them again, the cop remained. There'd been a time, she remembered, when cops drove cop cars, a time when plain, old, everyday vehicles didn't suddenly sprout flashing lights. Taking a deep breath, she glanced at the speedometer and tried to control the urge to flee.

Every time she saw a cop, she wanted to floor it and veer out of sight. Since she *usually* obeyed the speed limit, the cop always went around her in pursuit of some other offender. But, no, not this time. The speedometer and rearview mirror informed her that this time, this cop was definitely after her.

She hesitated a moment too long. The traffic signal in front of her switched from yellow to red. She hit the brake and only her seat belt kept her from serious injury.

Run the light!

Now!

Her fingers gripped the steering wheel. There'd be no time to get to the trailer and grab her suitcase. No time to pick up her cat.

Checking the rearview mirror again, she watched as the patrol car gained on her bumper. Instinctively, she adjusted her hat, trying to cover her face, and watched the cop motion her toward the side of the road. He was that close.

No, no, no.

Her foot, already poised for the escape she so desperately desired, brushed the gas pedal.

Floor it!

But there was always the chance the cop would just hand over the speeding ticket and be done with it. She slowly pulled off the street and into a deserted grocery store's parking lot. The front passenger tire bumped over the curb.

Great, just great.

She willed her fingers to cease trembling as she turned off the engine and slipped a bulging manila folder under the passenger seat. She carefully opened the glove compartment and took out the Arizona driver's license which displayed the likeness of Lucille Damaris Straus complete with a tight smile and short, choppy, black hair.

Please let this be a speeding ticket.

She should never have purchased this car. Statistics showed that red cars were pulled over for speeding more often than cars of any other color. And a Mustang just begged for attention. The car had gotten away from her today.

Why hadn't she been born an economy car kind of girl? Life sure would have been simpler.

She'd spent the last two years being careful, watching the speedometer, stopping longer at red lights than necessary and making sure she never forgot to use her turn signal. Then, somebody at work fell behind on car payments, house payments, child support, whatever, and needed to sell the Mustang cheap. She half purchased the vehicle in order to help the man. She'd half purchased it because she liked the car. But, no matter, truth was she'd messed up, started feeling safe, given in to impulse and a lead foot.

Bad timing.

The cop finally stepped out of his vehicle. Great, he wasn't even in uniform. Lucy didn't want to follow his rigid movements in her rearview mirror. What she wanted to do was stomp on the gas and leave him coughing in exhaust fumes. But, if she did that, there *would* surely be a problem. If she waited, there *might* be a problem.

He strode toward her, adjusting his sunglasses and walking ramrod straight. No doubt about this man's physique. He looked sort of like the Ken doll she'd had as a child. A second look told her that Ken did not hold a candle to this cop — the muscles of his arms about burst out of his sleeves.

Great, and probably he had that Ken doll good-heartedness, too. He wouldn't fall prey to tears, apologies or coy looks. This one had already started filling out some sort of ticket and most likely had radioed in her license plate number.

The driver's license stuck to her damp palm as she took a deep breath. Of all places to get arrested, Gila City was on the bottom of her list, and it was a long list.

The cop rapped on her window. "Ma'am, step out of the car, please." The afternoon sun bounced off his mirrored glasses, giving him a peculiar insect sort of look. She wondered if the glasses were protection against the come-hither attitude of females who wanted to avoid speeding tickets. Well, she wasn't one of them. She opened the door but didn't step out. Swallowing before speaking, she tried to sound in control. "Is something the matter, Officer?"

"I need to see your license and registration."

"I have them right here."

"I'll take them." His voice was textured steel. "Please step out of the car and take off your glasses."

She complied with the "step out of the car" order but ignored the "take off your glasses" command. Again, she tried to keep her hands from shaking. This cop was after something more than enforcing the It's-Our-Town-Please-Slow-Down request. She stuck her hands behind her back. "Why do I need to step out of the car?"

He opened his mouth to answer, but a thud against the side of her car drew his attention.

And hers.

Glancing in the direction the bullet had come from, she saw dark-haired men, big dark-haired men, three of them. The Santellises. She hit the ground, knees hard to the pavement, and pressed against the side of her car.

This *really* wasn't her day.

Glancing at the police officer she noticed

that he looked as surprised as she did. So, maybe, he wasn't in cahoots with the Santellises who were taking serious risks shooting at her while a cop — maybe an honest cop — was issuing a ticket. This made them all the more dangerous. The realization sent her heart slamming to her throat.

The next thud landed so close to her knee that tiny flecks of red paint settled like drops of blood against her white pants.

"Lady, move!" He pushed her around the car and down. In his eagerness to remove her from the line of fire, he knocked her hat and sunglasses off. His fingers tangled in her hair.

"Just let me —" Her knees hit the pavement as another bullet whizzed over the car. The pressure from his fingers disappeared, and Lucy brushed the hair out of her eyes, slipped her driver's license and registration in her back pocket and murmured a quick prayer while she tried to scoot back toward her vehicle. Maybe she could still get away. Maybe she —

This time the bullet hit the back window of her car, sending glass raining down.

Months of confiding in the Lord opened her mouth. Her lips moved, but to her sorrow, she couldn't form the words to pray.

Sam Packard edged to the front of the Mustang, crouched, with gun drawn. "Police! Put your weapons down!" He grabbed the radio from his belt and called a Code One Thousand. The assistance he requested better hurry. Right now, the odds didn't favor him. Three men ducked behind the aged, brown Chevy that sheltered them a short distance away. One of them, idiot of idiots, had a cell phone pressed against his ear, even as he took aim. Sam couldn't make any of them.

But the shooters weren't his only problem. He flinched as a gun's report rendered him momentarily deaf. Only the sight of one of the gunmen stooping, as a bullet ricocheted off the roof of his car, kept Sam from covering his ears.

"What the —" Sam looked down the length of the Mustang. The woman his scanner identified as Lucille Straus, the woman who moments ago seemed to be praying, was now pressed against the back bumper and taking aim.

She had a Beretta 21!

Without blinking, lips tight, she pulled the trigger. The passenger's side window of the

Chevy shattered. One of the men yelped.

Two steps had him by her side. The lady could handle a gun; she'd been aiming at the man who yelped. No matter, she was a civilian butting into his turf. A civilian who might accidentally shoot him. He wrenched the Beretta from her hand, emptied the chamber onto the ground, set the safety and tossed the weapon through the open passenger window of her car.

"Hey!" Her fingers followed the gun, much as a child chased an errant balloon. The look she shot him was pure venom. With one hand he restrained her from crawling through the passenger window to retrieve the weapon. With his other hand, he kept his gun trained on the Chevy.

Sirens wailed in the distance. Sam pushed the woman behind him. The three men jumped into their car and with tires screeching raced behind the grocery store.

He released her arm. "You stay here!"

She nodded.

Taking the radio from his belt, he sprinted toward his vehicle. Two cruisers pulled into the lot. He motioned toward the back.

Behind him, the engine of the Mustang turned over, revving to life even as the woman put it into gear.

Sam didn't bother to yell stop. She clearly

had no intention of sticking around to answer questions. Looking at the passenger seat of her vehicle, he realized she'd managed to retrieve her gun. Biting back irritation, Sam hoofed it to his car, hit the siren and burned rubber.

Intuition pointed him in the direction of the female instead of the three men. He trusted it, but that didn't mean he had to like it. Felony flight was just one of the things he would charge her with, unless she had one whopper of a story.

Gripping the steering wheel, he inched closer to her bumper. She made a sharp turn, zigzagged past a small park and entered a residential area. He closed the distance, and a school bus did her in. A load of what had to be grade school children spilled onto the sidewalk and meandered toward the center of the street. The Mustang swung left. Both right side tires went over the curb, and the car stalled. Miss Straus disappeared from sight, and Sam wondered if she'd been hurt. Then, her head popped up. She didn't check the rearview mirror as she exited the car.

His fingers fumbled as he stopped his vehicle, grabbed the keys, clicked the lock and took off after her. Quickly he scanned the area, locating her easily. She crouched between two bushes, stock-still for a moment, one hand patting the ground as if she'd lost a set of keys, then leaped the fence of a small, stucco home.

His peripheral vision took in the kids, parents and bus driver frozen in the background. Then, he took off and followed her over the fence. "Police! Halt!"

A dog trotted by her side, not yapping, not nipping, but seeming to enjoy the sight of a woman charging through its backyard. Lucy Straus. How did he know that name? Now that the ridiculous hat was history, he could see facial features that didn't deserve to be hidden.

She didn't crouch or hesitate before climbing this next fence and landing in yet another yard. Maybe she'd gotten her bearings. Sam scrambled over the fence and lunged. His fingers touched the material of her shirt, but the fabric slipped through. She slowed, looking left, then right. Her eyes were wild, like a caught deer. Her indecision gave him the opportunity he needed. His momentum tumbled her down with him right alongside.

Sam scrambled off the ground and yanked her to her feet, grabbed his handcuffs and secured them around her wrists. Then, he relieved her of the gun that was once again

18

stuck in an ankle holster. "You have the right to remain silent —"

Her foot hammered down on his instep. His grip loosened. She pulled away and managed to assume a position of flight. He had her on the ground in two seconds and finished giving the Miranda to the back of her head. She muttered a response, but since her mouth was jammed into the grass, he didn't catch the words. Had she cursed or begged?

He pulled her to her feet.

Sweat dribbled down the hollow of her neck. Her chest rose and fell with indignation. Finally, she spoke. "I'll pay you a thousand dollars to let me go."

A bribe! She'd offered him a bribe! Sam's eyes darkened. "Lady, it's worth a thousand dollars just to find out what's going on." He pushed her toward the street where his cruiser's lights still flashed. Some of the kids and their parents had disappeared; others hovered at the edge of the sidewalk mesmerized by the chase. Lucy went willingly until they neared her car. Then she bucked. Sam followed her eyes. Four bullet holes formed an erratic L shape in the driver's side door. The woman went to her knees so quickly that Sam lost his hold, but she wasn't running.

"You're safe. Gila City's finest are taking care of the shooters right now."

She clamped her lips together, and Sam knew he'd get no information from her at the moment. He secured her in his back-seat, radioed his location and returned to her car. Before stepping in, he glanced back. No movement. Sam liked challenges, and right now, the woman — who smelled like peaches and shot like John Wayne — promised to be an entertaining puzzle.

He straightened her car and turned off the ignition. Then, Sam exited the Mustang and started walking toward his vehicle. He had questions; she had answers. He doubted a liaison would be formed.

He opened the driver's side door and slid in. "Ma'am, do you want to tell me why you took off?"

At first she looked the other way, and then with short, jerky motions she turned to glare at him.

All thoughts of getting the answers to his questions fled.

Watching her chin jut out in defiance, Sam felt a righteous anger himself. Because the three men had involved him in the exchange of gunfire, Sam thought he had every right to know why they'd been shooting at her.

■ ■ ■ ■

Police stations always smelled the same: sweat, cigarettes and fear. Gila City's was no different. The last time she'd been in one, the precinct had been painted this same pond scum green. Somewhere, someone must have found quite a sale on pond scum paint.

Lucy looked at the entrance and then scowled at the man at the desk. A few Christmas cards hung on the wall behind him even though the holiday was weeks past. The handcuff securing her left wrist to the bench clanked as she fidgeted. She'd already raised a welt trying to tug free.

Once, way back when she'd still been an emergency room nurse, they'd brought in a convict who'd needed more than twenty stitches because of how seriously he'd ripped his skin while trying to escape the handcuff.

She hadn't understood back then; she understood now.

No way would she let them see the fear. If the fear showed, she'd have to accept it. Still, it roiled in her stomach, a constant reminder of a never-ending battle.

Fear wasn't the only emotion battling for

her attention. Guilt tapped her on the shoulder, reminding her that she'd shot a man today. Took aim and pulled the trigger.

Her teeth started to chatter, but she wasn't cold.

The bench creaked as she shifted her weight. She could not stay here! Tentatively she inched upward. Was anyone looking? Twice she'd stood, and twice the officer at the desk had glared at her. As if she could do anything!

"I have to go to the bathroom." She leaned forward, her words matter-of-fact. Too bad her heart didn't beat as calmly. The duty officer picked up a phone and barked a few words. Moments later, a female — the same cop who had earlier searched her and taken her belongings — removed the handcuff and escorted her to a windowless, closet-size excuse for a restroom.

Anger burned while helplessness whispered threats of *what if.* The nausea rose, but she controlled it by closing her eyes. This time when she tried to find the words to talk with God, they came. Finally, she finished praying, opened her eyes and looked in the mirror.

Surprise, surprise, a normal reflection.

The female officer called, "You all right in there?"

"Fine, just washing up."

"Hurry."

She took her time, trying to control her breathing, and was still wiping the water from her palms when she stepped out and almost bumped into the officer who'd arrested her.

He'd taken off the glasses, giving her a good look at him.

She knew who he was!

The day took a turn for the worse. He stood, one foot tapping a restless beat of discontent on the blue-speckled tile. "Lucille Damaris Straus?" He looked at her and through her.

The female officer handed him the handcuffs and disappeared.

Lucy took a breath. "Look, either charge me with something or let me go." She willed him to dismiss the charges, apologize, something, before she lost it.

He didn't. Instead, as if this were a normal day, as if she were a typical citizen, he stated, "Nothing's that simple, lady. I have some questions."

"Look, I don't have the answers. Give me the speeding ticket. I don't care. I just want out of here." She held out her hand, palm up. She almost smiled. It wasn't shaking.

"You had a concealed weapon." His voice

rose with each word. "I doubt you have a permit."

As if realizing he'd gotten too loud, he lowered his voice. "I want the names of the men shooting at us. You hit one of them, by the way."

"In today's society, a woman needs a gun."

"I'd agree, if not for the fact that I was there to protect you. Where did you get the Beretta 21?"

"From my father."

"And he is?"

Without flinching, she ground out, "Earl Warren Straus."

He blinked and shook his head. "Go ahead and sit. I'll be right back." Before she could protest, the bench caught her behind the knees and guilt wrapped tightly around her.

She hated lying and resented that she'd become so good at it. Not good enough, though. When ole Officer Friendly, real name Sam Packard, ex-partner to Cliff Handley, a man she wanted very much to avoid, ran his search, nothing would surface — at least on any Earl Warren he could attach Lucy to. Then, he'd have even more questions. Cops hated to be lied to. They took it personally.

Before she had time to contemplate the

absence of the handcuffs, he was back.

Lucy felt her control slipping. She had to get away from him. She stood. "Look, I've done nothing wrong. If you hadn't pulled me over, I'd never have gotten involved in that exchange of gunfire. I could have been hurt!"

He leaned close, backing her up. "Care to tell me who they were?"

"You didn't catch them? You said Gila City's finest was taking care of them." Her voice raised an octave.

His eyes scanned the room. Lucy followed his gaze and shut up. It was a small station. The last thing she wanted was to be the center of attention in a police station.

He guided her down some stairs, into a small office, and motioned for her to sit. The green plastic chair put her at a disadvantage. She saw that immediately. When he settled in his own scarred, wooden chair, he was able to look down at her instead of eye to eye. She gracefully tucked one leg under her and sat up straight.

His eyes glittered, as if he knew what she was thinking. He pulled some papers from his desk. "Name?"

She leaned her elbow on his desk, rested her chin on her palm, cocked her head and stated, "You know my name."

"Humor me."

She pulled her driver's license from her back pocket and slapped it down. "Lucille Damaris Straus."

He fit the license under a paper clip on his page. "Age?"

"Twenty-two."

"You look older."

Her eyes narrowed. She glanced at the form he was filling out. A simple information sheet. That was good. She took a pen off his desk and suggested, "I can fill that out for you."

He reclaimed the pen.

Nervously, she scratched at a shoulder blade. She needed to keep talking. Divert him. Figure out what he wanted. He still looked like her Ken doll. Except that the cop was having a much better hair day. Irrationally, she wished his hair wasn't so wavy, so chocolate-brown. Why couldn't she have gotten arrested by an ugly cop?

Okay, she could handle this. "I was on my way to the store. I was probably going a little fast. You pulled me over. Next thing I knew bullets were flying. Now, I'm at the police station, and you're asking me questions like I'm guilty of something."

"Are you?"

"Am I what?"

"Guilty of something?"

"I confess. I was speeding. What else are you charging me with?"

He didn't even blink. "Name?"

"I've told you my name. Three times."

Detective Samuel Elliot Packard, Robbery Homicide Division, tapped his pen on the form. "Place of employment?"

She knew most of his life story: when he'd graduated, when he'd served time in the military, when he'd joined the police force, when his mother died, when he'd broken up with his last girlfriend, and when he'd stopped attending church.

"Liberty Cab Company." She barely managed to answer his question. Of all the officers who might have pulled her over, this one could cause more trouble than any other. She should have recognized him back when he first pulled her over, but the glasses hid his face.

If he still looked like his earlier photos, she'd have floored it when he started walking toward her car. Of course, she wasn't prepared for a detective to be making a routine traffic stop. Just her luck, a slow day in Gila City and she finds a detective looking for something to do.

She never should have stopped, at the abandoned store or on the street. She never should have taken the risk of letting him see her without her hat and glasses.

Nervously, she started to reach for the pen again.

He moved the pen. "Are you a cab driver?"

"No, I do dispatch."

"How long have you worked there?"

"Almost six months. Why are you asking me all these questions?"

"You tell me."

"Are you bored? Too much free time?" She wanted the sarcastic words back as soon as they left her lips. She needed his sympathy, not his ire.

Briefly, the corner of his mouth twitched, but not enough to be sure of. He shoved the paperwork aside, took a sip of what must have been hours-old coffee and frowned at her. "Why were those men shooting at you?"

"At me?"

"Yes, at you."

She shook her head, acting indignant. She had to keep him from thinking that maybe she was the target, keep him from thinking she was more than just an ordinary civilian. "They weren't shooting at me."

"Lady, those three men were aiming at you. Not only that, but you carry a gun, because for some reason men shooting at you doesn't appear to be out of the ordinary. A gun you use with some proficiency." He resumed tapping, this time on a manila folder. "According to this file, you have no right to own a firearm." He leaned forward. "And according to this file, Lucy Damaris Straus doesn't possess the mental capability to know how to fire a firearm, let alone which end to aim. Do you want to tell me your real name?"

"I've gotten much better. The medicine I'm taking —"

His mouth became a single thin line.

"Have I done something to offend you?" She hated this. How dare he make her feel vulnerable! She tucked an errant strand of hair behind one ear. Normal movements, she reminded herself.

"Lying offends me."

"You've seen my driver's license. I'm Lucille Damaris Straus." She checked her watch. "May I go? Do you have the right to keep me here?"

He clutched the well-worn file, with a blue-edged white label and uneven typing, proclaiming a misspelled Lucy Stras.

She could imagine what was inside and then some. After all, Lucy's first introduction to social services came before she could even walk. Early on there'd been physical and mental abuse at the hands of an alcoholic father. Later on came the truant officers reports. Finally, when Lucy reached legal age, there were misdemeanors: accessory to fraud, shoplifting, public intoxication, until finally the more serious offenses, such as riding in a stolen car and possession. And, of course, there were the hospitalizations. Mental illness ran in the family. Why should Lucy escape the gene?

A paper slipped out of the file and landed faceup on the floor.

A photo.

Well, she'd always known that was a possibility.

This was not what he needed for an end-of-the-week finale. The woman kept her cool better than most. But she was scared. A few times her retorts had had an edge to them, a raw fear that threatened to erupt.

Detachment, a God-given gift most cops prayed for, left Sam. He'd never been as hard-edged as Cliff, his first partner. What had he stumbled onto here? What secrets did she so fiercely guard with fake identification and a Beretta 21 concealed in an ankle holster, no less.

He studied the photo. "Lucy Straus is a five-foot-three, twenty-two year old, Native

American. Who, by the way, I've hauled in a few times. She's been a street person for the last four years. You —" he laid the photo down, faceup "— are about five foot eleven and probably have thirty well in sight."

She didn't answer, but her eyes narrowed.

"I'll have your real identity within minutes. It's the hard way, but you give me no choice." He waited.

She shrugged.

Sam gave her time to change her mind. She couldn't possibly think he was going to go away! The minutes ticked by. "Okay, you had your chance."

Whatever secrets she harbored made her unreachable and unreasonable. Her shoulders tensed as he took her arm. Did she hate the touch of a man or was it just that he was a cop?

He guided her out of his office, down the hall, up the stairs and into a room where she gave her prints without argument. The mug shot would depict a woman with chewed-off lipstick and wise eyes. Sam leaned against the wall and watched Lucy wash the ink off her fingers. It didn't fit. Women usually did one of two things when they were fingerprinted. They cried, meaning they were scared. Or they glared, meaning they were angry about being caught.

Lucy — what else could he call her — did neither.

But he recognized the look. He'd seen the same expression on the face of a death row inmate. Walter Peabody had been the man's name. Sam had been a rookie, just twenty-two, invited to his first execution. He'd witnessed the final step of an arrest his partner Cliff had made years earlier. Sam had thrown up after the event. And it was an event. Peabody, convicted of murdering two policemen, had walked to the chair a mere three years after his arrest. He'd never denied the crime, but he'd never acknowledged it, either.

And Cliff had used the arrest to further his career. He'd quickly risen through the ranks and eventually transferred to a Phoenix precinct.

Peabody's widow insisted her husband was innocent. Peabody's daughter told newsmen that Peabody couldn't talk because proving his innocence about the murders would only point to a different crime. Sam still wondered what crime could invoke a punishment worse than the one Walt Peabody had been dealt.

Sam's hair was no longer Ken perfect. He ran his hand through it every time she gave an answer he didn't like.

They were back to this? She focused on a stain on the wall behind his head — if she stared hard enough she could make out hand-size angel wings right behind Officer Friendly's head. Except for that, the interrogation room had about as much personality as the ladies' restroom.

Periodically, cops peeked in, as if they needed to see the prize fish Officer Friendly had snagged. She took a breath. "I've told you my name. You've brought up the file on the wrong Lucy Straus. That's all. I liked your office better. Can we go back there?"

"No." His hand hit the table, rocking the chipped, brown cup that held his coffee, and spilling tiny drops that looked like mahogany tears onto Lucille Straus's folder. "Do you realize the seriousness of this situation?"

"I need to call my place of employment. Don't I get one phone call?"

He sighed audibly. She felt some of the control return. She might actually enjoy sparring with him, if something other than her life were at stake.

The female officers brought in a phone and mentioned something about a delay in obtaining the fingerprints. Lucy dialed Liberty Cab and quickly, without telling them why, begged off her next shift. When she returned the phone to the cradle, she looked at the two-way mirror and exaggeratedly mouthed, "Thank you."

"Why didn't you tell them you were being detained by the police?" Sam laced his hands behind his head, pretending to be comfortable.

Lucy ignored his new tactic. "I'll tell them tomorrow."

Tomorrow? Even the word sounded doubtful. Lucy stopped herself from fidgeting. With effort, she met the cop's eyes. It wouldn't do to let him know she was afraid.

He nodded agreeably and leaned forward. "I'm interested in who taught you how to shoot?"

"Well, Earl Warren, that's my —"

"Lucy Straus's father's name was John."

"That must be the other Lucy."

"You realize I can verify that?"

"You could try, but Earl was born on the reservation. I'm pretty sure he had no birth certificate. He was named after Hector Warren, who delivered him. Hector was one of those traveling salesmen. You know, they sold elixir. It's quite a family story. Earl never really held much of a job. Manual labor, mostly."

"You're amazing."

"Thank you."

"It wasn't a compliment. You're wasting my time. This lying is just prolonging the inevitable. Earl Warren!" He almost spat. "There is no Earl Warren. Of all the names to come up with! Tell me, are you going to commit perjury when you go before the judge? Why can't you tell me the truth?"

"You wouldn't believe it." Her words were low, deadly and displayed the faint hint of desperation.

"Try me."

A hmm of mirth was the only honest answer she could give him.

Then you will know the truth, and the truth will set you free.

When she studied her Bible the words sounded so comforting. Too bad they weren't always true. In this situation, she was the only one who knew the truth, but no matter how she tried, she couldn't fathom that sharing it would set her free.

Taking a breath, she said, "Earl Warren died suddenly under suspicious circumstances. It got a bit uncomfortable being around the family after that. Mama had a mental breakdown. She really missed Earl Warren —"

"Enough of Earl Warren!" His chair almost fell over as he jumped to his feet.

Lucy turned an innocent smile to the two-way mirror.

The female cop walked back in, righted the chair, turned it around and straddled it. What was this? Good cop, bad cop?

"I'm Officer Ruth Atkins. You really need to let us help you, Lucy." Atkins's voice was no-nonsense.

Lucy should have been prepared to see Ruth, but she wasn't — *like she hadn't really been prepared for Samuel Packard.* Of course, her research hadn't focused on Ruth Atkins. It had focused on Ruth's missing husband. Dustin Atkins had disappeared more than a year ago, the same week Lucy's parents had died. He was probably dead; they were definitely dead. He had probably been murdered by the Santellises; they had definitely been murdered by the Santellises. From what Lucy could glean, Ruth had become a cop to fight the kind of criminals who had cost her a husband. Lucy had become a fugitive to fight the kind of criminals who had cost her *everything.*

"I'm pretty sure you have no right to detain me." Lucy started to stand, but Officer Friendly put his hand on her shoulder and gently pushed her back down.

36

This cop had also pushed her down in the parking lot and that bullet had whizzed over her head. She owed him. She owed him not to talk. He wouldn't enjoy the mess she could lead him to.

Atkins spoke again. "We're obtaining a search warrant now. What will we find in your home, Lucy?"

"Nothing, but you'd better not let my cat out."

"Do you realize that you face up to thirty days for carrying a concealed weapon?"

If they'd let Lucy Straus do time, without any more background probing, that'd be fine. She'd do it. There were worse places than the county jail.

But, they'd taken her fingerprints.

The moment the cops identified her, she was good as dead. Police stations weren't safe for her now.

She had to get out of here. "I'm sure any intelligent judge will take into consideration bullets were first aimed in my direction."

"We have plenty of intelligent judges in Gila City. One thing we do need is your real name for the search warrant. What is it?" Officer Atkins asked.

Lucy looked at Officer Friendly. Why had he been so quick to boil over? She'd bet, when it came to interrogation, that he was more gifted than the female officer.

A gravelly voice came from the doorway. "Sam, I hear you picked up a —"

It was as if a vacuum suddenly sucked the air from the room. Adrenaline pressed against raw nerves, and although it was the last thing she wanted to do, she turned.

She knew the voice; it haunted her nightmares.

"Cliff, what is it?" Officer Packard slowly stepped toward the door. Tension became palpable.

Lucy figured he sensed the same thing she did, that the air in the room was about to implode, and that the victims would lose more than a piece of themselves. She being the biggest casualty.

He didn't have time to make a difference. It only took two steps before Cliff Handley's hands reached toward Lucy, opening, closing, as if he couldn't decide whether to hit her or choke her.

"Rosa Cagnalia. I'm going to kill you."

Two

Suspicion turned to incredulity as Sam realized whom he'd arrested.

As Cliff wrapped beefy hands around her neck, Rosa Cagnalia became a Tasmanian devil of movement even as her face turned the color of blood. Cliff went down to one knee as a well-placed kick connected.

Sam let go of the breath he'd been holding.

He'd found Rosa Cagnalia.

Atkins reacted first, grabbing Cliff by the waist and trying to tug him away.

Sam added his weight to Atkins's and wrenched Cliff's fingers from around Rosa's neck. Another officer hurried in and used his baton as a wedge. Using the wall as leverage, Sam managed to get his hand between Cliff and Rosa. His ex-partner emitted a sound, much like an angry bear, and rammed Rosa into the wall. Her head flew back, solidly connecting with the solid structure. Sam expected some noise from her then, but all she did was sink into the chair.

Executing a headlock, Sam pushed Cliff into the restricting arms of two fellow officers. Shoving them out of the room, Sam slammed the door shut, barely noticing that Atkins left with the crowd.

Rosa remained in the chair with her knees pressed together, her hands clutched at the edge of the seat, and her face full of a combination of disdain, fear, regret — so many emotions that Sam couldn't even begin to know which ones predominated. The only indication she gave of fear was the pale tinge of her skin.

She hadn't been this white when he pulled her over.

His eyes went to her neck. Cliff's fingerprints were there. Rosa Cagnalia, aka Lucy Straus, should be gasping.

But why should he care? She straddled a line he didn't dare approach, and the majority of her weight wasn't on his side of the law.

And, as much as Sam understood Cliff's pain, he sure didn't, *couldn't,* support his actions. The grief spilling from the man explained why video cameras sometimes caught America's Finest using extreme force. Cliff hadn't seemed aware that he'd been choking a woman. All Cliff knew was that he'd found one of the people responsible for his son's death.

They were alone in a room that now reeked of hate and anger. Sam stared at Rosa for a long time, waiting for her to move, speak, do something! This woman was partly responsible for the ruination of Sam's mentor, one-time partner, and full-time friend, Cliff Handley.

How could she look so ordinary?

She'd been there when Jimmy Handley, a rookie, a third-generation police officer, forfeited his life in the line of duty. Jimmy had been a mere Boy Scout when Sam teamed up with his father: a twelve-year-old carbon copy of his father. Jimmy had been sixteen when, thanks to commendations and promotions, Cliff had moved his family to Phoenix. Jimmy had been twenty-one when he put on his own badge and twenty-four when the coffin lid closed.

The funeral had been just two years ago this month: a cold, gray January day.

Sam took a deep breath. Contemplating what he had in front of him. Finding Rosa Cagnalia was tantamount to finding gold, fool's gold. She didn't look like a woman who could sit back while —

Well, this certainly explained her marksmanship this morning. And that answered another question. Now that Sam knew who she was, it explained who the men in the parking lot were. The Santellises. How had they stumbled upon her on the same day Sam had? But since she was supposedly on their side, why were they shooting at her?

And Cliff being in Gila City was just as coincidental. Just three weeks ago, Cliff retired and returned to his hometown. He used his limp — he'd been injured striving to bring justice to those responsible for Jimmy's death — as a crutch and bore no resemblance to the once-proud police officer who had bagged Walter Peabody.

Luck had turned her back on Rosa Cagnalia and dumped her in Sam's lap. Of course, in many ways, it was her own fault. What was she doing in Gila City: Cliff's hometown and a known haunt of the Santellis family?

Her chair was still flush with the wall. Her hair hung in her face, and she didn't move a hand to pat it back into place.

"You're Rosa Cagnalia?" Disgust accented his words. How could someone so beautiful be so flawed?

She flinched and unclasped her grip on the rim of the chair, folding her hands in

42

her lap. "No." The word was directed at her hands. She wove her fingers so tightly together that the skin turned white, and then she looked up at him and whispered, "You have to let me be Lucy."

"It's too late for that."

Her eyes blazed, and for a moment he remembered what had attracted him.

"Do you realize that by finding me, you've signed my death warrant?"

"You did that yourself, lady. You chose your way of life a long time ago."

"Oh, were you there?" She glared at him. "You know the choices that came my way?"

He frowned. "I've read the files."

Atkins poked her head in. "You need to back off, Sam. News travels fast. The feds want her."

"I brought her in." He stared at Rosa. No way would he be delegated to gofer by special agents. This was his turf. He was responsible.

"I'm sure they'll thank you."

He thought for a moment that the words came from Atkins, but they hadn't, and he was reminded why he had thought Rosa might be a cop. Wisecracks rolled off the tongues of those in blue, partly in jest, and partly as a shield from a daily routine that took them into the armpit of Gila City.

Female officers tended to verbally raise their shield a bit more than Sam was used to.

Atkins added, "Sam, I mean it."

"It's my case."

By all rights, he should hate this woman. She had been there when a drug bust spiraled so out of control that Cliff was emotionally crippled, and his son was killed.

She had been there, and she had left without making any attempt to help Cliff or save Cliff's son.

Funny way for a one-time registered nurse to act.

If she had shown compassion, Jimmy Handley might still be alive and Cliff would wear his badge with pride and determination instead of with grim need. Instead Rosa Cagnalia stepped over the bleeding body of Jimmy Handley, picked up a bag full of money, and in the chaos of the moment, managed to disappear.

Atkins rolled her eyes and backed out of the room. Sam looked at the two-way mirror. So the feds wanted Rosa. Having the FBI take over a case was something like inviting the class bully into your backyard. If you stayed, you got beat up. If you left, he destroyed your yard. Sam didn't relish turning Rosa over to them, but she deserved whatever she got.

He had nothing to lose by washing his hands of this woman.

And nothing to gain by hesitating. So why was he? He flipped the handcuffs from his belt. "Stand up."

She stood, muttering under her breath.

"What did you say?"

"I need someone to feed my cat."

"Your cat! Lady, do you realize the trouble you're in?"

"You keep reminding me."

"Your cat is the least of your worries."

She didn't say anything, just looked at him.

"Ms. Cagnalia, surely there's someone in this town who you can contact to feed the —"

"No, there's no one. I didn't make any friends. I was afraid to."

She meant it. Her face was as serious as a funeral director and just as pale.

"My cat needs food. There's a key hidden under the garden gnome behind my trailer."

He waited for a please. It didn't come.

Reluctantly, he left her with Henry, the duty officer who handled admissions. Feed her cat! Of course, he'd do it. She'd just given him permission to enter her home. He'd probably have to search long and hard for the cat food.

He could hardly wait.

Rosa awoke to more pond scum green. On television they always showed rickety bunk beds and open toilets, but Rosa's cell didn't look that domesticated. Last night, after hours of questions, when they'd finally shoved her in here, she'd been too tired to care.

Gingerly pushing up from the ledge she'd been sleeping on, Rosa tried to focus on what all had happened. She gingerly touched the back of her neck. A dull headache and a slight sore throat remained a souvenir of Cliff Handley's wrath. It could have been worse.

Stupid, stupid, stupid. Of all the dumb places to give in to the itch of a lead foot! She deserved to feel the bitter tightness when she swallowed. Stupid, stupid, stupid. She'd given a cop permission to enter her trailer. She didn't dare hope he'd simply feed Go Away and leave, that simply wasn't a cop's nature.

But she had no one to ask. She'd been careful at work to build up a reputation as a loner. She liked her coworkers too much to put them in danger. She'd been even more careful at church to distance herself and that hadn't been easy. She dropped off casseroles at potlucks, crocheted pale pink or blue blankets for baby showers she didn't dare attend, anonymously donated money for catastrophe relief, and all the while managed to convince the friendly folk of the Fifth Street Church that she was too busy to get involved more than a church service hello.

She didn't dare call Wanda Peabody.

She'd been so careful, except for the cat. Oh, she'd tried. When the stray showed up outside her trailer, she'd refused to feed it. She'd said "Go Away" every day for a week. Then, when she found her next-door neighbor Seth tormenting it, she'd gone all indignant.

She brought attention to herself, made an enemy of Seth and his girlfriend, and she'd wound up with a pet she didn't dare keep. Once she brought it into her trailer, cleansed its wounds — oh, it felt good taking care of a living being again — and had given it some food, well, the cat stayed.

Officer Friendly *should* feed Go Away. It was his fault Rosa was in jail. He was already involved, and nobody was likely to kill him as a way to get back on her. Plus, everything she'd discovered about Sam Packard while she'd been researching Cliff Handley suggested he was an honest, hardworking cop.

And a wayward Christian.

His name was in the directory of her church: the one he never attended. Hadn't attended since his mother died. Well, before that, really. Yet, everything about him shouted believer. He was the Gila City cop who spoke about choices at the local high school. He was the Gila City cop who actually helped parolees find jobs — two of the cab drivers at her company owed Sam thanks. He looked to be a decent man, a giver.

Pretty amazing since he'd first been assigned Handley as a partner?

Handley was a taker.

Still, even before she'd realized the name of the cop who had pulled her over, her first impression had been one of honesty. *Dear Lord,* she was scared. Clasping her hands together she prayed and tried to get a handle on how she should be feeling, what she should be doing, what Jesus would do.

Worry wouldn't add one moment to her life. God knew about the sparrows so he knew about her.

Oh, she so wanted the concept to work for her. But, she never seemed to be able to cease the internal dialogue that constantly played in her head: the dialogue that listed her sins.

One, she was partly responsible for Jimmy's death. She hadn't pounded on his chest, tried CPR or anything. She had no doubt he was dead, irreversibly dead. Still, it had been against her moral code to leave him there — *and her a registered nurse.* The cops had no problem reminding her about that little detail, over and over, yesterday.

Two, because of her, her family had forfeited any hope of old age. An inadvertent-seeming car crash — just one year ago — severed the last ties to anyone who would, could, believe her. Cliff and the Santellises knew how to punish people who got in their way.

Three, her best friend Eric was in jail because she wasn't able to find the evidence that would clear his name. Guilt by association. Nobody cared that an innocent man sat in jail. They only cared that his last name was Santellis. In Arizona, Santellis and crime were synonymous.

And, four, she had taken more than half a million dollars in drug money and didn't know how to make things right.

Okay, feeling sorry was allowable but not for long. She couldn't hope to get out of this mess if she gave in to self-pity. What were the positives?

Yesterday, she'd managed to ditch the evidence. That cop had been so close, she had hardly dared breathe as she grabbed under her seat for the manila envelope, vacated the car, and hoofed it through the residential area. And, thank goodness for the rosebushes by that first fence.

What if it rained?

What if some little kid found the envelope?

What if Samuel Packard remembered her hesitation and returned to the fence and found her pile of documents linking Cliff Handley to the whole mess.

What if —

No, she had other things to worry about. The folder was hidden, for now.

At least now she could start thinking of herself as Rosa again which was another positive. When she had first taken Lucy's identity, she'd taped the name and played it over and over on her cassette player. As she drove her car, as she lay in bed, even in the bathroom, she had listened to the name over and over, until she claimed ownership of it. She couldn't afford to think of herself as Rosa. It had taken weeks, but she'd learned to turn automatically when someone said Lucy's name.

She couldn't think of any more positives. Then again, she had heard of fugitives, who when they were finally apprehended, only felt relief. She wasn't one of them. She had thought Gila City safe enough for a very careful stay — a stay designed specifically for gathering evidence to prove to the world what Cliff Handley really was. She'd done all she could on the Internet. Now, she needed to casually speak to people off the record, find out what he'd been doing before his stint in Phoenix.

For almost six months, she'd felt safe enough here. She'd shopped in the dress shop his mother owned, managed to meet some of his friends, and when she had nothing, when her life was as empty as could be, she'd entered Cliff's church looking for someone who might point suspicion his way. She found something besides evidence. She'd found God.

He was the only one on her side in this dismal cell. A cement ledge protruded from the wall, a jutting giant step that had been her bed. Instead of a cell with bars, she was in a room with a door. An unyielding green door that bore the wrath of previous occupants whose names and insults were scraped into the paint. A small window gave a blurry view of an inner room with an aged picnic table. She could hear a washer and dryer humming. A television blared to the left. Men's voices came from the right.

How had things gotten so out of hand? The Santellises, Eric's brothers, had been in the parking lot! Did they just luck upon the scene of Rosa Cagnalia getting a speeding ticket? If so, coincidence had a sick sense of humor.

She really hoped Officer Friendly had taken care of Go Away. If she had any insight into the character of Officer Friendly, he would find a way.

Sighing, Rosa sat on the cement ledge and tried to piece together the events of the last twenty-four hours. She'd crawled out of bed at ten, a little earlier than usual. Mondays were her favorite day for getting things done. She'd dropped a handful of bills off at the post office, found her favorite computer at the library and again scanned old *Gila City Gazette* papers looking for any mention of Cliff Handley's name, any early instances of drug dealings, who was involved and possibly still alive. Then, finally, she'd headed home. She'd wanted to spread out the few new tidbits she'd uncovered. She wanted to read them at leisure, see if she'd missed anything.

She'd been hurrying home.

Could somebody who knew the Santellis family have seen her, recognized her? She had put on fifteen pounds since running. Weight put on intentionally. She wore jeans and T-shirts instead of the designer clothes she'd once thought necessary. Her hair, once long, wavy, and streaked with high-lights the color of burgundy, now flowed jet-black and straight. The real Lucy Straus had short, uneven midnight hair. Rosa had copied Lucy's style, and she still felt surprised when she washed her hair. Since childhood, it had been down to her tail-bone.

She had cried when she cut it. Then, she had cried because cutting her hair was actu-ally the least of her concerns.

A gray blanket was folded at one end of the cement ledge. She pulled it toward her, wrapped it over her shoulders — ignoring the stains — and leaned against the wall.

Mildew and strong detergent wafted to her nose. Throwing the blanket to the ground did nothing to end her frustration.

Now might be a good time to call a lawyer.

Unfortunately, the only lawyer she knew was Eric's lawyer.

Sam circled the trailer park twice before parking in Rosa's carport. The place was fairly empty. Most had already left for work, school or other vices.

Excessive paperwork and a need for sleep kept him from getting here last night.

In some ways, showing up to feed her cat was a stupid move on his part. Not even twenty-four hours since her arrest and already his life spun out of control. Still, he felt propelled by a continuous nagging that there was something he should know but didn't.

Her mobile home was nothing to get excited about. The first contradiction he could account for was the comparison of where she lived to what she drove. Now, to Sam's mind, a guy might pay out major bucks for a vehicle and live in a dive, but few women seemed to prefer first-rate wheels to a first-rate address.

He had searched the interior of her car. Nothing, not even a gum wrapper. Rosa kept no spare change, no tissues, not even a map of Arizona for the glove box. The Owner's Manual for the Ford lay in the glove box along with a slim wallet carrying more Lucille Straus identification. The spare tire, a tow chain and jack were in the trunk. She could walk away from the vehicle, and no one could trace it to her — especially since a quick search showed it still registered to a guy she worked with at Liberty Cab Company.

Not even a breeze tried to interfere as he snagged the key from the garden gnome. She'd picked a residence — it wasn't a home — where neighbors were not neighborly, where lawns were replaced by rock, and where a cement wall kept the world at bay.

As Sam put the key to the mobile home, he wondered if the inside would be as barren as the outside. He pushed the door open. The cat yowled and brushed against his foot.

"Back." His word didn't affect the cat. Judging by the torn ear and jagged scar that zigzagged down to its eye, not much should affect this cat. A feline tail shot straight up in the air as its owner circled Sam's legs. He should have gotten the feline's name from Rosa.

"Back, Cat."

It was a rectangular box, encased with paneling. And even with the overfed black-and-white cat, who seemed to think that continual rubbing against pant legs was an expected greeting, the place was a residence not a home.

Room one: a combination living room-kitchen. Inside the refrigerator was a six-pack of diet soda and two apples. Outside the refrigerator she had taped a scripture:

Listen to my cry for help, my King and my God, for to you I pray. In the morning, O Lord, you hear my voice; in the morning I lay my requests before you and wait in expectation.

The kitchen table didn't look as if it had been used. Not even a crumb graced the surface or the floor. There was also a couch, a television and a coffee table. Next to the couch was a basket of sewing. Picking up the sampler, he realized that Rosa seemed addicted to the words on the refrigerator. She was halfway finished with a cross-stitch bearing the same verse.

No knickknacks gathered dust. No pictures graced the walls. Sam opened two cupboards before finding hard cat food and filling the bowl on the floor.

The cat quickly lost interest in Sam and became devoted to its food.

Room two: a bedroom-bathroom. Her bed was made, no surprise. The closet held only a few outfits. If he had figured anything about the woman from her mannerisms, he figured that lack of clothes probably was a real sacrifice. She had a dresser, but only one drawer was utilized. There were a few piles of library books, stacked neatly on top of the dresser. A phone book and well-worn

Bible were on the nightstand.

Sam picked up the Bible. Flipping to the personal pages, he found the dedication page.

Presented to: Lucille Straus
By: The Gila City Fifth Street Church.
On: The occasion of her baptism, November 12th

She'd been baptized just two months ago at Cliff's old church. At one time, it had been Sam's church, too. Frowning, Sam wondered if he needed to consider that prayer he'd witnessed earlier as a true plea for divine intervention. Or, was there another reason Rosa attended a church where Cliff and his family were well-known even if they had seldom crossed its foyer in more than a decade.

The more he thought about it, the more he wished he'd never pulled her over.

The bathroom was stuffed into a small corner of Rosa's room, wedged between the closet and the dresser. The shower couldn't accommodate a big man; the sink had a continual drip. A small bag of makeup spilled out next to the faucet. Sam smelled toothpaste and peaches. Ah, the real woman.

Returning to the bedroom, he got down

on his knees and looked under the bed. A durable, green suitcase shadowed a back corner. He dragged it out, plopped it on the bed and opened it.

One outfit, a change of underwear, two cans of cat food, two bottles of water, toiletries and an envelope with five hundred dollars.

No, wait.

Another envelope was pushed behind the money. A set of keys tumbled to the bed, and Rosa's picture smiled out at him from identification belonging to one . . . Sandra Hill.

She was prepared for flight. If she had to run, all she had to do was crash open the door, shove her makeup back into the bag, nab the cat, grab the suitcase, and the police would have been left with little or nothing to prove that the mobile home had actually provided shelter for Rosa Cagnalia, aka Lucy Straus, aka Sandra Hill.

He closed the suitcase. His hand paused on the handle. What was he thinking? He needed to leave now. The feds could be pulling into the trailer park right this minute, and they would be anything but happy at a local cop tampering with evidence.

He felt a twinge of guilt. He was actually considering taking the suitcase, plus the

Bible, and working on the case without the knowledge of, or permission from, his superiors. This was not his usual method.

One mistake and his pension and retirement fund would become a distant memory — not to mention the wear and tear on his conscience.

Sam replaced the suitcase. When he got back to the station, he'd plug Sandra Hill's identity into his computer and find out what the connection was.

A couple of hours after a dismal breakfast of oatmeal — she'd eaten every bite and asked for more — they'd shoved a short blonde into Rosa's cell.

So much for solitude. Just her luck to get arrested during the busy season.

"Name's Marilyn Youngblood." The blonde blew a bubble and sat down on the ledge as if it were a well-worn recliner. "Whatcha in for?"

Whatcha in for? Rosa wanted to laugh. Yeah, that's right, a mere twenty-four hours in jail and here was a stranger acting as if sharing personal history was a given. "Speeding."

Marilyn raised an eyebrow. "I didn't know they arrested people for speeding. They always just give me a ticket."

"Must be a slow month," Rosa acknowledged.

"They stopped my boyfriend for speeding." Marilyn inspected her nails. "When he went to pull out his license, a joint fell out." Her voice turned sarcastic. "I didn't know he had a joint." Her tone indicated that she was more annoyed about the prospect of her boyfriend not being willing to share than about being arrested.

"Bummer."

"Yeah. So, this your first time in?"

"Yeah, you?" Rosa wondered if Marilyn realized that her blond wig contrasted ridiculously with her dark eyebrows.

"No, this is about my fifth. And all of them because of my boyfriend."

Rosa had never spent time behind bars, but during her friendship with Eric, she'd learned how to spot undercover police officers. She had little doubt about this blonde's true identity. Still, she knew the game, so she said, "I'd think about getting a new boyfriend."

"I really should." Marilyn inspected her nails again, then asked, "So where ya from? Me, I'm from Texas."

Okay, so the woman was persistent. That was to be expected. "I'm from here." Rosa recited her Lucy Straus history, pleased to note the disbelief in Marilyn's eyes.

"No kidding. You don't look Indian."

"We prefer Native American. And I'm only half."

The door creaked. The mumbler peeked in. His expression hadn't changed since he'd escorted her to the cell. This man made the old Maytag repairman look energetic. Rosa didn't understand his words, but Marilyn perked up. "Lunch."

The mumbler marched them to the wide room outside their cell. The picnic table had been scooted away from the wall. Two bowls, with slices of bread covering their lunch's identity, waited. Milk, from a miniature carton, was to be the drink of choice.

"Noodle soup," Marilyn said disdainfully.

After a few minutes, Rosa sopped up the last of the broth, left the picnic table and went to look out the window. She could actually see a functioning washer and dryer but nothing else. A door next to the picnic table led to the outside. On the off chance, Rosa tried the knob.

"There's no way out," Marilyn said. "I've been here before. And the television you hear, that's in the men's area. They get to have noodle soup and watch reruns at the same time."

Rosa leaned back against the wall.

"So is anybody coming to get you?" Marilyn asked.

"Nope."

"Have you called anybody?"

"Nope."

"When my uncle comes to get me, I could make a call on the outside for you."

"Thanks, but that's not necessary."

"Really, it's no problem. I know what it's like to be in here and not know what to do."

"I know what to do."

Marilyn leaned forward. "What are you going to do?"

"Absolutely nothing."

Sandra Hill's past history was a carbon copy of Lucille Straus's, only Sandra had a few more years under her belt. When the photo of Sandra popped up on Sam's computer screen, he sucked in his breath. He knew this woman, too. He'd picked her up for vagrancy more than once.

Rosa Cagnalia couldn't have . . . No, she wasn't capable of . . . She hadn't fired the gun that killed Jimmy Handley; she'd been there with her boyfriend Eric Santellis. The big question was who had pulled the trigger: had it really been Eric Santellis as a jury had ruled or an outsider?

Rosa knew.

And Sam wanted to know what Rosa knew. He wanted some sort of justice for Cliff. His ex-partner was a stranger now, a broken man who'd first lost Jimmy and then a year later his wife, Susan, divorced him.

He had a daughter, too, who looked a lot like Jimmy. Sam hadn't seen Katie since Jimmy's funeral.

He punched in Lucy Straus as a keyword and watched as more than twenty hits returned. Lucy had been a busy girl since Rosa assumed her identity. She'd rented a home, gotten a job, joined a church and donated to charity.

Was this how she was spending her stolen fortune: on sporty cars and the needy?

Sam pushed away from his desk, reached for his keys and barked at Atkins to get hold of the Tribal Police and have them be on the lookout for the real Lucy.

His phone rang before he could leave.

Within moments he'd been assigned to sit watch on Rosa's mobile home. Glancing at his watch, he figured he'd have time for a quick look for Sandra before he started surveillance.

If he found Sandra, there'd be questions.

If he didn't find Sandra, there'd be even more.

An hour later, Sam was no closer to the truth.

The homeless loved the park at the edge of town. It offered a sanitary, somewhat overly fragrant, bathroom, which never had toilet paper; a duck pond which drew children who often threw away a half-eaten Happy Meal; and enough trees to provide shade for any vagrant who wanted to slumber.

Sandra Hill was not there.

After a few minutes of questioning, Sam knew that Sandra hadn't been seen in over six months.

Exactly the amount of time Rosa had been in town.

One more piece to figure into the puzzle that was Rosa Cagnalia.

THREE

The Desert Caravan Mobile Home Park had a nightlife. Rosa's neighbors to the left had propped open their front door, and loud rock music boomed. The mobile home to the right had at least three carloads of visitors. According to the profile the feds had already gathered, neither of Rosa's neighbors could be termed "desirable."

Three jogging-suit clad women walked the drive that circled the park. One had weights strapped to her wrists; another mimicked an animated member of a marching-band; and the last strolled in between as if just along for the gossip.

Rosa's cat poked its head between the curtains for about the fifth time. Sam wondered if the feline was watching for Rosa's return and dinner. It would be a long wait.

The bright orange sun faded to a murky tangerine and began its slow disappearance behind the horizon. Sam blinked away fatigue. This was not where he wanted to be. He wanted to be back at the precinct, digging through records and trying to figure out what Rosa Cagnalia was doing in Gila City. She hadn't run far enough, that was sure. Gila City was too close to Phoenix. Rosa should have headed for North Dakota or Alaska, someplace far away from her roots and the scene of her crime.

Why was she hiding here?

It had to have something to do with that night and something Rosa had seen. If he remembered correctly, the bust and Jimmy's murder had resulted in ten arrests, one that stuck: Eric Santellis. In the aftermath, Rosa's description had hit the radio, and cops for miles went on the lookout. Sam remembered pulling over cars and shining flashlights into the interior of every vehicle driven by a dark-haired beauty.

Her picture still hung on one of the station's bulletin boards. Sam picked up his thermos and refilled the semiclean cup. He made a face, drank it anyway and stared at Rosa's home. Surveillance had never reached first place on Sam's to-do list. He'd sat with his first partner, Steve Conner, back in the rookie days. Conner had been two months from retirement and counting the days. He'd also been a religious man and started each surveillance job with a prayer for both criminal and victim. They spent many long evenings waiting for movement; some hint that the evening hadn't been a complete waste. Then, Sam got paired up with Cliff, and surveillance was still too long, stuck in limbo, with no proximity to a restroom. He had stared through the windshield at many a trailer. Some like this one, complete with repugnant neighbors.

In many ways, surveillance gave a man too much time to think. What Sam was thinking about now was Rosa, and her penchant for praying at the strangest times — like while getting shot at!

Sam had stopped praying during surveillance after he'd been assigned to Cliff. Although they went to the same church, Cliff didn't seem to need God. Sam hid his light under a bushel. Then, after his mother died, the light died.

Yep, too much time to think, otherwise Sam wouldn't be getting this melancholy.

A faint, unfamiliar sound interrupted Sam's meandering thoughts, a tinkling in the distance. He sat up, listening, alert. Laughter came from the space to the right of Rosa's. A man opened the door and stumbled out, holding up two beer bottles and laughing. Sam looked at Rosa's trailer and then back at the man.

Putting the beer bottles on the front step the man kicked at a hissing cat.

Rosa's cat.

Rosa's cat outside!

Sam's fingers twisted around the car's door handle even as Rosa's trailer shattered in a thousand pieces of aluminum and wooden paneling. A whoosh of sound billowed upward, swirling in flames and smoke to meld with the evening.

"What the —" Sam stumbled out of his car so fast he lost his footing and had to brace himself with one hand on the ground. Scrambling back inside, he picked up the radio and called dispatch. "This is Packard, I'm at 811 Elm, space 13. There's been an explosion."

The scent of heavy smoke and cinders scorched his nostrils as he hurried across the street. The sound of screams mingled with sirens. Fatigue disappeared as a gust of wind blew a piece of aluminum siding toward his car. Sam ignored the heat.

Rosa's neighbor was facedown on the ground. Sam's fist clenched as he hurried across the drive.

People poured out of the man's trailer. Maybe it was the shock of having their next-door neighbor's home blow apart, or maybe the drugs impeded conscious thought, but none of them had the presence of mind to deal with the fallen man. Sam dropped to his knees, pulling plastic gloves from his pocket and putting them on. A woman wailed and knelt beside him. Gingerly, after making an assessment of the injuries, he turned the man over. Blood gushed from a gash above the man's eye, but Sam doubted it was serious. Head wounds made the biggest fuss for the smallest affliction.

"Is everyone else accounted for?" Sam plucked glass from the fallen man's hairline.

"Yes, no, I don't know," the sobbing woman blustered. "Is Seth all right? He just stepped out for a moment. He wanted to —"

Through blistered, bleeding lips, Seth uttered, "Shut up, Margie."

A fire truck arrived. Neighbors drifted back, mesmerized by the excitement but as obedient as schoolchildren when Sam herded them out of the way.

Sam watched the firemen take care of Seth. Only a fluke kept the houses next to Rosa's safe. And the cat? Where was the cat? Too many people crowded the street. Sam set about separating potential witnesses from thrill-seekers.

The feds arrived and within moments were both talking into cell phones: their faces stone serious. A few moments of standing in front of them, waiting, told Sam they didn't have time for him.

The neighbor, Margie, huddled on her front step watching the ambulance attendants. Sam'd come back and talk to her later, when her mind wasn't distracted by the sight of her boyfriend's vital signs being taken — *when her boyfriend wasn't telling her to shut up.* Sam would play on her sympathy. After all, he'd been the Good Samaritan when Seth was moaning on the ground. She might not have made him for a cop.

Sam scanned the crowd, looking for the three exercisers. They might not even realize if they'd seen something, heard something. Anything. If statistics were to be believed, then whoever had set the explosion would want to view his handiwork. These women might be able to make identification. Unfortunately, if statistics were to be believed, then all three women would have different recollections.

His questions netted nothing. The women had been busy verbally dissecting a daytime soap. They'd greeted two park residents, and they'd noticed him. He, they specified, was the only stranger they'd noticed. Of course, maybe the man he wanted them to identify wasn't a stranger to the Desert Caravan Mobile Home Park.

Every question he wanted to ask, every detail he wanted to pursue paled in comparison to what he already knew. A beleaguered woman trying to comfort her man. The man who had stepped outside with *two* beers.

The feds hadn't been as rankled as Sam had expected. All in a day's work for them, he guessed. Of course, they'd treated him like a gnat that needed to be swatted away. He might very well be the only Gila City police detective to have a stakeout literally blow up in his face. This would be hard to live down.

It was after midnight when Sam pulled into the precinct's parking lot. He brushed a hand through hair dusted with soot. The need for sleep had disappeared along with Rosa's roof. He would look into the Lucy Straus, Sandra Hill — and the need for those fake ID's — angle later. Right now he wanted to figure out who Rosa's real enemies were and what she was doing in Gila City.

Sam snagged a bottled water from the

machine before heading downstairs. Sitting at his desk, he logged on to the computer and typed in his code. The scent of neglected cigarette smoke settled around him like a lonely cloud looking for a home. The desks outside his office were accusing in their isolation. Daytime at the precinct was a pulsating, heartbeat of energetic activity. Between 2 a.m. and 5 a.m. was a morgue of oppressive silence.

A picture of a much younger Rosa froze on the screen. She was one good-looking woman. Sam hit Enter a couple of times and finally the next file opened. Rosa's background was sketchy at best. She apparently had bypassed any youthful acting out. Although, Sam would call hanging out with the Santellises a crime. There were no reports of shoplifting, cruising violations or truancy. Now, her older brother was a different story. His name was cross-referenced with Rosa's, and Sam would need weeks to sort through Frank's file. Still, after what went down with Jimmy Handley, her fingerprints *should* have been on file.

Intrigued, Sam printed a few files and put them in a folder with a copy of the rest of Rosa's information. Her personal data had tripled since the feds arrived. They wasted no time. The fax machine had belched at about five, and Rosa's life story, as the feds knew it, was seared on paper for all to see by seven.

Sam separated the papers into three piles: personal information, newspaper clippings and FBI reports. The first pile chronicled birth through legal age. She'd broken an arm in third grade; she'd won a district spelling bee in sixth; and her wisdom teeth had been removed in eighth. This information was worthless. How could an arm broken in third grade be pertinent to Rosa's crime? The feds must be desperate for information about the woman. Sam had been right — she was older than twenty-two.

Sam scanned the newspaper clippings next. Her career as a news item started with Jimmy's death. One of the tabloids had a picture of Eric Santellis and her on the cover. The inside story said that she dated the drug dealer just for excitement. Hmm, interesting concept. The press had been hard up for photos of Rosa. Most seemed to be from a distant observer's sketchy photo album. Sam studied Rosa's high school graduation photo, and another of Rosa and Eric standing at the helm of a boat.

They looked happy, and for some reason

that bothered him. The last few photos were of the "Have you seen . . ." type.

Sam started at the top of the FBI's current file. Her GPA from high school earned her a scholarship. She'd taken a tour of Europe instead of going straight to college. This didn't sound like a girl who would date a drug dealer for excitement. A glossy photograph fell at his feet. He picked it up and turned it over.

"Wow." He whistled appreciatively and shook his head. Too bad the baggage she carried had organized crime stamped on it. Sam guessed this was what she looked like about two or three years ago: a bit skinnier, her hair somewhat curly and with that deep reddish shade so many women seemed to covet. Her eyes maintained a glimmer of innocence.

How could the woman have innocence in her eyes? It must be a trick of the camera.

Resolutely, he put the photo down, took a paper out of his desk and began charting a time line for Rosa. He figured out that up until age twenty-one, Rosa's only flaws had been a wild big brother and her connection to the Santellises.

Her family had moved during junior high school, right after her older brother died of an overdose, and that seemed to have been enough to sever her and Eric's adolescent romance. Chalk one up for Papa Cagnalia.

A snitch reported seeing her with Eric Santellis a month after her twenty-fifth birthday. Jimmy had been shot right after Rosa's twenty-sixth birthday.

This scenario wasn't making a whole lot of sense.

What happened after Rosa turned twenty-five? Why had she hooked back up with Eric?

He brought up Jimmy Handley's file. Grabbing a pencil, he jotted down the names of the people present at the shooting. Sam didn't bring up Eric's file. He knew it by heart.

Eric was doing twenty to life in the state prison in Florence. The Santellises were, for the most part, well-known in the Gila City area — their father legitimately owned a used car lot there. Illegitimately, the man laundered money in his establishments, operated a chop shop, was a known associate of drug dealers — probably more, and was so slick nothing could be pinned on him. The file on Eric wasn't as extensive as his big brothers. Both Tony and Sardi were more than well-known, and theirs rated as epics. Little brother Kenny's file indicated a desire to catch up but nothing major, yet.

75

There was a sister, too, Sam remembered. Most of her file could be blamed not on her brothers, but on her husband.

Until Jimmy Handley's murder, Eric had been the least-known Santellis. Of course, he just might have been better at hiding his sins. Sam could attribute the same skill to Rosa.

Sam punched in the name of Terrance Jackle, Tony Santellis's newly paroled best friend. It had been Jackle's apartment where all had gone wrong. The photo whirled onto the computer screen. A sentence blinked on, and off, bright green, before freezing. Jackle had bought it a few weeks ago, in the back of his head.

Strange.

Frowning, Sam punched in another name. This one wasn't a Santellis, just a hanger-on. Jason Hughes hadn't done hard time for being present at Jimmy's death. But that didn't matter, hard time might be preferable. The man had been dead for sixteen months, drug overdose. A suspicion hovered and then took over Sam's thoughts.

Two corpses.

Okay, time to try another name. Sam chose Mitchell Trent, a small-time dealer who'd never chosen friends wisely.

Three corpses.

Trent had been dead for almost a year. Trent apparently drove a vehicle with a brake problem. The report mentioned Trent's girlfriend, Lindsey, had also died in the crash.

Four corpses.

The news didn't surprise Sam. She'd been present at Jackle's the day of Jimmy's death, too, the only female besides Rosa.

No, no way.

Eric Santellis was the only one still serving time. It took Sam twenty minutes to ascertain that besides Rosa, Eric was also the only one still alive.

And now, thanks to Sam, Rosa had a known address, albeit currently the Gila City County Jail.

And her previous address had blown up a few hours ago.

Pushing his chair back, Sam stood up and stuck the files in a drawer. It was almost three-thirty. Time to head home. After a few hours of sleep, all this might make some sense, although he doubted it.

The brown sedan would have to suffice as transportation since one of the memos on his desk reminded him that the Exxon station had called at noon saying his truck was ready. A lot of good that did him now.

He flipped the light switch and headed

toward the stairs. This time of morning in the Gila City precinct meant solitude and paperwork. Sam glanced out the window. Cliff's car was now parked between a palo-verde tree and a trash receptacle. Suddenly, Sam doubted that sleep was anywhere in his near future. Rosa and Eric the only ones alive?

Cliff was behaving strangely.

What were the odds?

The women's area occupied the left corner of the station. It had one cell that opened into a type of foyer. They'd turned it into a women's holding area back in the sixties. A few female picketers had gotten carried away at a peace march and suddenly the town needed a separate cell for women. Sam didn't know, or care, what it had been used for before that.

The duty officer's radio played to a non-existent audience. Sam curled his fingers around the handle of his gun. This was his station, his home, his turf. Why was he feeling that some outside force had violated his space?

He heard Henry's voice, a low mumble even in a quiet night. Okay, that meant at least one person was where he was supposed to be.

Supposed to be?

That's what had been bothering him.

Cliff's showing up this morning.

Cliff had only been back in Gila City a few weeks. He'd told Sam that haunting his old precinct wasn't something he intended to do. Something about out with the old and in with the new. And this morning had been the first time he'd entered the doors. This morning, of all mornings, the morning Lucy Straus, Rosa Cagnalia, was apprehended.

And now he was back.

More than coincidence?

Cliff had said, back when he and Sam were partners, not to believe in coincidence.

For the first time, Sam truly understood what his ex-partner had been trying to teach him.

FOUR

The police station represented family to Sam, but, right at this moment, he felt out of place. Something — make that someone — he'd believed in was proving to be a crumbling cornerstone. Cops weren't supposed to take things personally. Cliff was, and who could blame him? But he seemed to be trying to get revenge on Rosa at any cost.

Sam decided to walk around a bit, try to shake off the disturbing feeling. Three women were in the dispatch room. Two detectives were on the second floor, staring at a wall of photos and arguing. Each photo was marked with large, red, chronological numbers. The number of cars stolen in Gila City had increased from fifteen a month to more than thirty. The mayor promised action; the police worked longer hours. The car thieves probably laughed.

He settled back at his desk and picked up

her file. No way should he feel obligated to keep an eye out for her. He had arrested her, but he'd arrested lots of people and figured most — if not all — of them were guilty. Maybe that was the problem. The more he investigated, the more he heard about the interrogation the feds had conducted yesterday, the more he wondered about what else she was guilty of, besides making off with drug money. There had to be something else involved here. The number of corpses certainly supported that theory.

And maybe there'd be one less corpse if she adhered to the Good Samaritan law by sticking around and helping Jimmy. She was a registered nurse. A few minutes of her time might have meant the difference between life and death for Jimmy.

What made her turn her back on a young man dying, literally, at her feet? She could have saved Jimmy, copped a plea and continued life as she knew it. She had no priors and almost every deposition taken after the bust painted Rosa as one of the good guys. She was well liked at work and by her neighbors. Her family supported her. Something was very wrong with the whole picture. If she was such a nice girl, why did so many people want her dead?

"Sam."

If he were inclined to give credit, he just might thank God for sending him the accomplice he needed. But he'd stopped asking God for anything a long time ago, so there was no need for thanks.

Ruth had dark circles under her eyes and looked as tightly wound as Sam felt.

"What are you doing here at this hour?" he asked.

"I can't sleep. We arrested someone connected to the Santellises," she said softly. "I don't think we asked her enough questions before the feds took over."

Sam nodded. "Not only did we not ask her enough questions, but we didn't ask her the right questions."

"Do you think she knows what happened to Dustin?"

"No." Sam gathered his notes and a few printouts. "I don't think she knows anything about your husband's disappearance. And I think I can convince you that she's a pawn in somebody else's game."

Ruth hadn't been on the Gila City force during Cliff's tenure. She'd still been in high school. She might be able to stay unbiased. Especially if she thought it would bring down the family she blamed for her husband's death. She took the seat that

Rosa had occupied, and just like Rosa, she picked up a pen and started fidgeting. Finally, she asked, "So, what's going on?"

"I'm putting two and two together and I'm not getting four. Someone's out to kill her."

"She's connected to the Santellises. That's why I'm here. And, someone's always going to be out to kill her." Ruth set the pen down and for a moment Sam thought she might leave, might turn her back on what she didn't want to hear.

Swallowing, he voiced the words that might begin to hammer the nails of his onetime friend's virtual coffin. "I don't think Cliff showed up by accident this morning. I think he knew she was there."

"What?"

"Whoever was shooting at Rosa, probably the Santellis brothers, I think they somehow got a hold of Cliff and told him she'd been arrested."

"You're jumping to conclusions. He's feeling raw. It's to be expect—"

"*He* knew we had her before *we* knew we had her."

Atkins shifted. "I don't think I buy that."

"Stay with me for one more thing, then tell me what you think. I've been going through the files. Everyone who was present at the shooting of Jimmy is dead except for Rosa and Eric Santellis. *Three* of the people present at Jimmy's death have been killed in drive-by shootings. What are the odds?"

"How many dead in all?"

"Twelve."

"Twelve." Ruth sounded incredulous.

Sam continued, "Five went down within the first three months after Jimmy's death. All in the Phoenix area. The rest were spread out a bit. Think about it. Eric's alive but in prison, and Rosa dropped out of sight. Now, Rosa's back in the picture, and Cliff immediately tries to kill her. That's a pretty bleak picture even without her mobile home blowing up."

"What Cliff did was purely an emotional reaction. I can't believe you're implicating him."

Sam watched her chin come up. He knew this woman. He'd been friends with her and her family since before she'd joined the force. Her late husband had caught Sam's pitches way back when Gila City High only had two hundred students and a baseball team with no uniforms. Ruth had changed his mind about the abilities of female cops.

And although she was protesting, he knew she was starting to believe.

Her fingers beat a tune of irritation on the

desk. "So who you going to tell? Not the captain."

"No, he's too close to Cliff. He'd be fair, but it would take too long to convince him there was a need to be suspicious."

"Who you going to tell? The feds?"

"I don't think the feds would listen, especially after her mobile home blew up during my watch. I'm thinking about talking to Mitch Williams."

Ruth stood. "Mitch is a good idea. This is one time when Internal Affairs might prove to be a blessing. And I think I'll bow out of this. It's too much. I'm —"

"Ruth, please, sit. I want you to look at what I've pieced together."

"I can't. This is scaring me."

"*This* is why you became a cop."

"I know, and suddenly I'm as frightened as I was the day Dustin disappeared. Sam, what about my daughter? Rosa's friends killed her father. I'm glad you're telling Mitch. Now, tell someone with even more authority. How about the mayor? Can he do something?"

"Sure, I can tell you exactly what Mayor Ripley will do. He'll arrange for photos of Rosa being led from her cell and use them for his 'No Mercy' campaign."

"She is guilty. Instead of helping Jimmy,

she took the money and ran." Indignation flushed Ruth's cheeks a high pink. She sat, clearly intrigued, but not quite on the side Sam wanted.

He rushed on. "I dug through her background. Until she turned twenty-six, there wasn't a blemish on her record."

"That's not enough. She was there when a cop bought it, Sam. That's hard to forgive."

"Are you saying you think she pulled the trigger? Do you think she knew a murder would take place in front of her eyes? What do you think she's guilty of?"

"She's guilty of dating a Santellis." Ruth almost spat the word. "I'll bet she knows where lots of people are buried." Ruth's voice dropped, and Sam knew she'd purposely left off *where Dustin is buried.* "And the families of those people mourn," Ruth continued. "I can't help you, Sam. I want her to pay."

"And I want to find out what she knows. I want to keep her alive."

"What do you think she's going to tell you?"

Sam almost laughed. Ruth kept throwing his questions back at him.

What did Rosa know?

Why was she in Gila City?

"Do you think she's here because of Cliff?" Ruth said carefully.

Sam nodded.

"Okay, why?"

"This is Cliff's hometown, she would be able to —" He stopped. A hazy memory surfaced. The Mustang pulled over, Rosa's head disappearing from sight as if she had fallen to her side, then her hasty exit. His next thought was a long shot. Rosa had needed to bounce up and down to gain momentum to carry her over that first fence. He'd thought her out of shape, but now thinking of it, there was nothing out of shape when she'd jumped over the second fence, and she'd barely lost her breath when Cliff had manhandled her. The woman was in shape. She'd paused by the first fence for a reason.

He'd been so intent on the chase, he hadn't noticed the discard.

Quickly he stood. "Take a little road trip with me."

"Where?"

"Just trust me."

"I don't need this, Sam."

"Neither do I."

For a moment, Sam thought she would turn him down. Then, her lips went together in a frown, and she led the way to the door.

"You owe me big-time."

The brown sedan purred to life. He could really start to like this car. It only took a few minutes to return to the residential street that had witnessed Rosa's arrest. The area lazed in the early-Wednesday-morning grayness. He parked near the indentations left by Rosa's car. The mournful sound of a train echoed in the distance. Sam grabbed his flashlight and headed for the fence. Ruth followed.

He found the envelope wedged behind a rosebush. Fate seldom gave in this easily.

"What is that?" Ruth whispered.

"A hunch that actually played out."

Together they hurried back to the car, turned the inside dome light on, and unclasped the envelope. The stack of papers probably measured a full inch. The top printouts had yesterday's date. He gave Ruth half and skimmed what he'd kept. After a moment he muttered, "These are all about Cliff."

Ruth's hands shook as she went from one page to another. Five, ten, twenty minutes passed before she cleared her throat and said, "Lots of names, some I recognize."

Sam passed over a stack of stapled pages. "And here's a record of all his collars."

"Is there more?"

"Yes, quite a bit. We need to go feed some of this information into the computer."

"Now?" Ruth rubbed her forehead, a pinched look replacing the incredulous, scornful look of earlier.

"Now." Sam started the vehicle while Ruth continued reading under the faint glare of the dome light. He wanted to peruse the papers, too, but he obeyed the traffic laws; the thought of speeding somehow didn't appeal, and finally, he pulled in to the station's parking lot.

In a matter of minutes, they were settled in his office, poring over Rosa's envelope, the information the feds had left, and Sam's chicken-scratch time line.

For Rosa Cagnalia, all it took for a jailbreak was hot, soapy water. Scalding water.

An overweight officer handcuffed her and then shoved her past the picnic table. Her leg hit the edge, and she tumbled. He yanked her to her feet, hard, and pushed. She flew out the door and into the arms of yet another man. Tangled, unwashed hair blew across her face as a slight wind joined the morning. A cruiser waited.

She doubted the duty officer, the one who'd legitimately been in charge of her, knew the police officers who'd thrown the bucket of water in his face. She doubted he'd be able to describe them. They were on either side of her, and she hadn't managed a good look yet. It had happened so fast. She'd been heading for the shower area. They'd been inside waiting.

Stupid, stupid, stupid.

The handcuffs bit into her wrists. They restricted her arms behind her back. A tubby cop opened the cruiser's door. He pushed her head down and secured her in the backseat. She shimmied over, and an officer scooted in beside her. The front passenger side door opened and Tubby got in.

The driver turned around to stare at Rosa.

Cliff Handley.

FIVE

For a woman who for the last hour had claimed, I can't help you, Ruth had suddenly become willing to explore. She hit the print button and said, "Eric Santellis has no criminal record. Not even a speeding ticket. The month Jimmy Handley died, Eric's address was a dorm at Arizona State University."

"Thugs go to college, too."

"It was his final semester."

"What was his major?"

"Criminal justice."

"Ah." Sam paused, digesting the taste of irony. "So instead of finishing his final term at ASU, he's serving a life term at Florence. That's poetic justice."

"I don't think so. Look."

She laid a Polaroid on the table. "This was in the bottom of the envelope."

Sam picked the photo up, squinting at the three figures smiling into the camera. This, again, was Rosa before the change to Lucy. She had long, wavy hair — streaked with highlights the color of burgundy. This picture must have been taken right before Jimmy died, roughly two years ago, but already Rosa had the haunted Walter Peabody look in her eyes.

Funny how often Walt Peabody had been coming to mind lately. Death row inmates were best forgotten, especially by cops. The other two men were also well-known to Sam. Eric Santellis had the black hair and olive complexion of his siblings. He was, however, made of slimmer stock. He had an arm around Rosa's shoulder. A loose grip, not possessive. Not the hold of a lover.

Jimmy Handley also had his arm around Rosa's shoulder.

"They were friends," Sam stated.

Sam fingered the documents retrieved from Rosa's envelope. "We need to find out what else and who else they were involved with back then and maybe the pieces will fit together."

Ruth turned back to the computer and started typing in dates. Sam stared over her shoulder. She'd obviously been researching all the crimes the Santellises were suspected of, her husband's included. Dustin's name remained in the keyword box. An officer killed in the line of duty. Another unsolved crime. This one with no body. Just a smear of blood found on the driver's side of his deserted cruiser on a desolate road in Broken Bones, Arizona.

I'll bet she knows where lots of bodies are buried. That's something else Ruth had said about Rosa.

Three years ago Dustin had been investigating a lead concerning Kenny Santellis. Rosa was connected with a Santellis.

Sam patted Ruth's shoulder. "I'm beat. Think I'll head home."

She nodded, intent on the screen in front of her, and obviously willing to spend more time researching.

Sam picked up one of the folders and paperwork and headed down the hall and then outside to the city vehicle he'd used for the last two days. At only 5 a.m. in the morning, traffic was practically nonexistent in Gila City. Sam saw a police cruiser up ahead. It turned toward the highway.

He yawned. It would be good to get home, strip down to his shorts, eat some cereal and sleep in his bed.

Before he made it more than another block, his cell phone rang. "Packard," he answered.

"You're not going to believe this," Ruth

said. She'd been saying that a lot tonight. "Rosa's escaped. Someone threw scalding water on Henry as he was taking her to the showers. Captain says she's been missing about twenty minutes."

Sam thought of the cruiser, heading toward the highway, just fifteen minutes ago. Coincidence? Maybe. Rosa's kidnappers? Probably. After all, who'd think to stop a police cruiser. "Don't tell anyone you told me about Rosa. I'll call you as soon as I can."

It was a long shot, but one he had to take.

It was an old police car, one that didn't even have the barrier between the front and backseat. Or, maybe the barrier had been there and Cliff removed it just so nothing would obstruct the dirty looks he sent her way.

Hateful, venomous looks.

Oh, Father, Rosa closed her eyes and prayed. *I'm not strong enough for this. Please, let us get in a car wreck — a rollover. I'll climb free and run. I'll . . .*

"Are you sure you know what you're doing, Cliff?" Tubby asked. "I don't like all this —"

"Shut up!" Cliff glanced back at Rosa, his lips curling.

She paused in her prayer and clenched

her fist. The three men, her persecutors, acted as though she wasn't there as they discussed their plans. Twice the name Tony popped up. *Tony* would meet them. *Tony* would take care of everything.

Rosa bit back bile. Tony took care of Tony. Eric rotted in jail because of his brother Tony.

Tubby was right to question Cliff's motives; Tubby was wrong to render assistance.

The men were silent for a while. Rosa stared at the back of Cliff's head. A crown of hair highlighted a shiny, bald circle. He ran his fingers agitatedly through the remaining, artfully parted strands, each time stopping as if surprised to find that part of his mane was missing.

It was a full half hour before he addressed Rosa. "I've planned for this day, you know."

She'd planned for it, too. Mostly how to avoid it. Her hands, cuffed behind her back, cramped. "Yeah, well you know what they say about the best-laid plans." She meant to sound defiant, instead her words were more of a squeak.

The officer in back laughed.

Cliff shot him a dirty look, and then glared at Rosa.

"You need to keep your eyes on the road," the man muttered.

And suddenly, he looked familiar. She'd seen him before. Where? Gila City? Phoenix? Eric's house? Did he know Eric? Did he know Jimmy?

The cop uniform confused her. Even after all the grief cops had caused her, the uniform still symbolized trust.

"This is taking much too long." Cliff's fingers gripped the steering wheel. His knuckles were red from exertion. Those same knuckles had been around her neck.

The man growled, "Now, Cliff, you knew the risks."

"I'm gonna finish what I began, Jeff."

Jeff growled, "You've gotten revenge, many times over. Let it lie."

"Yeah," Tubby added. "These last two come with connections. And until we get the rest of our money, we need to keep everyone happy."

And they had no clue where the money from that night was.

For a moment, Rosa wondered why they weren't asking her questions. Then, she remembered. They were taking her to Tony. He would ask the questions. He would give the death sentence.

When Jesus had been crucified, he'd been surrounded by both friends and enemies. It looked as though only enemies would be invited to Rosa's execution.

Sam spotted them easily. They were doing the speed limit, and they were heading for the town of Broken Bones. No doubt they felt perfectly safe. At this stage in the game, everyone save Sam and Ruth would suspect the Santellises of breaking Rosa out of jail. Most would assume they were protecting one of their own. Only a few would worry about her safety. Sam was one of the few.

Broken Bones was a town that attracted trouble, especially this early in the morning when nobody was around to be a witness.

January in this part of Arizona might not rate snow, but the mornings could inspire use of a heater. He slowed down. Now that he knew where they were heading, he didn't want to risk notice.

He thought again of Rosa and how she'd bowed her head to pray at such an inopportune time — when everything she'd worked to hide was about to be exposed.

Didn't look as if God answered her prayers.

He hadn't answered Sam's last prayer, either. Sam hadn't even realized he missed prayer until witnessing Rosa's.

Now was not the time to think about prayer. Unless Sam missed his guess, the

97

Santellises had to be involved, and they had a cabin here in Broken Bones. They knew the area, the places that drew criminals and cops alike. Yes, Sam could almost guess where the men would head.

A nerve knotted in Sam's stomach as he drove a stretch of road as familiar to him as the back of his hand. A wooden sign advertising Broken Bones read two miles.

Sam turned onto the dirt road. This is where Dustin Atkins's cruiser had been found. He doubted they'd head to the one-street town. He thought maybe the river bottom. More dead bodies were rumored to be buried in the river bottom than in the Gila City Cemetery. But Sam didn't make it to the river bottom. They were risking the edge of town, the wrong side of the tracks. He saw his quarry just past Palo Verde Street.

It was a perfect setup. Palo Verde Street fed into a rural route that led right into Phoenix. When escorting prisoners, sometimes RR-1 was preferable to the freeway. There were no traffic jams to slow the police down.

This morning, there was no one to see what they did to Rosa.

No one but Sam.

He eased the car off the road, not wanting

a trail of dust to give him away. Things were happening too fast, and Sam had a front-row view from where he was parked. The car pulled into the parking lot of the Last Chance Bar.

Luckily, the white car came from the opposite direction, and Sam didn't need glasses to recognize the three men who had shot at Rosa yesterday: The Santellises.

The hole-in-the-wall called The Last Chance Bar was the sole resident of a dead-end street. She'd been here many times. Listening in on late-night conversations had given her insights into the seedy side, and seedy people, of Gila City and Broken Bones. Cliff wasn't mentioned often, but Tony and his brothers — save Eric — were.

Tubby glanced at his watch. "Right on time."

Rosa stared out the police cruiser's windows at the diner's unpaved parking lot. So, this was to be the meeting grounds for the final conflict. Rosa shivered. In order for there to be conflict there had to be two sides. There were only bad guys here today. A white SUV pulled into the parking lot.

Eric's big brother, Tony, stepped out of the vehicle first. The other brothers followed. They looked more like a contingent of bodyguards than family. Kenny yawned and looked bored. Sardi carried a suitcase and sauntered.

His saunter didn't look so suave when one noticed the bandaged left hand. Too bad her shot hadn't been a little higher, like where his heart beat.

Irrationally, Rosa wondered if David had felt any emotion, any guilt, after slaying Goliath. Suddenly, she was cold again.

Cliff and Tubby exited the cruiser and went to meet the Santellises. Tony was talking, but she couldn't make out his words. His hair was longer, and he wore sideburns, like a bad Elvis impersonator.

Yeah, he thought he was king. Rosa almost laughed. Tony blamed her for almost every disagreement he had with Eric starting in fifth grade. Even back then, Eric had refused to play the games his brothers considered their right. He didn't bully little kids or steal their lunch money. He didn't think homework beneath him.

She had attended private school with their sister Mary. She could still hear their fifth grade teacher's voice preaching about right versus wrong choices. Sister Clara's eyes bore down on whichever fifth grader had currently incurred her wrath. Rosa and Mary had been fast friends, against the wishes of Rosa's family. But, then, neither of them was any good at letting other people tell them what to do.

Where was Mary now? The two girls had spent hours on the playground, designing their future homes and naming the children. Last Rosa heard, Mary had married one of Tony's friends.

Who knew, in those fifth grade days, that Mary's brothers would be the ones to steal the dream away from Rosa? Or that at one time, another brother would come so close to fulfilling it. From fifth grade up until seventh, Eric Santellis had absorbed every moment, every thought, every dream, Rosa had.

Of course, her schoolgirl crush ended when Frank died. Rosa's family moved, and Rosa hadn't looked back until Eric showed up in the E.R. one night along with an undercover drug enforcement officer going by the name of Jimmy Harms.

His real name had been Jimmy Handley.

Unfortunately, the minute Eric came back into her life, Tony did the same. And here he was yet again. Larger than life, words pouring from his mouth while he gestured with his hands, anger tensing every finger. This man could snap her neck without working up a sweat. He'd enjoy it.

She kept one eye on the men while she repeated the same prayer. *Oh, Father, I'm not strong enough for this. I'll leave Gila City. If only* — The minister at the Gila City Fifth Street Church had preached against bartering with God. But how could you not when you were this close to dying?

Finally Cliff Handley nodded, and his lips curled downward in a grim sneer as he accepted the suitcase. He gestured toward Rosa. Tubby came around and opened her door. He yanked her out, his tug allowing the handcuffs to viciously tear into her wrists. She would have bruises by nightfall. That was, if she lived that long. He shoved her over, and Sardi grasped her by the upper arms.

Tony gave her the once-over. "You've filled out nicely."

"You're as ugly as your father." If she could bend down, she would pick up a handful of dust and throw it in Tony's eyes.

Sardi's fingers dug into her elbow. Their vehicle loomed closer as he pushed her around to the back and opened the trunk. He looked at her a moment, as if waiting to hear a whimpered plea. No way. She would not give him the satisfaction. With no expression, Sardi picked her up and shoved her in.

■ ■ ■ ■

Cliff Handley shook Tony Santellis's hand. Even as Sam shook his head in surprise, he admitted to himself that surprise and disbelief were very different.

Sam believed what he was seeing.

The Santellises' tires squealed as they headed back in the direction they'd come from, with Rosa in their trunk. Cliff and his cronies waited a moment and drove off.

Any other day, any other time, Sam would be calling the precinct, asking for assistance, but not today. Cliff had just crossed the line from right to wrong, and at least two other cops were with him. How was this revenge? What was gong on?

It was the *at least* that kept Sam from calling. Who else was involved? Sam had trusted Cliff completely. His mother used to say that only God could be trusted. Well, maybe she'd been right.

Suddenly, distrust of his fellow officers was a tangible entity, in the car with him, making him *doubt* the actions he should take.

Sam started his car. For the first time, in years, he felt the urge to pray. Maybe because he was thinking of his mother, of her words. Maybe because he figured that's what Rosa was doing, there in that trunk, knowing she was about to die.

Six

The road the brothers traveled was seldom used. The only witnesses to the crime were motionless tractors and an old baler. Sam kept his foot on the brake. He needed to wait a moment, avoid detection, but he wasn't worried. They'd chosen a rural road with one entrance and one exit. He knew exactly where to intercept them.

He grabbed his cell phone to call Ruth. He needed to know what was going on back at the station, needed to know if they figured out what he'd done or *not done.*

But, here, in this desert, there was no service. Sam was truly alone. What would he do when he found them? Arrest them? These weren't ordinary kidnappers. No matter how many ways Sam rewrote the ending, the final curtain demanded a price that was more than he wanted to pay. Unfortunately, to do nothing was not an option he could live with.

He finally eased up on the brake and headed toward destiny. Miles past The Last Chance Bar was a mixture of homes that ranged from tin sheds to campers to two-story log cabins to stucco ranch style. Some were occupied by weekenders who wanted as far away from civilization as possible so they could ride their ATVs and shoot their paint guns in peace. A few were homesteaders whose families had been in the area when the mine was open. Others housed crazies who didn't want their social security number traced or the sound of their ammo to bring undesirable attention.

Quite a few miles past the final, fading mobile home lay the river bottom. If Sam were intent on committing murder, that's exactly where he'd go.

He parked the car behind the rusted shell of another car, this one long deserted by the thieves who'd stripped it. Since he had no clue what he was doing anyway, jogging to get there was as good an idea as any.

Sam exited the Ford and started jogging. The dirt road had grooves cut deep from irregular weather. Rocks and cactus appeared in unlikely places. Sam ran every morning, but not in these conditions. And he wasn't really jogging. Jogging would be preferable. He started out in a dead run. Heading west toward a dust cloud that gave away the Santellises' location, he considered that in all his years of fieldwork, he had never gotten involved in anything as bizarre and unbelievable as this.

He saw the car and stopped so quickly he inadvertently kicked up dust himself. Ducking behind a cactus, he tried to regain his composure. His side hurt and he doubled over while he waited to see what the man leaning against the car door would do.

Nothing.

Sam inched closer, careful not to disturb any desert life. He swallowed, painfully, and only succeeded in pulling more dust into his throat.

They had parked off the beaten path. Sam had to account for three men plus Rosa. There was a man asleep in the front seat. That would be the youngest brother, Kenny, the lazy one. Sardi leaned against the car door, a gun held loosely at his side and a bandage on his arm.

Tony had forced Rosa more than a mile from the road. Sam could see her red shirt bobbing in the distance like a beacon. Sam crouched, angled to the left and started following, keeping behind the rock formations and jojoba bushes. They weren't moving fast, so he caught up in just a few minutes.

Rosa's head was high. Her white pants were now two-toned brown. The shirt was torn at one shoulder, and Sam saw blood dripping down from the jagged tear.

Sam could shoot Tony. The brothers would hear the gunshot but might assume it was Tony shooting Rosa.

That really wasn't the best scenario. Somewhere down the line Tony had crimes to answer for, and he needed to be alive to do the telling.

Sam wished he could get closer, hear what the two of them were talking about. He narrowed the distance between them, took his gun from the shoulder holster and held it. If Tony took aim, Sam would take aim.

Saliva dried in Rosa's throat. Her elbow throbbed with an erratic pulse.

"Tony, what are you doing?" Her feet were burning and felt like fifty-pound weights. Her toes cramped; the urge to sink to the ground beckoned. The prodding of Tony's gun was as effective as a whip.

"You turned Eric against his own brothers."

"That's bull, and you know it. Eric had already started helping the police before I came along." She stumbled, careful not to step in a hole. The rolling, brown dirt stretched on forever, interrupted only by shrubs hardy enough for the desert.

"He hadn't turned into a snitch yet. You encouraged that."

"And it's enough to kill me over?"

Tony knocked her to her knees. Her pants protected her from the first harsh onslaught of dirt and sand, but jagged edges still left their mark. A strange look transformed his face, softening his features, making him look almost human, then the hard mask of a hardened criminal returned. "I'd kill you bad, Rosa, but Mary asked me not to."

She spat, and he didn't even flinch. No doubt he enjoyed knowing her throat was so firmly powdered with fine Arizona grit that she could barely swallow.

Mary asked me not to.

Only Tony could believe there was honor in his current actions.

Suddenly, Rosa had an epiphany.

"You didn't kill my parents." A statement, rather than a question, and one that momentarily made her forget that death had a hand around her neck.

A hand connected to Tony Santellis.

Tony stopped, no doubt surprised by her words, and maybe surprise is what inspired him to respond. "No, I had nothing to do with their deaths."

She wanted to look back at him, see what expression he wore but he tightened his hold. His fingers dug into her hurt shoulder.

How long had it been since her last drink of water? Thank goodness it wasn't summer or she'd suspect Tony of hoping she'd die of thirst. She wanted to look back, see how far away the car was, but last time she had tried, Tony hit her with the gun so hard she still felt the blood dripping down her shoulder blade. Her shirt stuck to the spot and with each step it pulled so that the material rubbed against the open wound.

"What are you going to do, Tony?" She made the words soft. "Eric won't like this."

"Eric will never know."

"Don't you want to know where the money is, Tony? The drug money?"

"Sure I do, and in a few days, if you're still alive, you'll be more than willing to tell me."

"A few days? What are you planning to do?"

"Because of Eric and Mary, I'm not going to *kill* you." He shrugged. "Right now, I'm just going to make you pay."

"Pay! How?"

"And if you should die while I'm gone, well, that was an accident, and there are things more important than money."

His foot kicked out viciously. "Like revenge."

Rosa went to her knees, the pain in her shoulder searing as she hit the ground. She saw the hole, knew what it was, and tried to think of something to say, something to yell, something to do. Her fingers felt splintering wood. She clutched. The dirt betrayed her and moved.

She clawed at the ground, but the handcuffs didn't allow a single inch of maneuvering. From a distance this old, decrepit mining shaft had been hidden. It blended in well with the stark beauty of brown dirt, bent with aged cacti and gravel.

Then, she was falling, a jarring, skidding kind of fall that had her bumping into hard walls and sharp, protruding timbers before finally landing with a thud. Her mouth filled with dirt. Tony's laughter echoed through the darkness. The air changed, became colder.

The back of her head knocked hard against something. A rock? Her feet were sticking straight up, one shoe gone.

She'd only thought it was dark. Tony's laughter echoed down as a dim — so dim she hadn't realized it existed — light vanished. He covered up whatever hole he had thrown her down. Sheer horror enveloped

Rosa as the dank air filled her nostrils.

She wiggled into a semisitting position. Hot rage swelled into a lump of nausea in her throat. She would not cry. Her father said Cagnalias did not show weakness. The advice had been directed at Frank. Rosa listened.

Her oldest brother hadn't. Drugs had been his weakness.

Rosa closed her eyes and banished the memory of family. They were dead, partly because of her. Feeling guilty over their murder only hindered her from making sure their killers received justice. Of course, justice would be hard to achieve down here in this hole.

Funny how so many meandering thoughts took root when a person felt trapped.

She was Jonah in the belly of the whale.

Trapped.

Just a month ago a visiting preacher visited the Gila City Wednesday night Bible Class. Jonah and the whale took up a whole enthralling hour. The pictures of Jonah in the whale's belly always showed a fairly clean-looking man, dressed in colorful robes, sitting on a bone or something.

In truth, at least according to this preacher, Jonah had been imprisoned in a dark, tight space that allowed very little movement.

Like Rosa's hole.

He certainly wouldn't have been clean looking. More than likely his clothes would have been gone, and not only would he have been covered with smelly fish goo, but the acids from the whale's belly would have sucked the pigmentation from his skin and turned him murky white.

Rosa figured she was pretty pale herself, and instead of fish goo, she was covered with sweat and blood.

Jonah, too, would have had plenty of time for meandering thoughts. And prayer. She waited a moment, hoping her eyes would adjust. They didn't. There were too many shades of black.

Once, when she was little, her brother, Frank, had locked her in a closet as a joke. Her screams alerted him, and the whole family, as well, that she didn't think it funny. Strange she could remember that now. She hadn't *really* been afraid of the dark — of anything — until two years ago.

This darkness was so black she could feel it. It was cold, palpable, with an offensive scent that reminded her of Go Away's litter box.

One thing for sure, she didn't intend to lie there with her feet in the air and her head gathering dirt. Her hands clutched at the ground, dirt gathered under her nails. Small, hard, bits of gravel — whatever — crumbled under the force of her palms. "Don't cry." The words echoed off the walls. She hadn't meant to say them aloud. Where was she? And how was she going to get out? This was not where she intended to die!

Die.

She was going to die.

Alone, in the dark, without anyone knowing.

Her nose twitched. Maybe from the cold? No, it was just one more annoyance. With her hands cuffed behind her back, an itching nose was destiny.

The first tear slid down her chin when her hand smushed something gooey. Rosa jerked away, the cuffs again biting into her wrists. As another tear drifted into the corner of her mouth, she wondered what bothered her more: that her hand was in gooey stuff or that she didn't know what the gooey stuff was.

Or that she was going to die down here.
No. No. NO.

Panic turned up the beating of her heart. Breathing became audible. Every time she moved, something bit into her skin.

"Great, just great." What she guessed to

be small rocks imprinted her palms. Jagged edges of wood, or maybe a small tree — who knew? — took the skin off one of her ankles. Hopefully, the scrape didn't come from the sharp end of a rusty nail. One more thing to worry about. The least of her worries, actually. Why should she lie here and imagine lockjaw when dehydration was a more imminent foe.

Rosa wanted to rub the yuck off her hand, but maybe if she laid her palm down, she would just place it in the gooey stuff again.

She deserved this. She'd made her choices. Eric cooled his heels in Florence for a crime he didn't commit, and in two years she hadn't managed to find enough evidence to help him.

And then there were her parents.

Finally, in between disjointed prayers, she let herself scream. Her throat, too dry to really belt out her frustrations, managed an embarrassing squawk that echoed through the darkness. If her white knight was out there, he'd mistake her cry for that of a loud, dying, overwrought turkey.

Another thing her father had preached was the senselessness of lost causes. Who was out there to hear her scream? She needed to save her breath, her energy.

She screamed again.

The pitiful sound choked off as her throat constricted. Screaming wasn't going to help. She needed to get out of here on her own. And to do that, she needed these cuffs off.

Okay, first thing, get her hands in front of her. Even with a throbbing shoulder, she should be able to stand and maneuver — Dust flew from overhead and settled in her hair, on her hands, in her mouth. Coughing, she looked up and saw light seep in. Tony coming back again?

She choked back a cry.

"Are you all right?"

A familiar voice?

"Yes, yes. I'm all right! Who are you?"

"It's Detective Sam Packard. I'm going to get you out!"

So Cliff's ex-partner was to be her hero. At first, he'd thought her biggest crime to be speeding. Was he involved, as well? Had he been sent to make sure she was still alive? Alive so Tony could come back in a few days and torture her until she gave up *his* drug money.

"Wait a minute, while I find something to use as a rope or ladder. Are you sure nothing's broken?"

Would he be concerned about broken bones if he only wanted to finish her off?

"I'm not sure. There's not much room for

movement down here, but I don't think anything's broken."

"I'm going to have to go back for my car. I have a flashlight and some rope in the trunk. It's going to take a while. I'm parked almost a mile away."

She could just make out his silhouette at the top of the hole. Panic swelled. More than anything, she didn't want to be left alone. "No! Wait! Maybe I can climb out."

"Okay, go ahead and try. I'll reach down a hand."

She could see the top of the hole. Unfortunately, what she couldn't do was stand. Her shoulder throbbed. Without free movement from her hands, she could neither brace herself nor push upward. She fell back, hitting her shoulder on the wall behind her and feeling such pain that she cried out. Yeah, and to think she was trying to convince him to let her *climb* out.

"Let me just —" He sounded impatient.

"No, wait a moment." It was unrealistic, she knew. But she didn't want him to leave. What if he didn't come back?

"You are so far down —" his words had an edge "— that I can't even see you."

"Well, think of something."

"I have thought of something and that something is in my car."

"What about your belt?"

"I'm not wearing a belt."

"Is there any wood, something I could use for a ladder?" She'd climb with her teeth if she had to. Anything to get out of this premature grave.

"Will a cactus do?"

"Great, I'm being rescued by a comedian," she muttered.

"What did you say?"

"Nothing, just thinking out loud."

"Keep thinking out loud. I'm going for the car."

"No!" More dirt fell in her mouth.

"What is it? Are you going to faint?" He stepped back to the rim of the hole.

"Can't you just think of something else?"

"No."

"Maybe if I stood up, you could see me. Give me a minute."

Smushy stuff or not, she was going to stand. If he could see her, maybe he could reach her.

One foot pressed against a solid structure. The one without the shoe, of course, and ragged edges of something grabbed hold. Luckily, her hours at the gym paid off. She managed a handless sit-up. Now, how to get onto her feet. Twisting her legs to one side, she wiggled until she managed to get to her knees. "Hey, are you still up there?"

"I'm giving you one minute, then I'm going for my car."

She lodged one foot under her and pushed up with the other. "I'm standing! Can you see me?"

"No."

She could jump without the use of her hands. But only once. Her first leap, in darkness, had her stumbling against the wall. She froze. When she'd had a goal, standing, the darkness had lost its power. Now she felt vulnerable again as the pitch blackness returned.

"I can't see you. This won't work. I'm going to the car. It shouldn't take me more than a half hour to return."

"Are you sure," she whispered, "that nothing else is possible?"

"What?"

She cleared her throat. "All right. Go, but hurry."

It was so quiet, she thought he'd gone.

"Rosa?"

"What?"

"I'm pitching down my radio. I've switched it on, but reception is hit or miss. You'll hear static. Don't even try to mess with the buttons. Right now we don't know who's listening. When I get to my car, I'll say 'Packard, signing off.' Maybe it will come through, and you'll know that I'm on my way. Does that help?"

The radio landed near her feet. She sat back down on the ground as close to the static as she could get. "Yes, it helps."

He didn't like leaving her any more than she liked him leaving. What miner would choose this forsaken piece of land to dig a hole? Had the land been that different back before they'd built the Hoover Dam? On the other hand, it did make a perfect grave for a woman everyone wanted to disappear.

It had been a long time since he'd gone more than twenty-four hours without sleep. He had already run this stretch of land once. Doing it a second time wasn't any easier. Thirty-six was too old for boot camp regimens. Maybe because he wanted to get to his car so bad, it seemed to take forever. He cleared his mind and focused on what he would do with the rope once he got back to Rosa.

She had sounded panicked, brave, irritated and in charge all at the same time. He couldn't help but be impressed. His original attraction was turning into a grudging respect. She was a woman to be reckoned with.

When he finally reached his car, he checked the trunk and decided that the tow chain would suffice. Jumping in, he started the engine and pulled out onto the road, keeping the car at a certain speed.

"Packard, signing off." He hoped she'd heard him. He wanted her sane and rational for all the questions he had.

Glancing in the rearview mirror, he was pleased that no other cars were evident. Though the chances of him being seen were slim, he still wanted to maintain a low profile. The Santellises were probably well on their way to Phoenix by now, so really, no need to worry. They lived in a home that cost what Sam would make in a lifetime times four.

The car's tires dug into the dirt and spun as he left the road and traveled open terrain. What he needed was a four-wheel drive. The saguaro he'd hidden behind while watching Tony finally came into sight. Good thing for him that he'd found a cactus bigger than Godzilla. He backed the car up, as close to the hole's edge as he dared. Then he threw the emergency brake and climbed out.

"Sam?" Her shout came immediately, breathless and frantic.

"Yeah." He lobbed the end of the tow

chain to the rear bumper. "If I lower a chain, can you climb out?"

Silence.

"Rosa, what do you think?"

"Well, if I wasn't handcuffed I'd say yes."

He'd forgotten about the handcuffs. No wonder she sounded frenzied. "I'm going to lower the tow chain. Watch for it."

His estimate of a nine-foot hole was off.

"I don't feel it." Rosa's voice echoed. "It's not anywhere near me."

The flashlight's beam fell short, also. Sam pulled the tow chain up and headed back to the car's trunk. The police vehicle had a first-aid kit, water, leftover D.A.R.E. T-shirts, flares — D.A.R.E. T-shirts? They'd do for the end of the tow chain. He wove two of them together, secured them between links and lowered it once more.

She yelled, "That works! It's right to the top of my head. Now what?"

Now what? Good question. He had never rescued a person from a deep hole. If her hands weren't cuffed, he'd have her loop the tow chain and climb up while he slowly guided the car forward, giving her momentum.

The only thing for Sam to do was climb down there. "Can you cover your head?"

"Why?"

"I'm dropping my flashlight down. I want you to situate it so the beam heads upward."

"Go ahead. Throw."

He didn't hear an ouch. A few thuds and incomprehensible words later, the beam soared upward. Sam grasped the chain and flung his legs down the hole. It was just wide enough so that he could brace his back against one side while levering himself down the other side step by step. Rosa didn't say a word. He glanced down. She was pressed against the side, her hair blending in with the blackness, but her face a pale orb. His hands were damper than he wanted them to be, the tow chain not as hospitable as one might hope. He let go of the chain and jumped the rest of the way.

In the tight quarters, the first thing Sam felt was the proximity of Rosa. It was a tangible sensation, overtaking the mustiness of the long-forgotten mine shaft.

She broke the spell. "I sure hope you know what you're doing and can get me out of here."

"Stand still."

She froze. He picked up the flashlight and fished his keys from his pocket. A moment later, the cuffs fell to the ground making a clacking noise that caused them both to jump.

Rosa rubbed her wrists. "How'd you find me?"

"We'll do the small talk bit when we get to the top."

Her face tilted upward. "Okay."

"You can climb?" He shouldn't have been surprised. She'd almost outrun him the other morning.

"I think so."

"With that shoulder?"

"I can do it."

"Okay, up you go."

Sam would have preferred a longer tow chain himself, but he knew the cotton would hold. Rosa hauled herself upward, slowly. This was *not* going to be a quick venture.

He held the flashlight, waited until she'd climbed a good four feet, then he stuck the flashlight in his shirt and grabbed the end of one of the D.A.R.E. shirts.

"What are you doing?" Rosa stopped.

"Climbing to the top."

"I'm not there yet."

"No kidding."

"Are you sure the car won't —"

As if in answer, the tow chain jerked.

"Climb faster," Sam said.

SEVEN

She muttered again, reminding him of the backyard chase. Then, she lost her grip. He felt her coming, braced himself and cradled her against his knee. "You going to make it?"

"Yes." She spoke softly. This time he heard a "Thank you."

He had to push her from the hole and help her stand up, but he'd half expected to carry her so he wasn't complaining. With one hand on his cuffs, he paused. In the dark, he hadn't gotten a good look. Now the gash on her shoulder stared him in the face. So did the burn marks on her left arm.

"We need to get you to the hospital for stitches."

She swayed a bit. "No."

"You're already under arrest. What have you got to lose?"

"What I just about lost a minute ago. My life. Are you forgetting that a policeman had me thrown down that hole?"

"Tony Santellis is no policeman."

She put her hand on her hip. "You're not that stupid."

He had expected her to argue, to get indignant, not to come back with a personal insult. "Tell me why the Santellises want you dead?"

"Tell me how you found me in that hole?"

"I left work and saw the cruiser you were in. A few minutes later, Officer Atkins contacted me about what happened to the duty officer watching you. I put two and two together and followed."

"Who else knew you followed?"

"Nobody." It was true. He hadn't told Ruth, yet.

"I don't believe you."

"Doesn't matter."

She swayed.

Sam put away the cuffs. "Get in the car."

"Where are you taking me?"

His hand went to his forehead, and he brushed back his hair. "I wish I knew."

Obediently she occupied the front passenger seat, gingerly pushing aside his baton. He stuck it under the seat, his side, away from her reach.

He concentrated on not hitting any cacti as he maneuvered the car from the desert.

Once on the road, he asked again, "Rosa, what do the Santellises have against you? Do they blame you for Eric being in jail?"

She didn't answer. Her eyes were closed, but she didn't look asleep. If anything, it looked as if she was meditating. Half of him envied her. Half of him wanted to shake her and force her to answer, but a second look stilled him. She'd be asleep any minute, and she looked as though she needed it more than he did.

The blood from her shoulder seeped onto his car's seat. She'd really suffered very little from the scalding water. Henry, the duty officer, had been the target. Rosa had merely been splashed.

He checked his cell phone. Just as he feared, drained, no more power, and the charger was in his other vehicle. Broken Bones and The Last Chance Bar would be the closest telephone, but Sam didn't want to go there. Instead he turned on the radio and listened to the news as he traveled the extra half hour toward Phoenix and chose a busy truck stop off the freeway.

Ruth answered on the first ring. Sam let out his breath.

"The precinct's going nuts," she whispered. "They've put out an all points bulletin. What's going on? Do you know?"

"Yes and no. How's Henry? Are they questioning my whereabouts?"

"Henry's at the hospital. It's not pretty, but he'll be fine. The feds asked about you, but they've got other things on their minds. Now, you tell me — what's going on?"

He had no intention of lying to Ruth, no intention at all. Ruth was already involved, and telling her the truth would keep her alert, keep her on guard — *against Cliff.* Words Sam never expected to say spilled out of his mouth so quickly that Ruth had to ask him to repeat. Then, he ended with, "You need to start researching Cliff. He . . . he —" Sam stumbled over the words, almost choking "— it looks like he sold Rosa to Tony Santellis."

Silence.

Ruth was never silent.

Finally, in a quiet voice, she muttered, "Oh, Sam, what have we gotten ourselves into?"

He could imagine Ruth's face. Since Dustin's death, she'd hated surprises. She wanted every procedure to go by the book. When they didn't, she agonized over decisions.

"You're never going to believe this," Ruth said. "This stuff she's gathered is amazing. You know what she stumbled upon? She traced Tony Santellis's actions here in Gila City back twenty years. Tony worked at his dad's used car lot."

Before Sam could say anything, Ruth continued, "Guess who owned the gas station next door?"

Sam loosened his hold on the phone, realizing he'd been gripping it so tightly he'd almost lost the feeling in that hand. He sensed he wasn't going to like what he was about to hear.

"Walter Peabody."

Sam had known that Walter Peabody owned the gas station. That information had been part of record. He'd forgotten its proximity to the Santellises' used car lot. That the Santellises and Peabody worked together *was no surprise.*

That just a few hours ago Tony was in proximity to Cliff and looked pretty comfortable *was* a surprise.

Theirs wasn't a new relationship.

Yet just how old was it? It was that connection Sam had started to fear. Tony Santellis had at one time lived in Gila City. Walter Peabody owned a gas station cops often frequented — to keep an eye on the used car lot.

All Sam could do was shake his head. Finally, he cleared his throat and went on.

"Look, we need to pay more attention to when Tony's and Cliff's paths crossed. Find out who else worked at Yano Santellis's used car dealership twenty years ago. Let's find somebody willing to talk."

If she thought helping would solve the mystery of her husband's whereabouts, then Sam knew she'd willingly ferret out the information, through whatever means, honest or hack.

"I need to go. Rosa's in my car right now, and —"

Actually, she wasn't. As he said the word *car,* Sam glanced at his vehicle. He just made Rosa's white-clad leg hoofing past a gas tank.

He dropped the phone so fast that it whacked him in the knee, and he yelled, "Freeze!"

Two housewives, one pizza delivery man and an attendant hit the dirt. Rosa peeked over the top of a Volkswagen. Then, she bolted. Tired as he was, Sam managed to scramble over the Volkswagen as if it were a Matchbox car. Rosa disappeared around a used furniture store. Sam went to the opposite side of the store.

As planned, Rosa ran right into him. She tumbled and took him with her. Her elbow rubbed into his gut.

"Let go of me." Her words were uttered into the dirt.

Sam hoped she swallowed a mouthful.

"Rosa, I suggest you ease up before you make me mad." He handcuffed her, trying to ignore her wince of pain as her shoulder came forward. "You made me do this. I want you to remember that."

He lifted her from the ground, surprised at how easily she came. A smudge of dirt smeared one cheek. Without thinking, he brushed the dirt away.

She didn't thank him.

Handcuffed again!

It was futile to try to pull her wrist through the bracelet-like clamp, but Rosa tugged anyway.

Next time she escaped and created a new life, she was going to spend more time running the two hundred meter and reading Houdini's biography.

Would there be a next time? She'd barely escaped with her life two years ago. She had been caught twice now in the space of a week.

Sam Packard stood fifty feet away with his back to her. What was going on with this cop? This onetime partner to Cliff Handley. He finished one call, and then he dug in his pocket for more change and made yet another. This man had saved her life. Still, the desire to trust him, unburden her soul to him, or be in close quarters with him, was an uncomfortable consideration. She had personally known him just over forty-eight hours and besides saving her life, he had arrested her, harassed her, and, yes, made her notice him the way a woman should notice a man.

Normally, noticing a good-looking man — especially someone with Sam's magnetism — might be something to smile about. Being attracted to Cliff Handley's ex-partner was definitely not. He could very well be the same Jekyll-Hyde that Handley was. Good versus evil. And she wasn't smart enough to tell which he was.

Okay, thanks to him she was still alive, but that didn't mean she *had* to trust him. Unpredictable, he was way too unpredictable. Even now, as he spoke into the receiver, he gripped the phone as if to crush it. Was he irritated at the person on the other end, or just her? Maybe it was both of them. Who was he talking to, anyway?

She *had* to get out of here.

Looking down, she grimaced at the confetti marks of burned skin. Why somebody hadn't come running when she'd screamed, she'd never know. Maybe female prisoners screamed so often that nobody paid attention. Next she stared at the red welt that circled her wrist like an angry tattoo. Her Houdini attempts at escape proved ineffective.

She was stuck and at the mercy of this cop. At least she wasn't dead. Climbing that tow chain had taken every ounce of strength she had. Maybe that's why she hadn't outrun Packard. Of course, her desire to get out of the hole had provided an adrenaline boost that surprised even her.

She couldn't just sit here. Doing nothing. She yanked at the handcuff. She had to get out of this car! Her leg hit the glove compartment. It flopped open and banged her on the knee. The pizza delivery man at the next pump stared. Rosa flipped the glove compartment shut.

Sam Packard didn't frown, he scowled as he headed back to the car. Once again, Rosa really noticed this cop who wouldn't go away, noticed him as a man instead of a cop. He filled the gas tank, then opened the driver's side door, slid in, started the car and pulled into traffic.

"They're reporting you as an escaped convict. Your picture is going to broadcast from here to Timbuktu. I'm supposed to

133

hide you."

If he hadn't been driving, Rosa could imagine him hitting his head with frustration.

He continued, more to himself than to her. "What was Cliff thinking?"

The words reminded her that she couldn't, didn't dare, forget that she was sitting in a vehicle with Cliff's onetime partner. "Are you and Cliff still close?"

The look he shot her answered that.

"If you're still so close, then why are you helping me? That is what you're doing, isn't it? Helping me?"

"Lady, how can I be helping you when you won't tell me the truth."

"My name is not lady, it's Rosa."

"Yesterday you were Lucy. Where is she, by the way?"

"Here. Phoenix."

"You're kidding."

"No, that's where she wanted to go. When she needs money, she comes back to Gila City, and I give her money."

"How much money?"

"Surprisingly little. In exchange for her identification, I take care of her whenever she asks."

Sam grunted. Looking at him, Rosa almost wished he still wore sunglasses. His eyes were much too honest. Right now they looked straight ahead, zoning in on the freeway's entrance and the traffic. His whole demeanor spoke of purposefulness. His lips pressed together in annoyance. Rosa watched for a moment. She didn't think, this time, his ire was directed at her. More likely, he didn't like where his thoughts were leading him.

Welcome to my world, buddy.

It was well past noon. The time was verified by the digital numbers above the car's radio. Maybe this was one of Packard's ways to deal with the people he arrested? He starved them until they talked.

McDonald's. She wanted McDonald's. And she wanted a hot shower, two shoes, her Bible and a bed. Mostly she wanted her Bible and a bed.

Staring out the window as the road narrowed to one lane because of road construction, Rosa figured her life was much like this road, once smooth and functional; now rocky and dysfunctional.

Funny, she really hadn't known Jesus back when her life was smooth and functional, but she sure couldn't manage a day without him now.

Sam turned onto the freeway. Rosa probably told the truth about Lucy. What homeless person wouldn't turn over their identity for limitless financial support?

"And what about Sandra Hill?" he asked.

"Is there anything you don't know?" Her face turned wary, but was that grudging respect he saw in her eyes?

"Why Cliff wants to kill you."

She stared out the window.

Okay, he had to earn her trust. After all she'd been through, he could understand that. "You were going to tell me about Sandra Hill."

She directed her answer toward the swiftly passing electricity poles. "You were asking about Sandra Hill, that doesn't mean I intended to tell."

"You might as well, it's not like you can use her identification any longer."

"Sandra has a mobile home in a retirement community in Florida. She has enough money to keep her there for a decade if she's careful. How do you know about her?"

"I found the suitcase under your bed."

"Oh, good. You fed Go Away." She looked at him with hopeful eyes, and it pleased him, which made no sense.

"You named your cat Go Away?"

"Yes."

She had a sense of humor. It had probably been stomped on during the last few years, but it still existed. He almost wished he'd known her before. Right now, her hair clumped in one big mass of tangles. Fatigue added dark half-moons under her eyes. A trembling, bloody shoulder poked out of a torn, dirty shirt. For a solid woman, she looked amazingly small, vulnerable. She put up a pretty good front. Yet, if mannerisms were any indication, then this woman was more than scared. And it had started well before Cliff had recognized her.

"One more question. Why were you hiding in Gila City?"

"Gila City was as good as any place."

"I don't think so. Why choose the city where Cliff lived?" Sam watched her as he turned onto the freeway. Her expression didn't change. "You were there when his son died. More than anyone else, he has the right to hate you. Why choose his town?"

Sam purposely didn't mention that they'd found the envelope filled with photos and articles about Cliff. "Well?"

"Well, what?"

"Why Gila City?"

Rosa stared out the window. "Sometimes the best place to hide is the most obvious and the best place to start is the beginning."

Sam checked the rearview mirror. Phoenix disappeared into the distance. Two lanes took him away from endless flanks of concrete and commercialism.

"Where are we going?" She didn't look at him.

"It's probably better you don't know."

"Right. I was born here in Phoenix, remember? We're well past city limits. Payson? Why are we heading for Payson?"

"I need to keep you out of sight and out of danger."

"A little late for that."

"It's perfect timing. Right now, Cliff and the Santellises aren't worrying about you. They think you're buried and-or dead, and if we play this right, they won't need to know you're alive until it's too late."

"Do you think you could remove the handcuffs?"

"What do the Santellises have against you?"

"My brand of toothpaste."

"Ha-ha. Why did Tony throw you down the mine shaft?"

"What do you plan on doing when we get to Payson?" Her stomach growled.

"I guess I'll feed you first. I can't let you starve before you answer all my questions."

"Humph."

Traffic came to a halt. Sam strained to see what was ahead; after a few seconds he checked his watch, then looked at Rosa. He grinned mirthlessly. Any woman who could fall asleep while handcuffed deserved to slumber. And it looked as though this woman needed some uninterrupted sleep. Of course, now she was in a nervous doze that had her jerking awake every twenty minutes or so. Then she would stare at him, panicked for a moment, before shrugging and falling back to sleep. Her slender neck was tilted at an angle she'd regret later.

Sam's original plan had been to grab something to eat before turning down the Tonto Ridge Road. But now that she was snoozing, if they got the accident cleared up ahead, and if he drove straight through, she would have no clue as to where he was taking her. Maybe his family's cabin wasn't such a bad idea after all.

An hour later, he'd almost convinced himself he was right as he opened the first of the gates.

At the second gate — the one that opened onto the road where the Packards lived — snow bit at Sam's socks with a sting that made him remember why he stayed in Gila City. This section of Christopher Creek experienced little traffic during the winter months. It was private land, heavily guarded against errant vacationers. The padlocked gates were just one safeguard. This lock resisted. Sam checked to make sure he had the right key. He'd only been here a few times since his mother died. Rambling, empty times, where he'd battled his God, his conscience and his goals.

Seemed as if he'd lost more battles than he'd won.

The sign warning against timber rattle-snakes hung on the last gate. Finally, the lock gave, and the gate swung open. Sam pushed it all the way, ignoring the snow that pushed against him. Jogging back to the car, he wondered if Dad would be at the cabin. Well, where else would Dad be?

Rosa didn't move as Sam guided the car through the gate and then jumped out to close and lock it.

Tonto Ridge hadn't changed. The Bockers' cabin stood empty. They were friends of his father. Smoke billowed from the Dundees' place. They got along well with Elmer, Sam's dad. Most of the people in this area got along well with Dad. Quite a few of the neighbors had started their Arizona residency in Gila City. Elmer's father had been the first to buy a cabin here.

Neighbors and friends with money followed suit.

Sam hadn't called his father for more than two weeks. Somewhere between Elmer Packard's retirement and Sam's last promotion, they'd lost track of what to talk about. Or maybe it was the death of Sam's mother and then his faith that left them both tongue-tied.

During Sam's childhood, the family had spent every long weekend, every vacation, every major holiday at the cabin.

Sam breathed a sigh of relief as the road ended. Elmer's Jeep Cherokee was missing. Good: Sam wasn't prepared for a family reunion. Bad: Sam had less then twenty-four hours before his next shift began, and he needed someone he could trust to watch Rosa.

He hated to give his dad such a tough assignment, but Elmer had served in two wars. Once, during his childhood, Sam had watched Elmer down a man by just holding on to his ear.

Sam fumbled for his key, found it and finally opened the cabin's door. He hit the switch, relieved when light invaded the darkness. In Tonto Ridge, winter didn't always inspire working electricity.

Rosa woke up when he tapped on her

window. Her eyes held the haunted look even before cognizance dawned.

"We're here," he said unnecessarily.

"Where?"

"Just think of it as home."

She scowled, still not fully awake. "Great."

He unlocked the handcuffs and winced when he saw the raw, red circle that marked her wrist. She'd fought the clamp.

She made no move to check out her wrists, but her eyes met his. He knew if he looked away, she would look at her wound. A power play. He'd let her win, this time.

There were other more important battles ahead.

He followed her to the house, watching her hobble instead of walk. He shook his head before asking. "When did you lose your shoe?"

"Back at the hole."

"Why didn't you say something?"

"Oh, would you have stopped at a shop for me?"

He ignored her. "The bathroom is to your right. I'll get us something to eat while you shower. Towels are in the closet before the door."

She frowned at the melting snow forming a puddle beneath his shoes. "Last time I headed for the shower . . ."

"You're safe here."

"What about clothes?"

"I'll find you something."

"Can you do it now? I am locking the bathroom door."

"The door doesn't have a lock."

"Oh, be real."

"My mother disassembled the lock when my brother and I were little. Seems we had a habit of locking people out."

"Oh." She turned abruptly, heading for the restroom. He thought he heard a softly spoken "may she rest in peace," but he wasn't sure.

Sam plugged in his cell phone and went looking for clothes. The downstairs bedroom belonged to Dad. It hadn't changed in fifty years. Sam fingered the well-worn, leather Bible that rested on the nightstand. Funny, but Mom's Bible occupied a spot similar to Rosa's. Both wanted the Word of God within reach. Mom had read a chapter each night. She'd made it through the whole book that way. Took her more than seven years. His dad claimed to be using her method now. During their infrequent phone calls, Elmer would often mention where he was.

Sam thought about his own Bible. Where was it? The last time he remembered opening it had been for a reading he'd given at his mother's funeral.

He hadn't entered the church since. To his way of thinking, women always seemed to be able to find more comfort in the Word than men.

No, that wasn't true. Elmer had always known where his Bible was and often turned the pages. And Darnell, Sam's brother, a perfect oldest son, had at one time wanted to be a minister.

Sam was the only one who could be termed a hit-and-miss Christian.

The prodigal son who never returned home.

It was Rosa's fault all these memories were coming back. Most criminals who toted Bibles did it for show. Not Rosa, she actually bowed her head and obviously opened her Bible.

Sam left the Bible alone and went to the closet. Inside were neatly labeled boxes, most by his mother's hand. His father's scrawl marked the top three. Sam grabbed the one labeled "Clothes."

Unfortunately, what was on top wasn't clothes but a quilt. It was the one she'd made especially for Sam. She loved to quilt, though she seldom had the time. While Elmer and the boys had explored the ridge,

Anna quilted. She gave her finished products away more often than not, but not this one. Sam stared at the green square in the middle. It was all that was left of his favorite childhood blanket.

He carefully removed it from the box. A smell unique to long-forgotten clothes wafted upward. Sam ignored it. What would fit Rosa Cagnalia? And what was she willing to wear? Anna leaned toward cotton nightgowns and flannel shirts. Sam chose both, plus a pair of sweatpants and a robe. Then he headed for his dad's room and a thick pair of socks. The shower sputtered on.

In that moment, Sam wondered if he'd done the right thing back at the gas station. After connecting with Ruth, he'd dug out the quarters and as promised called Mitch Williams, the officer he'd dealt with every time.

Mitch *hadn't* been surprised to hear from Sam, *hadn't* been surprised to hear what Cliff was involved in, *hadn't* been surprised at the Santellis connection. Instead, Mitch said he'd have the brothers picked up, put a tail on Cliff, and told Sam to hang low, keep Rosa alive and talk to no one.

Very unusual.

Maybe Sam should turn Rosa over to the feds, no matter what Mitch said.

No, Sam was doing the right thing. If there was one thing he knew about Mitch, it was that the man was usually in the thick of — if not in charge of — whatever needed doing.

The aged floorboards creaked as Sam stepped in front of the bathroom. He laid the clothes on the carpet by the door.

A moment later, two cans of chili filled a pot. The gas stove perked to life as Sam turned it on high. He set the table and poured two glasses of milk. The shower still whined. He felt a pang of worry, but the window in that bathroom wasn't big enough for a cat to squeeze through.

He was going to have to tell her about her cat.

Pulling his dad's portable phone from its cradle, Sam stepped out the back door and leaned against a no longer used outhouse. He needed, no *wanted,* to call Ruth. She was his contact back in Gila City and if everything went haywire, she's the one Cliff would be after. She needed to watch her back. She needed to be forewarned.

Ruth answered on the first ring. "Where are you now?"

"Better you don't know."

"It's a mess here. Henry's got second-degree burns by the way. Have you been listening to the news?"

"No."

A rabbit peeked around the outhouse, took one look at Sam, twitched its nose and ran.

Ruth was talking again. ". . . at least three states."

"What? What did you say?"

"Rosa's been spotted in New Mexico, California, and Utah, all in the last hour."

Sam brushed a hand through his hair, feeling the dampness of snow. As tired as he was, it almost hurt to breathe, or maybe it was the whole situation, getting to him. "She's also safely taking a shower not twenty feet from me."

EIGHT

The gray sweats were about two sizes too big. Rosa had breathing room to spare in the musty garment. The worn flannel shirt was so thin it no longer offered warmth. Rosa wore two.

The socks, now, were perfect and warm.

"Rosa." She said the name slowly to the smudged mirror, then nodded. It felt good to admit to being Rosa again. The shower had been half blessing, half nightmare, as she strove to keep the spray from touching bruised and/or torn flesh: a difficult task since almost every inch of her bore some evidence of her three-day ordeal. The burns, at least, amounted to nothing. Her hands still trembled, and one bore the circular welt from the handcuffs. Her shoulder was a swollen lump of torn flesh and bruises were forming. Oh, well. She was alive. She was out of Gila City. And, for the moment, she was safe.

Safe with Sam Packard?

"I'm Rosa. I'm safe. *Thank you, Father.*" This time the words were almost calming.

Rosa tied the rope belt to an off-pink, furry robe. A quick check of the medicine cabinet failed to turn up any type of lotion for her skin, unless Old Spice was a contender. Cracking open the bathroom door, she paused. No sound came from the cabin. Was she alone?

"Officer Packard?" She spoke softly, not really wanting an answer. Not really knowing what she did want. Stepping out of the bathroom, she picked at the robe, rubbing the soft cotton between her fingers nervously and took a good look at her current prison: a well-made cabin that during any other place or time would be a picturesque retreat.

This two-story structure of rough-hewn planks reeked of comfort. Hand-painted studies of flower arrangements hung lopsided on every wall. Rosa stepped closer to note the artist's signature: Anna Packard, Sam's mother. Gingham curtains, the orange of the seventies, covered the windows. Intrigued, Rosa looked down. Green shag carpeting! Against her will, she dug her toes in and allowed a smile.

The rare moment of peace of mind was

interrupted by the smell of burning chili. She followed her nose to the kitchen: a single woman's dream. It was a room so small you could clean it without changing positions. The microwave oven took up all of one counter, leaving just enough room for an ambitious man to make a peanut butter and jelly sandwich.

After turning off the gas, she took a quick look into a freezer full of frozen dinners and a refrigerator crammed with milk, sodas, sandwich meat, bread and jelly. No, this kitchen was not a single *woman's* dream, but a *man's*. It definitely needed a woman's touch.

The open back door invited a chilly breeze. Rosa's toes curled against the cold. From where she stood, she could see Sam Packard clearly. He was a good five or six yards from the house and talking on a phone. Since his lost juice hours ago, or so he'd claimed, it must belong to the cabin.

One of Sam's hands gestured wildly in the air. So, once again, he was irritated at whoever was on the other end.

She could slam the door and lock it! She glanced back at the table that took up over a third of the living room. No car keys there. *Run.*

She couldn't even muster the energy to

get excited about the prospect. Then, there was her raw and seeping shoulder wound.

Stay?

If she ran, she would need money. Guilt prickled as she briefly considered where Sam kept his wallet? Unsure if she was making the right choice or not, and pretty sure his wallet was in his back pocket — too far away for temptation — she ladled slightly burnt chili into two orange, Tupperware bowls.

He had already poured two glasses of milk. Milk? If the cabin had milk, it meant someone lived here on a regular basis.

She took crackers from the cupboard and found spoons tossed carelessly in a drawer under the microwave. Then, after setting the table, Rosa stepped to the back door. Sam still spoke, make that argued, into the phone.

Carefully, she took one step out into the snow. The creak from the door sent a rabbit scurrying for safety. Sam broke off his conversation and said, "You're going to catch cold." He pointed at her foot.

Her sock was ridiculously white against the surrounding snow. They hadn't been cold until he brought up the possibility. "The chili's ready."

"Yum." His hand opened the door wide,

gripped her shoulder — the good one — and guided her back inside and to the table.

"Who were you talking to?"

"A friend. Now eat. Your stomach's been growling for more than two hours."

"We can eat and talk at the same time."

"Sounds good to me." He replaced his dad's phone, casually took a seat, finished his milk before picking up the spoon and spent the entire time looking at Rosa.

He certainly had presence. He dominated the room.

Rosa said her silent prayer, reminding God where she was and what she needed.

After she raised her head, Sam stared at her uncomfortably. The prayer had obviously disconcerted him. Good, it gave her a moment to enjoy the chili before he bombarded her with questions. Finally, she asked, "Why are you helping me?"

"I want to know what you know."

"It will hurt you more than you can imagine."

They ate in silence for a few minutes. Rosa stood, went to the kitchen and refilled her bowl. Sam didn't move to follow. When she returned, he shook his head and said, "You left Jimmy on the floor of that apartment, bleeding."

"I couldn't help him."

"How do you know?"

"I'm a nurse —"

"No, a nurse wouldn't leave a dying patient."

"He wasn't a patient, and he wasn't dying. He was already dead."

He blanched. "He was still your friend. So, tell me, why did Tony Santellis throw you down the mine shaft? Why did Cliff hand you over to be thrown down that shaft?"

Rosa took a bite, tried not to taste it and swallowed. The chili had a blackened flavor, sort of a misplaced New Orleans attempt at flavoring.

He finished his chili and carried his bowl back to the kitchen, returning with a stack of papers which he spread on the table.

"Ruth and I have pieced together quite a bit of your life."

She swallowed another chunk of chili and choked back a cough. Her high school graduation photo was on top, spread out next to the one of her and Eric on his father's yacht.

No more pretending to eat. Burnt chili on an already upset stomach was too much. "You're right. That's me."

"What made you hook up with Eric again?"

"I knew him from the time I was a kid."

"I'm specifically talking about after you were twenty-three."

She blinked; she couldn't help it. He knew too much, but then again, he knew too little. "I was working the emergency room at Good Samaritan. He came in with a broken arm. I was on duty."

"And you just took up where you left off?"

"No, not really. A lot had changed after my family moved out of the neighborhood."

Sam settled back in his chair, one hand wrapped about the empty milk glass. "So, Eric Santellis passed through your emergency room and suddenly you no longer date —" Sam shuffled through his papers, found the one he wanted and continued "— Michael Long."

"It wasn't that simple."

"That's an understatement."

"Eric wasn't, isn't, like the other Santellises."

"Oh, and that's why he's serving twenty to life in Florence Penitentiary?"

Rosa finished her milk and stood up. The chili was a giant lump in her stomach, and nausea returned.

Sam didn't move. He held up another one of the papers and looked at her expectantly.

Leaning forward, Rosa took the paper. She

scanned it, and then spread the rest of the papers out on the table, selecting one. "You spent a lot of time on me, didn't ya?"

"Yes."

"Because of what I did, or didn't do, when Jimmy was shot?"

"Yes."

She gripped the piece of paper and then pointed it at him emphasizing every word. "How many of these deal with Jimmy?"

"He's mentioned quite a few times in documents relating to you."

"But only in documents relating to me?"

Sam nodded.

Rosa placed the paper back with the pile, smoothed it out and tried to make it past her fear. There was so much to say, so much to do.

Why did her hero have to be Cliff's ex-partner?

Why!

"I suggest you research Jimmy as carefully as you think you've researched me. Maybe use his alias, Jimmy Harms. Then, come to me with your questions."

"Alias? Jimmy had an alias?"

"Yes." She was telling him more than she meant to. She was telling him more than she'd told anyone else.

"Why should I believe you?"

"Because I'm telling you the truth."

"You're connected to a member of a crime family."

"I *was* connected to *one* person biologically linked to a crime family, and that doesn't make me a criminal."

"No, but making off with more than half a million dollars in drug money certainly did."

"Yes, I'm a thief," she admitted. "But we were talking about Jimmy, not me."

"I'm willing to talk about you. Why have you been hiding in Gila City for the last six months?"

"Looking for evidence." She swallowed. She'd just crossed a line, a most dangerous line. Telling Sam she'd been gathering evidence was one thing, admitting the evidence concerned his ex-partner was quite another. Of course, if he'd followed her from the police station, he'd seen Cliff Handley. He'd seen his ex-partner hand her over to die.

"If you're not connected to the Santellis family, not really a *criminal,* then why are you afraid to talk to me?"

"Chew on this, Sam Packard. You figured out I reconnected with Eric in the emergency room, right?"

He nodded, carefully, the anger in his eyes

disappearing.

"Guess who brought him in?"

"I don't know. Who?"

"His good friend Jimmy Handley."

She saw the last of the anger swoosh out of him, so fast he sat down. A shiver went up her spine as she recognized that he was contemplating listening to her, *believing* her.

Believing the truth.

"You mean his good friend Jimmy Harms. You said Jimmy used an alias. Eric wouldn't know that. He wouldn't know Jimmy's real name."

"Oh, yes, he did. Just like I did."

The fingers circling her wrist loosened. She yanked her arm away and then flinched, as sharp pain shot through her shoulder.

Raw emotion, bordering on tears, highlighted her next words. "I am not a criminal, but I trust criminals about as much as I trust the police. Figure that one out! Now, where do I sleep?"

"You can sleep after I take care of your shoulder." He gathered their bowls and carried them to the kitchen.

Rosa tried to turn her head enough to assess her shoulder's damage. "It's all right. It's long past the point where stitches were necessary. I cleaned it thoroughly while I showered."

"It's still seeping, and the simple maneuver of you eating chili irritated it. It needs stitches, and you know it." He disappeared into the room next to the bathroom. A moment later, he returned with a sewing basket. "What color?"

"I'm not going to like this." Rosa hesitantly took a spool of white thread.

Sam picked out a needle and went back into the bathroom. Rosa could hear the water running. Then, he headed for the kitchen before returning to her with a bottle of rubbing alcohol tucked under his arm. "Thread broke so I'm using dental floss."

Rosa bit her lip. "I can't believe I'm letting you do this."

"You obviously can't see the full scope of the damage." Sam handed her the bottle.

She poured some of the alcohol into a glass and took the needle from him and immersed it. After a moment, he took it back from her and threaded it. His fingers were huge, yet the endeavor took him little to no time.

"Hmm, you're pretty good at that. Sew much?"

"I used to thread needles for my mother all the time. Bare your shoulder."

"First, you need to take a match and heat

the end of that needle."

Sam nodded, found an old lighter in what must have been a junk drawer, and followed her directions. Then, he dipped the needle in the alcohol again. A moment later his fingers were warm on her cold flesh and without thinking she flinched.

"Scared?" he asked.

"Yes," she admitted, but didn't add that his touch unnerved her.

"I think you'll only need about five stitches."

The prick of the needle pierced through her like a bee sting. Rosa pitched forward and hit her forehead on the table.

"Great," Sam said. "Now, you'll have another bruise."

"What's one more?" She tried to joke. Inside, she recited God's commands: *Do not be afraid . . . Do not be terrified . . . Do not be fainthearted . . . Do not tremble . . . Do not be troubled . . .*

After the first penetration, the needle didn't feel quite so sharp. Sam worked quickly and neatly. He was tying a knot before her hands started shaking. He set the needle on the table in front of her and went back to the kitchen. A moment later, Rosa heard the telltale sounds of their dishes being done. Who would suspect that Officer

Friendly would know the right time to leave a woman alone?

She closed her eyes, willing herself to be strong. Finally, she calmed down enough to take one of the folders from the pile of papers. Before she could open it, she felt him behind her. Still giving her space, he checked the back door's lock and then turned off the kitchen light. She pushed the folder away.

He moved beside her. "Do you need something for the burns?"

"I took care of them while I showered."

What she'd done, he hadn't a clue, but they already were fading, and so was she. "We're both exhausted. It's time to get some sleep. I'm giving you my room —"

"I'll take the couch."

"Yeah, right," he said wryly as he helped her to her feet. "You'll take the couch that is so conveniently located near the front door. No, I don't think so. It's my room, and I'm sure you understand why I have to handcuff you?"

"You've got to be kidding."

"I don't want to handcuff you, Rosa. But, you'll run, and I need to sleep, too." His hand was a hot spot on her back, guiding her toward the stairs.

"Don't rush me." She tripped over the

narrow bottom step. His hand left her back and took her elbow.

She stumbled, attempting to get away.

His fingers imprinted proprietorship against the soft skin of her arm. Her body tingled, but surely that was the side effect from the earlier too-hot shower reviving a too-tired body. Opening her mouth, she started to protest, but he interrupted.

"Rosa, I'm letting go of your arm now. Try not to fall down the stairs."

She stomped the rest of the way up the stairs. Her steps resounded in the quiet cabin.

"Scaring the ghosts away, Rosa?" The words fell against her ears. He was entirely too close.

Her mistake was in looking at him. His hair was still slightly damp from the winter's snow. A bead of moisture glimmered on his brow. He grinned, as if reading her thoughts and liking that they were about him. Brown eyes stared deeply into her own until she had to blink.

"I've got nothing to say to you," she snapped.

He stepped around her as if she were an ordinary guest. Pushing open a door, he swept an arm out. "Welcome to Hotel Packard."

The bedroom had a sharply sloping roof. Rosa took two steps in, and then halted as the sloped, planked ceiling met the top of her hair.

It was obviously the bedroom of his childhood. Baseball trophies littered the top of a scarred dresser. *Star Wars* posters stared down from the ceiling. A family portrait was shoved among more trophies cluttering a shelf. A few books, dog-eared and yellow, threatened to spill over and onto the floor. His bedroom? No way did she want to sleep here. "Why are you doing this?"

For a moment she thought he wasn't going to answer. Then slowly he admitted, "I found the envelope, Rosa. You're investigating Cliff, and for some reason, it looks like he deserves to be investigated. Until we figure out who else is involved, we're not sure who to trust."

Whoa. He'd found the envelope in the bushes. And instead of turning her in, instead of letting her die, he'd taken her to his private residence and was asking questions.

She opened her mouth. Dare she tell him. Instead, she asked her own questions. "We? Who is we?"

"Ruth Atkins, she frisked you remember? I'll bet you know the Santellises are suspected in her husband's disappearance. Right now she's trying to put together the connection between Cliff and you, Jimmy and you, *anybody* and you. I'll call her in a moment and fill her in about the emergency room. She's one of the few people I trust who might be able to figure out what is going on."

"Will she come here?"

"No." He rubbed his forehead. "She's sticking close to Cliff. According to the press, you've been spotted in three states so far."

"Huh?"

"To the world, you're an escaped convict. I'm glad you're being sighted in all these locales. As far as I know, no one knows you're with me except Ruth and my friend Mitch Williams. He's internal affairs, Rosa, and, at the moment, one of the few I trust. It's time for you to start trusting me, Rosa. Think about it — Cliff and the Santellis brothers *think* you're disposed of, they *think* they're safe. What better time to bring them down?"

He moved closer, his hair just a breath away from the ceiling. "What's really going on, Rosa? Why does all the paperwork you've gathered make Cliff look like a bad guy?"

Rosa sat on the bed, thought better of it and stood. He'd asked the question she'd never expected to hear from a cop, let alone Cliff's ex-partner.

Indecision turned to fear. She'd worked alone for so long. "You'd never believe me."

His face contorted as if a myriad of thoughts were battling for dominance. His forehead smoothed. He must have reached a decision. "I'll believe you."

Maybe, thought Rosa, she'd have been more willing to trust him if she hadn't seen a framed photo of Sam and Cliff — each laughing and clutching some sort of citation — sitting on an ancient turntable downstairs.

The lights were all turned off. Sam checked the doors, twice. She'd changed into one of his mother's old, flowered nightgowns, and then he'd handcuffed her to the headboard.

He'd just handcuffed a woman to a bed.

In all his years of law enforcement he'd never done anything so distasteful, so wrong.

Cliff should be the one handcuffed.

Sam wouldn't sleep a wink tonight. Not only would he worry she'd find some way to escape, but he'd also feel guilty about keeping her prisoner.

Well, she was his prisoner.

Did he have any other choice? Without the handcuffs, she'd leave. He'd declared his willingness to believe her. What more did she want?

This woman bothered him. Just like Walter Peabody. Again memories of the death row inmate surfaced. Maybe because Peabody died with a secret? Maybe because it looked like Rosa would do the same thing?

No, he didn't believe that. He went back up the stairs and paused by her door. He couldn't hear her breathing. He waited a few moments then slowly pushed open the door.

"I knew I couldn't trust you." She looked uncomfortable and wide-awake. "How am I supposed to sleep?" Grumpy didn't begin to describe her tone.

Protective custody seemed an oxymoron with her. The discarded robe slid to the floor as he settled himself on the hard, leather chest that still housed board games and action figures, as well as a few more Mommade quilts.

His mother would have loved Rosa Cagnalia, would have loved her stubbornness, would have loved how the woman slipped into silent prayers at the oddest times, would have loved her resourcefulness, would have loved that Sam had apparently met his match.

While they'd been eating the chili, Sam had been struck by the similarities between Anna and Rosa. Both were strong women, who protected what they considered theirs. Sitting across from Rosa, at the rickety table his mother had found at a garage sale, Sam had been taken back in time. How often had he sat in that exact chair, across from his mother, and dined on burned chili.

He couldn't afford to dwell on the past for too long. Rosa required *all* his attention. He didn't trust her. She slid her legs under the quilt on his bed. Sam leaned forward and straightened the bunched-up part by her feet.

She pulled her feet back. "You can go now."

"You said you weren't going to be able to sleep."

"That doesn't mean I want company."

With a toss of her head, she scrunched down and turned her face away.

Sam left. Already this woman made him want things he had no business wanting.

The aroma of bacon and eggs wafted up the stairs. Rosa's right eye opened, and she stared across the bed. *The nightmare contin-*

166

ues. She started to turn over but remembered the handcuffs. She'd awakened plenty of times during the night wanting to turn but held firm by the restriction, her shoulder stiff and cramping.

Wait.

She was on her stomach and comfortable.

He'd removed the cuffs. A fresh pair of sweats and a T-shirt lay on the chest next to the robe. She put them on.

Sam Packard had found the folder, read the contents and maybe believed what he saw.

As she hurried down the stairs, she both dreaded and looked forward to their morning conversation.

"Hope you like them scrambled." The voice that greeted her didn't belong to Sam, but there was no mistaking this elderly man. He belonged here. And while it was obvious that featurewise Sam took after his mother, Rosa could see the strength handed down from one generation to the next. It was in the set of the shoulders, the way the men held their heads, the size of their hands.

He set a skillet on a tabletop doily and held out a hand. "Elmer Packard. If you tell me what you like to eat, I'll see about getting it. I took the cuffs off you, but don't tell Sam."

167

"Thanks." She shook his hand.

He nodded toward a folder that lay in the seat of an antique rocking chair. "I've glanced through some of the papers about you. I agree with my son. Something doesn't smell right."

Actually, his breakfast smelled pretty good.

"Sam had to go to work. I'm pretty sure he'll be back this evening or early tomorrow morning. I'm supposed to guard you. I put a new toothbrush for you in the bathroom. Sam would never think to get ya one. Today's newspaper is on the table. You might want to look through it. You got lots of attention."

Running her tongue across her teeth, she decided she'd brush her teeth now before breakfast, then again after breakfast, and maybe a few more times later on just for effect.

Once she'd scrubbed on the pearly whites long enough to bring blood, Rosa returned to the living room, pulled out a chair and stared at the front page. The picture of her and Eric standing on the bow of a boat stared back at her. The bottom of page one highlighted her relationship with Eric and her presence at the murder of Jimmy Handley. A recent prison photo of Eric showed a much heavier man than she remembered.

His shared gene pool with Tony had never been clearer.

The lead story centered on her arrest, her escape and the recent death of her family, complete with their photos.

She'd not allowed herself to read about their deaths. She'd relied on the radio because she couldn't bear to see the family photos that might accompany a sensationalized story.

Tony Santellis rated coverage, too. They'd blown up a recent mug shot. Another photo, looking suspiciously like a driver's license, made Tony look like the thug he was. They'd even dug up an old Little League photo of him. He looked like a normal, little kid. Her dad had been his T-ball coach.

Nausea rose in her throat.

Funny, Rosa's dad had seen promise in Tony. Said the boy could be a major league player. Instead, Tony sold drugs, and Rosa's big brother purchased them. Respect for Rosa's dad hadn't overcome Tony's love of power and money.

And still, Tony had respected her father because of T-ball.

The newspaper trembled in Rosa's grip. She despised Eric's family. She'd despised them ever since her brother, Frank, died and she heard her mother crying every single night after they buried him.

But nothing compared to the last year while she blamed them for the murder of the rest of her family.

The difference in the way she felt had to do with her new faith. Leviticus, chapter 19, clearly stated:

Do not hate your brother in your heart.

Hard not to hate Cliff and Tony.

Do not seek revenge or bear a grudge against one of your people.

Could Cliff and Tony be considered one of "her" people?

"I'd kill you bad, Rosa, but Mary asked me not to."

She'd made a mistake. Like the media, she'd blamed Tony for the murders, but Tony wouldn't have killed her father. Tony had a warped sense of honor. He'd thrown her down a shaft so that he could claim clean hands to his sister. He'd done it because, in his own way, he loved his sister.

Tony had history with her father. He'd not have killed so brutally.

"Sir," she finally said.

"Call me Elmer."

"Do you have a Bible?"

It was more than twenty years old, yellow where it had once been white, and with extremely small print.

Rosa went to her favorite chapter in Psalms, for if Leviticus had added more guilt to an already guilt-ridden heart, then the book of Psalms had been her redemption.

Listen to my cry for help, my King and my God, for to you I pray. In the morning, O Lord, you hear my voice; in the morning I lay my requests before you and wait in expectation.

The minister at the church in Gila City said that often when men prayed for help and the Lord provided that help, for some reason the men who prayed refused to accept the help. Rothchild was the preacher's name, and he'd been one of the faithful sent to Louisiana after Katrina hit. Members of his church had donated money to help rebuild the homes of fellow Christians. And Rothchild had difficulty getting the Louisiana Christians to accept the money because they figured others might need it more.

Finally, Rothchild would ask them, "Did

you pray to God for help?"

"Yes," a Louisiana Christian would admit.

"Then he's sent help. Now take it!"

Maybe she should take the help Sam offered. It was just so hard to fathom that Cliff's ex-partner was the answer to her prayers.

"Did you find the comfort you needed?"

Rosa almost ripped a delicate page of Sam's mother's Bible when Elmer's question jarred her back to the present.

"What?"

"I said did you find the comfort you needed?"

"Yes, I found what I needed."

"Did you love him?" Elmer tapped on the newspaper image of Eric.

"No, not the way you think."

"Then don't waste your sighs."

Rosa looked up. A trick question? "He's not a murderer."

"A jury of his peers decided he was."

"Define peers."

"Honest, hardworking citizens who take time off from work to look at the pros and cons of a situation."

Rosa bit back a senseless retort. No doubt this man believed in justice. No doubt he was an honest, hardworking citizen.

He had no clue he was a minority.

Rosa couldn't remember the last time she'd viewed the world through rose-colored glasses. She closed the Bible and focused again on the newspaper. Turning the page, she found her high school graduation photo. Some enterprising young reporter had gotten quotes from her classmates. People whose names meant nothing and whose faces she couldn't recall gave statements implying that she'd turned away from their offered friendship. That sounded right. The whole family was still dealing with Frank's death while she'd been going to high school.

A boy she'd never met had a quote about a supposed date.

"The press feeds on a good story," Elmer remarked.

"It's not the first time my life's been turned into fiction."

Elmer sat at the table and ladled salsa onto his eggs. He motioned for her to sit down. "Eat."

She found ketchup in the refrigerator. She preferred her eggs that way. Elmer chuckled and cleaned his plate even faster than Sam had the previous evening.

The eggs stuck in Rosa's throat.

"Would you rather have cereal?" Elmer started to get up.

Rosa closed her eyes and shook her head.

She doubted this man would understand it if she told him eggs weren't the problem.

"The pictures brought it back, huh?"

She opened her eyes. "What?"

"Your family. The way I figure, you didn't dare go to the funeral."

"No, I couldn't go."

"I lost my wife a few years ago." Elmer stood and walked over to the turntable. He picked up the picture that stood next to the one of Cliff and Sam. "She was Navajo. She took such pride in clan. Knew her people from both parents to grandparents and beyond. Bitter Water, Coyote Pass, her connection to the Navajo clans all meant something to her. Sam speaks it like he was born to it. Me, I never could master it. Neither could my oldest boy, Dar. Anna got the arthritis. It bound up her fingers until they were so gnarled she couldn't hold a fork, turn the pages of a book, or quilt. I think she wished herself away."

"I'm sorry."

"We had a good life. Dar tells me to get married again, but I don't want to. Besides, I like living here, and it's too far away from them shopping malls for most women."

"I like it."

"Yeah, that makes sense. You remind me of Anna. She was always so independent."

Elmer downed the last drop of coffee. "You're not going to try to leave, are you?"

"Yes, after I do the dishes."

"I can't let you."

"You can't stop me." Surprised, she looked at her plate. She'd eaten every bite, and nothing lodged in her throat. He'd managed to distract her with stories of his Anna. Quickly she gathered the dishes. He took the newspaper in his hands and smiled when she refilled his coffee cup.

The water pressure was low. Rosa whisked her hands through the lukewarm liquid trying to get the soap to bubble. The red welt that circled her right wrist objected to even that minute of contact. Her shoulder throbbed at the movement.

Ten minutes later she stood at the kitchen door. She'd taken a coat that had obviously seen better days and found a pair of boots that must have belonged to Anna.

"I really can't let you go out there." Elmer came to stand beside her. "Please, come into the living room. We'll play Scrabble."

"I don't have time to play Scrabble."

Elmer shook his head. "Sam told me you'd do this. I can't take care of you if you go stomping through Ellison Creek in the snow. Now, take off Anna's boots, and we'll find something to do until Sam gets back.

Oh, and by the way, he told me to remind you he believes you."

NINE

Captain Hull sat at a wooden table in the briefing room and waited for the noise to die down. Rosa was the topic of the day. Sam had been bombarded with questions by both the feds and by his friends. There didn't appear to be a cop in the room who didn't credit the Santellises with the escape. Sam leaned his head against the back wall and closed his eyes. There wasn't a word to describe the type of tiredness he felt.

Last night, he'd checked on Rosa four times. He couldn't sleep; he was so worried she'd somehow escape. After his dad finally got home, he'd also picked up on the worry and was soon right there with him, hovering at the bedroom door.

Rosa managed a lot of movement considering she had a wrist handcuffed to the headboard. Rosa, it appeared, did as much running in her sleep as she did in life.

If only, he thought, he could get a handle

on the right and wrong of the case. He would protect Rosa, with his life, if he knew what the *right* was. It was that off chance that he was *wrong* and thus part of the problem, not the solution, that troubled him.

His gut feeling told him he was doing right but never before had his gut feeling been contrary to the opinions of *so* many others. And, never before had he involved his father. Elmer had almost been excited at being asked to help.

Sam opened his eyes. It took him a moment to reenter the reality of the morning briefing. He focused on the captain, who didn't look happy — not that he ever did.

He'd really be unhappy when he found out the truth about Cliff. When had Cliff changed sides? Sam wanted to believe it happened after Jimmy's death. Cliff refused counseling and eventually his marriage broke up. If only Cliff had returned to Gila City right after Jimmy's death, Sam could have done something, lent an ear, something.

Prayed?

There'd been a time in Sam's life when he would have prayed for Cliff. And obviously the need for intervention had been well before Jimmy's death — probably had been needed about the time of Walter Peabody's death.

Well, the briefing room wasn't the place to catch up on sleep, meandering thoughts, or how much the sight of Rosa in deep prayer bothered him. Sam listened as the captain banged on the table and read the latest bulletins.

Captain Hull brought the room to attention. "Sam, you with us?"

"Sorry, Captain."

A moment later, Hull dismissed them, except for Sam. Chairs scooted into one another as the other officers prepared to begin their duties. The hum of activity seemed too normal. Never had Sam felt so alienated from the occupation he loved.

Hull waited until everyone left the room and walked over to Sam. "Lot of strange things happening, and now doesn't seem to be the time to loan you out, but I'm told I have no choice. Tamir has requested an interpreter."

Sam had been loaned out to Tamir, Arizona, before. The small town nestled at the Utah border near Canyon de Chelly and every once in a while they butted heads with the tribal council. Tamir's entire police force was a two-man operation; neither spoke Navajo.

Sam nodded. "A change will do me good right now."

Good old middle-of-nowhere Tamir. Two years ago Sam had signed on for a day that turned into two weeks. That investigation took place mostly on horseback. Who knew how long this assignment would be, especially since it would have nothing to do with Tamir.

Mitch had arranged this. On the phone last night, he'd said he'd take care of freeing Sam up. It was perfect and would infuriate the feds to no end. While they didn't want to include him in their investigation, they did want him at their disposal.

"Okay, clear your desk. Give Atkins anything pressing. They want you in the morning." The captain squinted. "And get some sleep. I don't want them complaining that you were next to worthless."

Sam went to his office by way of the restroom. The reflection in the mirror proved the captain right. Sam looked like a street bum. Splashing water on his face, he tried to shake the feeling life as he knew it was about to change.

Ruth sat in Sam's office, and she'd already cleared his desk of everything they'd been working on when he took off after Rosa. She blinked owlishly and glanced at her watch. "I've never been so scared in my life. What are we doing? What am I still doing here and on my day off?"

She answered her own question. "Working on a case that might end my career and/or solve my husband's murder."

Before he could respond, she held up her hand. "Don't say it. You were right. I've been up all night going over this stuff. Your friend Mitch Williams was here. He's a wealth of information. I'm more than impressed with IA. We, I should say, he, dug up some real details about Jimmy. Did you know that he'd been handpicked by the DEA to go undercover? Apparently, he was quite good at fitting in, squirreling out informants and finding ringleaders."

"Which is why he was at Terrance Jackle's, under the name of Jimmy Harms."

"You knew already!" Ruth went indignant.

"I just found out. And, he worked alongside Eric Santellis."

"Yes," Ruth said slowly. "With Eric and Rosa both. I've spent some time researching Eric, too. You know, if it weren't for the fact that he's Yano's son, and brother to the rest of those yahoos, there's really little to nothing about him. To think I've spent all these years blaming him for Dustin's death. You gotta read some of this, Sam. I never thought I'd feel compassion for a Santellis but talk about being railroaded. Eric Santellis didn't stand a chance. Then, there's Cliff. He has a lot of money, Sam. A lot."

"Well, he always talked about investing."

"If he'd made the money by investments, I don't think he'd have accounts in the Cayman Islands or so many properties titled in his wife and daughter's name."

"He's involving Susan and Katie? How'd you find all this?" Sam felt the beginning of a dull headache. It was true, all true, everything Rosa had put together, starting with Walter Peabody.

"Your friend Mitch again. We spent most of the evening here. Another guy was there with us, some kind of computer guru. Sure impressed me. It took him about six hours, but we've linked Cliff to more than two millions dollars in various accounts, various locations."

Sam nodded. "What next?"

"After our phone conversation, Mitch and I made a list of people to interview. Our goal is to link Cliff and Tony. Mitch is in Phoenix trying to figure out who the two cops who helped Cliff are."

"And, where do I start?"

"Wanda Peabody is still in town. Maybe she can tell you why Rosa is so fascinated with Walter's execution. Then, I'd say either Mary Graham —"

"Eric's sister?"

"You got it. Then, Cliff's ex-wife."

"Oh, man. Visit Susan? I think I'd rather visit a Santellis."

"Look, what to do is simple. Visit Wanda on the way out of town. Then, visit Susan. She bought a house in Phoenix two years ago, just after she divorced Cliff. Mary Graham lives somewhat in the same area. Visit both of them, it doesn't matter what order, then detour through Florence and question Eric."

"You think Eric will talk to me?"

"I've already called Billy. He'll set it up."

Billy, Dustin's brother, was a guard at Florence. No doubt Ruth had hinted that this might help them find out what happened to Dustin.

"I think Eric will talk to you once you tell him that you have Rosa."

"I'll do it."

Ruth picked up a box filled with printouts, yellow tablets and records. "I think what I hate most is that I'm stuck here trying to pretend it's a normal day when I most want to be helping you. Man, I've been awake all night, watching the news, reading the reports, doing Mitch's bidding and realizing just how much information is, well, quite frankly, ridiculous. Then, Cliff shows up this morning, the captain's barking as if he were a terrier denied a bone, and you're re-assigned to Tamir."

Ruth shoved the box of papers into his hands. "You were on the force during Walt Peabody's case, what happened?"

"He killed two cops," Sam said the words slowly. "Cliff broke the case and made his career."

Atkins picked up her purse and took a couple of steps toward the door before turning. "You know, I've been on the force now almost six months, and this is the first time I've felt like I'm making a difference."

Sam could only nod in agreement before asking, "Could you give me a ride to the Exxon station? I need to pick up my truck and get out of here."

Scrabble, with Elmer Packard, was more a mind quest than a game. Rosa challenged his words twice and both times he won.

"You know," she said. "It's safer for everyone if I leave."

Elmer didn't respond, so Rosa continued, "Do you know who I *really* am? What I've supposedly done?"

"Yep, I read the newspapers."

Rosa rubbed another smooth tile. "You know about Eric?"

"I know all about the Santellises. They've been dealing in Gila City for fifty years. Back when I was a young man, I ran into the father a bit more than I wanted."

"How well do you know Yano?"

"Not well at all. First time I met him, wife and I were just getting started. I was a fireman, but I drove a delivery truck on my off hours. Anything to earn money. I met Yano Santellis at a company picnic."

"What did you think?"

Elmer chuckled. "I thought he was young. And I thought he was a smooth talker."

"When I met him," Rosa said, "he was old, but he was still a smooth talker."

"Why did you stop being a nurse?"

"You're as bad as Sam with the questions."

"Having you here is a bit of excitement."

Rosa put the final *T* to the word trust and added a measly four points to her score. She stared at the word. *Trust.* Maybe it was time to trust Sam. She'd start small. "I stopped being a nurse the day I stole half a million dollars in drug money. I became a fugitive. How can I get in touch with Sam?"

"He told me not to contact him unless it's an emergency."

"This is an emergency." Rosa scooted her chair back and stood up. It was all gone. All the control, all the careful planning. She'd messed up more than once, the red Mustang just a small part of it. "Look . . ." She turned, trying to figure out how this man worked.

He waited patiently. Liberty Cab would welcome him with open arms. He'd make a great cab driver. He liked small talk; he exuded trustworthiness and safety. And, there was his penchant for games. The cab drivers played checkers, cards, all kinds of games between shifts. Rosa had kept her distance. Sitting across from a coworker was too ripe an opportunity for some tidbit of information to slip.

"Look," she repeated. "If you let me make a phone call, I promise not to try to escape."

The older man smoothed imaginary hair and Rosa smiled. Her own father had often stood in front of a mirror rearranging strands. Her mother had kissed his bald head and joked about only so many perfect heads and the rest needing hair.

"I have your word." Elmer's fatherly stare made Rosa long for her father.

"My word."

Elmer pushed away from the table with both hands. His movements were slow and precise as if he wanted to give her time to change her mind, or to at least think about what she was promising.

He pulled a cell phone out of a desk drawer and punched in a number before handing it to her.

It rang four times before Sam answered. Rosa didn't waste time with a greeting. "Where are you?"

"How did you get this number?"

"Are you in Gila City?"

The question must have surprised him, for he answered, "Yes."

"Sam, I need you to go by my trailer and get —"

"Rosa." His words were soft, different from the irritated man who'd answered the phone. "Rosa, you no longer have a trailer."

"I know it's been cordoned off. But you're a police officer, surely they will let —"

"No, Rosa. You literally no longer have a trailer."

"Wait!" Rosa grasped the phone. It was small and didn't fit in her hand as easily as a phone should. "What am I missing here?" He was trying to tell her something. Something she didn't want to hear.

"I should have told you, but things were happening so fast. Someone blew up your trailer day before yesterday."

She felt her teeth go together, tight, hurting. She felt air fill her throat and hot tears pool in her eyes. She blinked them away.

"Rosa, are you okay?"

Sam was loud, his voice coming over the phone like a frantic radio announcer. "Are you crying?"

Rosa cleared her throat. It had been a while since she'd cried, and she certainly didn't want to cry in front of — make that on the phone with — him. He'd never understand what Go Away meant to her. "What happened? Why?"

"What happened?" His tone went back to brisk. "What could have been in that mobile home to make someone feel threatened enough to blow it up?"

The tightening of her throat almost turned into a tickle, a tickle of a laugh. Who would want to blow up her trailer? Who didn't? Her allegiance belonged to neither side of the law, which meant the only safe haven might possibly be a black hole in outer space.

"Rosa? I'm sorry about your trailer. No one was hurt."

"Why would anyone be hurt?"

"Your neighbor was outside when it blew —"

Seth? That creep. The slimeball who

moseyed over to talk to her when his girl-friend wasn't home. The slimeball who had held a lighter to Go Away's ear. She had him as number ten on her prayer list. The sad thing was he was most likely to reform.

"Were you there?"

"Yeah, I was on surveillance."

"You were watching over my trailer?"

"Yes."

"Like you're watching over me?"

He faltered. "Ah, yes."

"And while you were watching my trailer, it blew up?"

"Look —" he sounded more than annoyed "— it's not like you had turned it into a home or anything. It was just a place to hide out. The only sign of life in that tin can was a bag of makeup. Tell me I'm wrong."

The only sign of life! Her teeth hurt again. "They can blow up anything they want. You're right, I hated that cheesy trailer. But, Go Away was there!"

"Your cat." He didn't ask a question; it was more statement. "Rosa, your cat is not dead."

She clutched the phone so hard she accidentally hit the off button. Without missing a stroke, she activated Redial. "Are you sure?"

"I was there. I saw your cat outside.

Before the explosion."

It was clear the man thought she was nuts. She could hear it in his voice. He couldn't know, couldn't understand, that one little cat represented all that remained of family life to her.

"You saw my cat outside?" Rosa closed her eyes. "Where's he at now? The Humane Society?" She visualized Go Away in a cage. No one would adopt Go Away. He was ugly now, thanks to Seth.

"I don't know what happened to your cat. There were a few other major happenings that night. I radioed 911. I got to Seth. The feds arrived. The cat disappeared."

"You go find her."

She had to give him credit; he didn't laugh, although she figured he thought about it.

"I don't have time to get your cat. I've got a few stops to make before I come get you."

"Sam, I can promise you this. If you don't get my cat, you'll never hear the truth from me."

"Be real. Who do you think is in charge here?"

"And while you're at it, check out my car." Rosa smiled. She knew who was in charge. It was whoever pushed the off button on the phone first.

■ ■ ■ ■

Sam was so mad he could have cheerfully tossed the cell phone out the window. The last thing he'd heard was his dad laughing in the background.

She'd won his dad over.

Elmer spent too much time alone. Sam needed to find time to go fishing with his dad or something. Maybe Dar wasn't around as often as Sam thought.

Get her cat.

Check out her car.

Women!

One bit of good news, his Ford 250 sounded great. Larry's Exxon had gotten rid of the clicking sound in the transmission. Sam pulled off to the side of the road and rummaged through the files that Ruth had given him.

The depositions from her coworkers at the cab company were on top. The feds had handled the interviews. The general consensus indicated that Rosa was a good worker who said very little. No one had been invited to her home. No one knew about her family, real or make-believe. Her coworkers all said Rosa was a nice girl and couldn't possibly be involved in a murder.

The mobile home park manager admitted entering her trailer once to check on the swamp cooler. The man compared Rosa's "home" to a motel room: every piece of furniture in its place and impersonal. In his mind, she was the perfect tenant because he figured that when she moved her mobile home was rent ready.

Not now.

The man also mentioned how he'd had to stop a fight between Rosa and her next-door neighbor. An altercation over that silly cat. Still, the landlord seemed to think Rosa a victim not an instigator.

Most of her neighbors said she waved at them but didn't stop to chat. If they initiated conversation, she obliged but seldom acted enthused. They all said she was a nice girl and couldn't possibly be involved in a murder.

Her next-door neighbors, Seth and his girlfriend, who offered considerably shorter depositions than her coworkers, thought she was snobby and a troublemaker. No doubt Seth didn't like it that his overtures weren't appreciated, didn't like it when she made such a fuss that everyone in the trailer park knew he'd maimed a defenseless cat.

No doubt the girlfriend didn't like it that Seth made overtures.

It occurred to him as he parked in front of what remained of Rosa's trailer that he should have gotten some sort of carrier or at least a leash. Did cats go on a leash? He'd been raised in a dog family. Dogs served a purpose.

Already the debris had been swept up but cordon tape still blocked off the entrance. Sam gave a lingering glance at his truck's leather upholstery and frowned. One claw mark, and the cat was dead.

"Hey!" The lady from next door hurried out her torn screen door. Limp blond hair fell to her shoulders. A yellow sundress covered a body that begged for exercise. "I wanted to thank you for what you did for Seth."

"You're welcome."

"You looking for something?"

"The cat."

"I heard about Lucy going down. All this time I've been living next to a criminal." The woman gave an exaggerated shudder. "I told Seth she was trouble."

"Have you seen the cat?" Sam bent down and peered beneath the skirting.

"She's under there."

"How do I get her out?"

"Climb under."

Sam gave the woman a tight smile he

hoped signaled that he wanted her to go away. Instead she followed him to his truck.

"I'll call you if she comes out," the woman offered, "or I can call the Humane Society."

"Great." He got behind the wheel. The woman took the hint and went back inside. Grabbing the cell phone he called the cabin. "Get Rosa to the phone, Dad."

She came but the only proof he had that she was on the other end was a faint breathing. And she was a woman who knew how to insert anger into her faint breathing.

"Rosa, I'm giving you one minute to tell me how to get your cat out from under the trailer, and then I'm giving up."

"You're at my trailer?"

"I'm at what's left of your trailer — your cat is under that."

"Get a can of cat food."

"What?"

"Go to the store and get a can of cat food. Make sure it has a pop-off lid. Try to figure out roughly where Go Away is, then hunker down and open the can. Go Away will hear the lid pop off, she'll know it's food, and she'll come to you."

A few minutes later, he discovered that cat food cost almost as much as motor oil at the convenience store.

Back at the trailer, the woman next door

sat on the front porch smoking a cigarette. She offered him one but didn't offer to help get the cat.

Rosa was right. The pop-off lid had barely left the can before a cat's nose pushed its way into Sam's palm. Sam wiped a dribble of fish-scented gunk off his hand, scooped the cat and can up, and hauled them to his car. Content to be carried while dining, the cat didn't resist.

Dog food didn't smell this bad.

He laid the cat food on the back floorboard — hoping it wouldn't spill — and set the cat near the can of food and covered them both with a box he'd found near the trailer's debris. There, that wasn't so hard.

"That box ain't gonna keep the cat." The woman next door was at his elbow. Cigarette smoke overpowered the cat food.

"Thanks." He ignored her knowing smile. He'd caught the cat without any problem. The hard part was over. There wasn't that much room on the back floorboard, but the cat should be just fine.

Sam pulled out and headed toward the freeway. It wasn't even noon yet. He could fit in all the interviews today.

As Sam headed toward Wanda Peabody's nearby trailer park, he felt the first indication that Rosa's neighbor was right. The box hit the roof, bounced off Sam's head, and tumbled upside-down onto the front floor-board. Go Away climbed over the seat, squatted on the passenger side and glared. The strong smell of cat food wafted throughout the vehicle.

Sam's hand shot out, to knock the cat to the floor, but cats didn't knock nearly as well as dogs. Sam pulled and was rewarded with the discovery that cats, unlike dogs, could stretch with the ease of a Slinky. Go Away clutched at the leather with the strength of a mountain climber. Just as Sam was visualizing rolling down the window, Go Away let go. Sam almost took his eyes off the road, but managed to keep Go Away's head from exploring the steering wheel. Cat hair flew, as if magnetized, toward his nose and mouth. "Listen, cat, I *will* throw you out the window."

Go Away turned her body around, with her tail standing straight up in what must be a well-known insulted cat gesture.

YEOWLLLLLLLLLL. ERYEO-WLLLLLLLLLLLLL WOOOWOOOO-WOOOOWOOOO.

The cat's body performed what could only be termed extreme yoga followed by loud gags, and then the cat food smell was back, stronger than when he'd opened the can.

Only the vision of crossing three lanes of traffic and winding up on a stretcher, kept Sam from seeking out the proof of what he suspected. The vision didn't keep him from grabbing his cell.

Elmer answered the phone.

Rosa came on breathlessly. "Is Go Away all right?"

"Cats have nine lives, how many are left on this one?"

"What?"

"Your cat threw up in *my* truck."

"Oh, poor baby. I should have warned you. She gets carsick, especially if she's just eaten. Any minute now she'll crawl beside you and fall asleep."

As if lured by her owner's words, Go Away jumped up on the seat, stretched out, and with her chin on Sam's knee stared apologetically at the owner of the truck with cat vomit on the floor.

Sam hit the off button this time. Go Away burrowed her nose into the crease of his pants and laid a paw across his knee.

It was because the cat didn't feel good, Sam told himself as he scratched a furry forehead. "And don't think I forgive you, either," Sam told the cat. "Or your mama."

TEN

Using a handful of brown paper towels taken from the men's room of a convenience store located just down the road from Wanda Peabody's place, Sam cleaned up the mess. "You know, *cat,* I told Rosa I was bringing you home. I didn't say alive."

Twenty minutes later, Sam finally made it to Wanda's trailer. While Rosa had lived in motel room sparseness, Wanda more or less lived in what looked like a shed overflowing with collectibles.

Funny how the vision of the woman had stayed so firmly in his mind all these years. Although slender, Walter's wife had preferred the tentlike dresses that reminded Sam of a circus fat lady, one who had seen too much and liked too little. In some ways, it was like Wanda wanted to hide.

What had Wanda said, that last time Sam spoke with her? *Walt didn't kill those men. But he fessed up to it. If he didn't, he faced a worse fate.*

That was it exactly, and Sam had wondered what fate could be worse than death.

He still wondered but figured the woman sequestered at his family's cabin knew the answer to that. Maybe even *lived* the answer to that.

Sam glanced at the piece of paper Ruth had given him with Wanda's address on it and wondered if this had been the Peabody address back when Walter was alive. Sam picked his way across a cracked sidewalk. Walt had owned the gas station he worked at. Surely their circumstances had been better. What had it been? Walt had been executed fourteen years ago, arrested seventeen years ago.

She opened the door before he could locate the doorbell.

"It ain't working," Wanda announced.

She'd aged since he'd last seen her. Well, hadn't they all. What he remembered most is that she and her daughter had been alone in Walt's defense. It looked as if she was still alone although looking past her he could see a dog sleeping on an old, green couch and a family picture of herself, Walter and their daughter. She'd run away during the trial, and as far as Sam knew, hadn't been heard of since.

"I'm Samu—"

"I know who you are."

"I'd like to —"

"You're the idiot who arrested Rosa." She slammed the door.

The Big Bad Wolf wouldn't even need to take a deep breath to cause this structure to tumble.

Sam simply knocked *again.*

"Go away or I'll call the cops."

He raised his hand to knock again, but instead yelled, "I am a cop!"

The declaration had no effect. Wanda still didn't open her door. Sam raised his fist; he'd knocked on more doors than he could count. It was a silence that stopped him. It was early afternoon, and there should be noise. Looking around, he saw that he'd been noticed. An elderly couple stood in their driveway, staring. A teenager on a bike had stopped on the sidewalk, far enough away to escape, close enough to draw a picture. Now was not the time to draw attention to his interest in Wanda Peabody.

So, he'd go away, and, he thought wryly, come again another day.

The cat slept the whole time Sam maneuvered the interstate and then navigated through Phoenix neighborhoods consisting of carbon copy stucco houses. Susan Handley's house reminded him of their home in Gila City with the children's bikes and swing sets. Odd, since Cliff had no grandchildren.

According to neighbors, Susan Handley and her daughter, Katie, had only lived in the house a month before moving on. None of them knew Cliff.

A few minutes later, Sam stood in the yard of another dead end. Mary Graham's house was missing the child's bike and swing set that should have been in the yard. Instead of toys, newspapers huddled around the front step like black-and-white fish come to a feeding. If Mary's house was any indication of how the Santellises took care of their sister, then she had been disowned. The house badly needed painting. The grass was brown. Mary Graham's next-door neighbor closed her front curtains before Sam even got out of the car.

Interesting that the two women — so far removed from each other in both lifestyles and family — were both missing. They were on different sides of the law but connected to the same enemy. The thought of who the enemy might be left a bitter taste in Sam's mouth.

It was time to move on. Besides, he had left Rosa with his father far too long. She was something, this Rosa, he thought wryly. If she weren't the prime suspect — a supposedly missing prime suspect — in an ongoing murder investigation, he'd be more than interested in her as a woman. Sam took a small notepad from his front pocket and made a note to stop off at Kmart and pick her up some clothes that fit.

Oh, and he needed to buy cat food.

Spilled orange juice from two years ago, maybe? Rosa dipped the dishrag into warm, soapy water and scrubbed at the bottom of the refrigerator and tried to convince herself she was doing the right thing. Elmer slept on the couch, a frown marring his pleasant features. Snores accompanied her cleaning spree. He'd serenaded her cleaning through two bedrooms, a bathroom, and now as she tackled the kitchen. Apparently, the Packard men counted dusting and mopping as lost arts. Pine scent permeated the cabin. Rosa preferred lemon, but settled for the only cleanser Elmer owned. At least she hadn't had to settle for Old Spice. The refrigerator wasn't a lost cause, only a few pieces of bread sported green spots, and the vegetable drawer was empty except for sticky ooze, which she'd scoured until her fingers turned red.

Then, the snores were accompanied by a sharp banging. Rosa paused, her hand gripping the wet rag. The front door! Would there ever come a day when fear wasn't a constant companion? She closed her eyes.

Already, they were here already?

She opened her eyes. *Her gun, she wanted her gun.*

Clutching the wet rag as if it were a lifeline, Rosa crept to the living room. If it weren't for Elmer, she'd hightail it outside and disappear into the forest. But no way could the old man face her demons and survive.

She looked for a place to hide. Could she fit under the sink? She inched toward the back door, barefoot, with a spoon substituting for a lethal weapon.

Elmer woke up just as snow blew in, followed by the two white-haired people who didn't wait for an invitation. After a harried moment of foot stamping and palm rubbing, the neighbors burst out with, "Everything all right? You said you wouldn't be here this week. We saw the smoke from the fireplace and got worried."

Elmer grinned and massaged his head. "Had some things come up." All eyes turned to Rosa. The neighbors smiled expectantly.

Silence, she could cut with the spoon, followed.

"Todd and Tanya Dundee," Elmer introduced, "This is Lucy . . . Lucy Packard." He cleared his throat. "Sam's new wife."

"Sam got married! When?"

"Last week." Mischief replaced hesitation, and Elmer's voice grew louder. "Very spur of the moment."

Conversation exploded. Elmer didn't invite the neighbors to stay, but they didn't need the encouragement. Without a moment's hesitation the front door slammed shut, coats were shed, and gloves removed. Rosa backed up. These people were touchers.

"I can't believe we weren't invited to the wedding. My goodness, after Michelle, I thought Sam had given up on women. I'm Tanya Dundee. Todd, just look at her. You a police officer, too? You look like one."

"Now, Tanya, slow down. Sam done real good." Todd smiled approvingly. "How did you two meet?"

"Oh, Sam started chasing after me the moment we met," Rosa offered, the lump in her throat growing thicker. "I've only known him a short while. We're figuring things out as we go."

Todd nodded. "I met Tanya at a Dime-A-

Dance. Married her the following night. Spent the next four years overseas. Spent the last fifty years trying to figure things out. You two will have fun."

"Where is Sam?" Tanya peered over Rosa's shoulder into the kitchen.

"He had to work."

"You mean over in Gila City, they can't give a man a couple of weeks off for a honeymoon. I know the mayor, I could call —"

"They're going to honeymoon. Sam just needed to tie up a few loose ends." Elmer was back to massaging his head.

"That boy works too much," Tanya said. "Especially since his mother died. You're the answer to so many prayers."

Great, thought Rosa, settling down on the couch for what looked to be a lengthy visit. *They think a lie is the answer to their prayers.*

An hour later, back on the interstate and fighting drowsiness, Sam digested that there hadn't been one minute of peace since he'd arrested Rosa. Even when he had her out of sight, she penetrated his thoughts with the finesse of a pit bull.

Would this quest of his end a perfectly good law enforcement career? And he was doing it all because of something he saw in a woman's eyes? Not just any woman, either. Rosa Cagnalia. Maybe Sam should just pin a Kick Me sign to his back and get it over with.

His thoughts hadn't improved by the time he arrived at the Arizona State Prison in Florence. It had been more than a year since Sam had set foot on the premises, but nothing had changed. Miles of fence, designed not to keep nature out, but to keep inmates in, marred the landscape. Built in the early 1900s, Florence had changed decor and politics more than once.

Parking in a reserved space, Sam stepped down on pavement and headed toward the last name on his to-do list and probably the only one he'd actually get to talk to.

Eric Santellis, prisoner number 255253, hadn't been incarcerated long enough to earn many privileges. And, as a convicted cop killer, he wasn't likely to be anybody's favorite. But as a Santellis, he would at least be safe from falling victim to an unfortunate accident or unexplained suicide.

One thing for sure, Eric Santellis wouldn't appreciate this unorthodox visit from the Gila City officer who'd brought down Rosa Cagnalia. He'd be annoyed, suspicious and probably angry. Getting him to talk would be a challenge, but Sam had no choice.

What Rosa didn't know or couldn't tell, this man knew and *could* tell.

He was doing life. He had nothing to lose.

Of course, Eric and Rosa had known each other for years. They'd been childhood friends and adult more-than-friends. He'd probably been the one to teach Rosa how to talk in circles.

Now Sam didn't have time to dance. He needed answers.

Ruth's brother-in-law, Billy, led Sam into an empty room — more like a corridor — with empty rows of chairs facing glass partitions.

"Fifteen minutes," Billy warned. "Any longer and someone will notice him gone."

Choosing a seat in the middle of the room, Sam waited for his introduction to Eric Santellis. It took only a moment for the hair on the back of his neck to prickle. He hated prisons. Pulling a notepad from his top pocket, he jotted down his questions. Nothing came to mind. After a few seconds he pushed the small notepad aside. He couldn't concentrate. Prisons were never quiet, yet today the visiting room was, and the silence was heavy with the ghosts of prisoners past. Every other time Sam had been in a visiting room, it had been hustling with the voices of lawyers, wives, girlfriends.

Sweat and perfume battling with gloom. And always there'd been a feeling of lost hope in the room — a room where real life intercepted prison life, only for a moment, and then the moment was lost.

Like the prisoner was lost.

Like Eric Santellis was lost.

But not so lost that he didn't need leg and arm chains. Not so lost that the room didn't explode with the sounds of a prison guard dealing with an unwilling prisoner.

The Eric who stood on the boat with Rosa was gone. His slender build had morphed into a shape Hulk Hogan would approve of. A prison-earned scar twisted like the Gila River down the side of his face. And his angry expression sent a tangible "Get lost" message.

Sam picked up the phone and waited for Eric to do the same. When the inmate didn't, Sam mouthed, "I'm Sam Pac—"

Eric's expression didn't change. Intent on intimidation, he stared at Sam until Sam almost smiled. Eric and Rosa were quite a pair.

Billy shrugged, pulled a sandwich from his pocket and moved away. A prisoner's privacy was a court-issued right. For the first time, Sam appreciated the courtesy.

Sam pointed. "Pick up the phone." Duh,

as if Eric didn't know what a phone looked like. Sam hadn't expected Eric to lay out a welcome mat, but, well, he'd expected some sort of response. Truth to tell, with all that was going on, Sam had entered the prison with little or no game plan. Gut instinct had been the mode of operation for this case from the beginning.

"Pick up the phone, for Rosa."

Sam had expected to get some sort of re-action out of her name, but Eric didn't budge.

"For her cat?" Sam meant it in half jest. A last-ditch effort playing a card not really part of the deck.

Eric blinked and his lips pressed together disapprovingly. Hatred transfixed his angry expression. Slowly, he picked up the phone but didn't say anything.

"I'm Sam Packa—"

"I know who you are."

Great, thanks to this case everyone and their mother knew who Sam Packard was. He was the idiot cop who'd arrested Rosa.

"Oh, good, then —"

"You're Cliff Handley's partner."

"Ex-partner."

Eric snorted.

Sam lowered his voice. "What I am now is Rosa's only hope."

If Sam had blinked, he'd have missed the haunted look that flickered in Eric's eyes. It happened that fast. Prison choked human kindness from the best of men, and since the best of men seldom went to prison, fate had to work doubly hard to wring emotion from the soul of a convict.

According to Rosa, Eric had been an exception in the Santellis clan. Even Ruth was inclined to believe it. Sam felt a stirring in his gut. Maybe Rosa was right. Because while Eric, who now looked like his father and brothers, had the ability to wither a foe with just a stare, what he couldn't seem to do was keep his hands from shaking.

As if sensing Sam's thoughts, Eric stretched his fingers slowly, as if trying to gets the kinks out. "Why did you say *her cat?*" Eric lips moved, but his body remained like granite. His voice was as deep as Tony's, but he didn't clip his words as his brother did.

"I have Go Away in my truck."

"Go Away? Rosa's cat's not named Go Away."

"Yes, the cat's name is Go Away. I picked her up this morning. Rosa's mobile home blew up, and the cat needed to be captured." Sam had Eric's attention now. The man still sat ramrod straight but every nuance of his body posture shouted tension. "Eric, when did you last speak to Rosa?"

No answer.

"Okay," Sam said. "We can both sit here playing games, or we can start a conversation. I'll go first. Three days ago, in Gila City, I stopped Rosa for speeding. When she tried to flee the scene, after your brothers tried to shoot her, I —"

"Wasn't my brothers," Eric interrupted.

Sam continued as if Eric hadn't spoken "— arrested her. It quickly became obvious she was using an alias. Lucy. Does that mean anything to you?"

Eric didn't respond, and Sam rushed on. "When I took her in for questioning, the trouble continued. First, we couldn't identify her right away because her fingerprints were smudged, then Cliff Handley —"

"Your partner," Eric interrupted.

"Ex-partner," Sam reminded.

"Sounds like you're the reason Rosa's going to be dead soon." Eric leaned forward.

Sam had always understood the need for a partition between a prisoner and the public, but he'd never *personally* felt grateful for the glass.

"No." Sam leaned forward, too, and whispered. "No, I'm the reason she's safe, *for now.*"

If hope were a tangible emotion, Eric's whole demeanor changed with it. Glancing at Billy, Eric leaned forward, this time a willing participant in a no-win conspiracy. "What do you mean safe for now?"

Sam stared past Eric, at the clock nearing six, at the backside of the guard still eating his sandwich, and peripherally at the prisoner so frustrated he about came off his chair.

"Tell me what you mean?" Eric repeated.

"I mean that yesterday morning I followed Rosa after Cliff Handley and two others broke her out of jail. Imagine my surprise when Cliff turned her over to your brother."

"Tony?" A look that surpassed worry crossed Eric's face. "Tony has her?"

"Had her. Now I have her."

Eric sat stock-still, staring at Sam as if daring him to go on.

"I'm telling the truth!"

"Hah! A cop *who speaks the truth.*"

Sam might have been angry had anyone else made the accusation, but Eric's last three words had not only been slowly spoken, they'd gotten progressively softer.

"You've known a cop who told the truth, haven't you, Eric?"

"Prove that Rosa's still alive."

"Jimmy Handley, *the cop,* was your friend,

wasn't he?"

"Yes. Now, prove that Rosa's still alive."

With Billy's help, Sam had managed to keep his cell phone. Praying the battery had enough juice for a quick call, Sam dialed his father's number. It took only a moment for Elmer to put Rosa on the phone. Glancing at Billy, Sam quickly held the phone up to his connection with Eric.

"Did you hear her?"

"I heard somebody."

"What are you doing?" Rosa hissed, loud enough for Sam to hear, but not loud enough for Eric to hear.

"Trying to find answers."

"You'll get Eric killed. Leave him alone!"

"You left me no choice, Rosa. You want to know where all I've been this morning. First I went to Wanda Peabody's — she called me an idiot. Then, I went to Cliff's ex-wife — she's disappeared. Finally, I stopped by your friend Mary Graham's house — no one's home and hasn't been for weeks if not months."

"Did you tell Eric that Tony is involved?"

"Yes."

"Idiot! You have no idea what you've done."

She might have rambled on, but he interrupted, "Me, an idiot! Well, then, I'm an

213

idiot risking everything, Rosa. Everything. My job, my friends, and all for a woman I think is innocent. But what I think doesn't matter because you won't talk to me."

A strange sound filled the room. It took a moment for Sam to identify the source. Eric Santellis's laugh barely sounded human. A pounding interrupted Sam's conversation. Eric rapped his knuckles on the Plexiglas. "Hang up the phone," he mouthed.

Sam hit the off button and put the phone back on his belt.

It almost immediately buzzed with an incoming call.

Leaning back, Eric looked Sam over much the same way a father should a potential suitor. "Tell me how Rosa wound up hiding with the partner of the man she should be hiding from?"

"I pulled her out of an abandoned mine yesterday morning."

"Who put her there?"

"Physically, your brother Tony. Theoretically, Cliff Handley."

Eric's hands stopped shaking. He clutched the phone and tightened his lips. "What do you want?"

"You're surprised that Tony put her down an abandoned mine?" Sam noted.

"What do you want?" Eric repeated.

"Who killed Jimmy?"

"I was facing the wrong way. The bullet sounded, I turned around, but there were too many people and it seemed all of them had guns."

"But Rosa saw."

"She did. I'll never forget how white she turned and how scared she was. I told her to run."

"Why didn't you run?"

"I'm a Santellis. There's always someone watching me."

Sam frowned. Eric was right.

"Okay, tell me what Rosa doesn't know. Tell me about Cliff."

"What are you going to do with the information?"

Sam paused. It would be so easy to say, *Put the people responsible behind bars, free you, free Rosa.* But at the moment, that seemed a distant possibility. Honesty seemed the best choice. "All I can do is add to the information Rosa and I have already gathered."

"Rosa and you? I thought she wouldn't talk."

"When I picked Rosa up, she had an envelope. Everything in it had to do with Cliff."

Eric didn't look convinced so Sam contin-

215

ued. "I've turned most of what I have over to Internal Affairs. Before we can accuse Cliff, we have to have enough proof to counter any doubt."

"You're trying to bring down Cliff?" Eric asked. The next words were more of a sneer, "You *were* his partner."

"I'm a cop, I'm supposed —"

"Cliff was a cop, too, and you're a cop working on your own dime. That only happens in books and on television. What's in it for you?"

No wonder Rosa and Eric were drawn together. Neither could answer a straight question. And Sam wasn't sure what to say. He'd been forcing the whys and what-ifs to the back of his mind since Rosa's kidnapping.

"I was Cliff's partner way back in my rookie days. There was this man, Walter Peabody. I didn't know enough back then to question why so many things felt wrong. I went to his execution. I remember the look in his wife's eyes. If the evidence Rosa's starting to put together can be proven, then the wife had a right to hate us, hate the good guys."

"Anything else?" Eric asked.

Rosa, Sam thought but didn't say.

Eric smiled, almost as if he could read

Sam's mind. "Yeah, she's gotten to you. She got to me before I was old enough to know better. You keep Rosa alive or I'm coming after you."

"I'd lay down my life for her."

Billy Atkins coughed. It wasn't because of a cold. Sam knew his time had to end. "Come on, Eric, give me something."

Billy coughed again.

Eric stood. "You need to leave, for Rosa's sake. The longer I talk to you the more likely it is that my brothers will find out. There are no secrets in jail."

ELEVEN

Rosa pushed herself out of the chair and set aside the Bible. She'd been reading Psalms, trying to come to terms with trusting the Lord, trusting Sam. She'd focused in on the fifty-sixth Psalm.

> Be merciful to me, O God, for men hotly pursue me; all day long they press their attack. My slanderers pursue me all day long; many are attacking me in their pride. When I am afraid, I will trust you. In God, whose word I praise. In God I trust; I will not be afraid. What can mortal man do to me?

It was as if God were directing his message directly at her. With that thought, she'd fallen into the best sleep she'd had in years.

And how long had she been asleep? Not long enough, she decided, checking the still-smoldering fire.

Even with the clean pine scent wafting through the room, the smell of maleness made Rosa pause. It was all too familiar and comforting: all too foreign and forgotten.

She missed her brother and tripping over his dirty laundry on the floor. She missed her father who had also favored Old Spice. She missed her mother who had purchased the cologne every Christmas and who never complained about picking laundry off the living room floor. Some of which had been Rosa's.

The headlights cast a glow in the front window and Rosa jumped up, turned off the light, and for a moment, terror tightened around her heart.

Who was out there?

She wasn't safe! Not while she had to depend on strangers. Not while she had to wait for others to let her know what was going on. She ran to the window and got behind the curtain. Was it Sam outside? She assumed it was Sam, but what if it wasn't? Could that old man snoring upstairs be any kind of a bodyguard? And, without her gun . . . Oh, if not for the snow, and her cat, she'd have left hours ago.

Elmer was too trusting. Why had she listened to him? Where was *his* gun?

The curtain brushed against her face. Fat

lot of good peeking out did. She couldn't see a thing, and now there was no more time. Whoever was coming in turned the doorknob. She wrapped the curtain around her and wondered what to do with her feet.

The door opened with a creak that only came with age. Whoever it was, he was a silent man. That could be Sam. The living room light went on.

Dare she look?

"What are you doing?" His textured steel voice always sounded accusing.

Rosa looked up, angry at the fear that had her clenching her fists and grinding her teeth. "I wasn't sure it was you."

"Oh, sorry. We probably should work out a signal."

"That would be nice." Rosa watched as he reached outside to pick up a box. Edging around the couch, she peered in. "Go Away!" The cat was out of the box and cradled like a baby before Sam had time to move. "I was so worried. Did Officer Friendly feed you?" She shot Sam a questioning look.

Sam finished bringing in gifts from outside. This time he retrieved a bulky basket and asked, "What's this?"

"I have no clue."

Sam tore open the card. He read it silently,

and then shot Rosa a startled glance. "It says Congratulations. For what?" He turned the card over and read slowly, " 'Here's to a long, uninterrupted honeymoon.' "

The card fell to the floor. The basket almost followed, but Sam managed to put it down a bit more carefully. "Rosa, you didn't tell the neighbors that you're married to my dad, did you?"

"No, I'm not that clueless."

"So, then what does this mean?"

"Actually, it was your dad's idea."

Sam sat on the couch, his legs sprawled forward and one hand idly strumming his forehead's frown lines. Snow dripped from his shoes and puddled on the clean floor.

He didn't look like a cop now.

The heat from the fireplace intensified. All this time she'd assured herself she wasn't attracted. She had been fooling herself. Why did he have to be a cop? And on top of everything else, she had the feeling that he'd just read her mind . . . and liked what he saw.

He feels it, too.

She turned away before he damaged any more defenses.

His voice sounded strange, half chuckle, half disbelief. "Well, are you going to tell me about the congratulations?"

"Thanks to your dad, the Dundees think I'm *your* wife." She wanted to be mad, but it was halfway funny. She was running from the cops and her best defense was pretending to be married to one.

When he didn't answer, she turned around. He still strummed his forehead, but now the frown was gone.

"They saw me. We had to think of something. It happened."

"It was a good idea. Sit down, Rosa." He sounded tired. She chose an old rocking chair. It was uncomfortable, but she relished the unyielding wood. It would keep her on guard; keep her from dwelling on the man behind the magnetic eyes, the man she was starting to rely on.

"I can't believe you went to see Eric! Are you nuts? You put him in danger. His brothers will find out!"

He kicked off his shoes, shed his coat and settled back in the couch. "His brothers have already been arrested." He made a face. "Except for Kenny. Seems he has no outstanding tickets, not even a parking ticket. And, you know, maybe if you were willing to talk, I wouldn't have to be jumping through all these hoops just to find a few answers."

He was right, but then, so was she.

He looked exhausted. Well, he had a right. Before she could say anything else, he looked around and inanely asked, "What did you do all day?"

"Read the newspaper, went over all the files you have on me, played Scrabble, wished you had an Internet connection and cleaned."

"Oh." The appraisal Sam gave the cabin suggested he didn't like it this clean. "Okay." Then, he settled down to business. "Mitch managed to arrange to loan me out to the Tamir police."

"Mitch? Tamir?"

"Years ago, I helped out in Tamir, a little town near the Utah border. They needed someone who spoke Navajo. I worked with them for two weeks. Mitch Williams is an Internal Affairs agent. At the moment, he and Ruth are the only people we can trust."

"You're going to Tamir?"

"No, it's a dummy assignment. My real assignment is you. Mitch is looking into Cliff's involvement in your abduction. So am I. Rosa, tell me what happened. And, why is Walter Peabody's name all over those papers you were carrying."

He acted as if it was simple. As if she could open her mouth, spill her guts, and all would be well. *Obviously* he had no clue whom the key players were or how many good guys had a price. *Obviously* he didn't get the gist of how long Cliff had been dirty.

Rosa had already trusted one cop. Cliff Handley's son Jimmy. He had been a good cop. That's what killed him. At least ten people were dead because she'd believed in the system, make that she, Eric and Jimmy had believed in the system. They'd forgotten that *both* sides of the law were controlled by men. Men who wanted money and power. Staring into Sam's eyes, she wondered what kind of a price tag would lure him.

She looked at him, really looked at him. He looked exhausted. He hadn't shaved, he was dirty, and he'd just told her that for two weeks, he was working with her.

With her.

Dare she hope he could really help?

Hope deferred makes the heart sick, but a longing fulfilled is a tree of life.

Now where had that verse come from? It wasn't one of her favorites. It wasn't even one she really understood. She'd been in Psalms all day working on building up a foundation of trust in Samuel Packard. Maybe she should have strayed over to

Proverbs and spent some time with hope.

"You're exactly what I need," she admitted.

"What?" He looked up, hope taking the place of exhaustion in his eyes.

"You're a credible witness. You can help me put Cliff away."

"I'll help you put Cliff away, but kidnapping, while a federal crime, isn't going to keep him behind bars for long."

"I don't want him to go to jail for kidnapping."

"Then what?"

She obviously didn't answer fast enough because Sam pressed his lips together so tightly his entire chin wrinkled and turned white. "What do you want him to go to jail for?"

He was off the couch before she could brace herself. The rocking chair tilted backward until Rosa thought she might fall, but his grip pulled the chair forward and her hands grabbed at his upper arms. Her eyes were even with his chin. Slowly she looked up, past the strong nose and high cheekbones. His eyes trapped her. She couldn't look away.

"I'm tired, Rosa. Tired of playing this game and tired of not knowing the rules." He smelled like wet snow, cat and male. The male overpowered everything else. It over-powered her.

She started to push him away, but the chair shuddered. She stopped moving, knowing that he kept her from falling. "I never asked you to play. What happens after your two-week dummy assignment is over? What happens to me?"

"Changing the subject, Rosa? You're good at that. I'll make a promise to you. The same promise I made to your friend Eric Santellis. I'll keep you alive." With all the finesse of a gentleman, he carefully positioned the chair so she no longer tilted.

He stood there and stared at her while Go Away — the Benedict Arnold — weaved around his legs. Finally, he backed off and went over to the couch.

She cleared her throat. He'd frightened her. Oh, not because she was physically afraid of him, more that she was afraid that he was the Joshua who could tumble the walls she'd so carefully erected. She grasped for a new subject, something safe. "How did Eric look? Sound?"

"He doesn't look like the guy on the yacht anymore. He's buff."

"Does he look like Tony?"

"Yes."

She couldn't help it. One side of her lip

curled at the thought. "How does he sound? Has he given up hope?"

He looked at her strangely. "I don't know. I couldn't tell."

"Did you tell him that I'm okay?"

"Yes."

"Good, I didn't mean for him to worry."

"He's worrying. Rosa, I'm worrying."

He pulled a small notebook from his pocket. "I spent all morning following leads — mostly dead ends. First thing in the morning, we're going to find Mary, Susan and Katie, and Wanda. I don't care in which order. Now, why don't you tell me about Cliff, about Jimmy, and about all this stuff you've gathered."

"And if I tell you, you'll believe me *and* keep me alive?"

"Yes."

"Tell me, why should I trust you to keep me alive when *you're* the one who put me in danger?"

"You were in danger of being picked up sooner or later. Just be glad I'm the one who pulled you over — I believe you, Rosa." He took a notebook out of his pocket. "Now tell me what you want Cliff arrested for."

"Dealing drugs."

He didn't even blink.

"You believe me," she whispered.

"Every word."

"I think I'll start at the beginning." She'd never shared the story before. She'd written it down. She had three safety deposit boxes scattered throughout Arizona, each with fake identification in case she needed a new life and each with an envelope containing a thirty-page explanation of the truth as she knew it. Each envelope was addressed to a major newspaper. Interspersed in the document were names and testimonies of the few others who had information on Cliff. If she died, Wanda Peabody was named as executor of each box. She had strict orders to mail the envelopes. Should something happen to Wanda, eventually a probate clerk would get involved, and Rosa could only pray that justice would be pursued. "My brother, Frank, died of a heroin overdose. Did you know that?"

"Yes, you were in seventh grade."

"My family fell apart. Dad knew Frank got the drugs from Tony, and, in his own way, Dad loved Tony. Frank and Tony had been good friends. They played T-ball together. Dad coached."

Sam nodded.

"On television, they make it look so easy. Cops come to your house, you tell them who the bad guys are, they investigate, and the bad guys go away, all in an hour's time."

"Doesn't work that way in real life," Sam admitted.

"We moved the day after Frank's funeral. Dad didn't want to stay in the same neighborhood as the Santellises. He wanted me away from Eric and Mary. And, he had been so vocal in blaming Tony that he became afraid that Tony would come after us."

"If Tony wanted to kill you, moving wouldn't have been enough," Sam said.

"No, and my dad knew that. I found out later, when I was older, that my dad also had a little chat with Yano, Tony's dad."

"I know who Yano is."

"I didn't see Eric again for almost fifteen years. I graduated high school, college, toured Europe, got a nursing degree and worked in the emergency room."

"And Eric showed up in your emergency room."

"He broke his arm playing baseball. He never was the athlete of the family, but he joined so that he could bring Jimmy onto the team. I found this out later when they recruited me to help them."

"Help them what?"

"Jimmy was Jimmy Handley, who was DEA, working undercover, trying to find the source of the drugs. Ironic, you know, that the dealer turned out to be his own father."

Rosa stopped talking. She could see how all this hurt Sam.

"They knew that I was the front line whenever anyone overdosed. I'd hear the ranting and raving. I'd hear the complaints and accusations from the families, girl-friends, boyfriends, cops. In an emergency room, people seem to forget that their every word is overheard. The ploy that I was dat-ing Eric Santellis again loosened the tongues even more."

"So the picture of you and him on the yacht, as a couple, was posed."

"And it broke my father's heart. I love Eric, like a brother. As for having a real relationship, Eric and I had, have, too much water under the bridge and hardly any of it clean. I admire him. He risked everything — the ire of his family. But he did it."

"Tell me about October thirteenth. Tell me about the night Jimmy died," Sam urged.

"We were at Terrance Jackle's apartment."

"He's dead."

Rosa nodded with resignation. "Isn't everyone? Anyway, at first everything was running smoothly. Our goal was to just home in on anyone we didn't recognize.

Eric, of course, seemed to know everybody. Jimmy had infiltrated quite a few gangs and was known. And I knew more of the players than you'd expect.

"We didn't even have time to do anything that night. We got there, I started to go hunt for the restroom, and the front door burst open. Tony and Sardi and another man."

Sam had stopped writing, captivated by her story. He believed her. He really believed her. "Strange that Jimmy was the only one to die that night," he said.

"That night," Rosa added softly and started laughing.

Maybe it wasn't healthy to laugh at the memory of watching a murder happen at your feet. Maybe it wasn't healthy to dwell on the fact that that first murder led to so many others, including her parents and younger brother, maybe it wasn't healthy but sometimes it was all that Rosa could do.

Because she was afraid if she allowed herself to cry, she would never be able to stop.

Sam didn't follow her up the stairs. No doubt tailing hysterically laughing women into bedrooms didn't fit in his job description.

TWELVE

If anyone deserved a meltdown, it was Rosa. She was wound up tighter than . . . Well, so tight he didn't know what to compare her to. She hadn't blinked when the duty officer smeared her thumb in black ink to take a print. She hadn't engaged in hysterics when Sam pulled her from a dusty, forgotten hole in the middle of nowhere. Then, again, Sam remembered the woman who sat so stiffly while he stitched her shoulder using only an old quilting needle and dental floss.

Problem was he didn't have *time* to wait for her to spill everything. She was quite a woman, this Rosa Cagnalia. Most women — oh, to be honest, most men — would have broken after going through all that Rosa had in the last few days. It seemed she prayed instead of cried.

At least she had an outlet.

He hadn't cried or prayed since his mother's death.

232

He'd also always considered himself quite a man, quite a police officer. He'd been wrong. Rosa, wanted by both sides of the law, knew more about justice than he did.

How could he convince her to fully trust him?

He almost considered praying about it.

Almost.

Mitch was doing all he could on his end: arranging for Sam's loan to Tamir, having the Santellis brothers jailed for outstanding tickets, looking for Cliff's accomplices, giving Ruth access to even more computer files than her clearance allowed and arranging for a meeting tomorrow at brunch.

She was finally talking, but not telling him everything — no, not by a long shot. Mitch could only do so much, and then Rosa needed to fully commit. Otherwise, they were spinning their wheels for nothing.

He adjusted the rocking chair again — more for something to do than need — and looked around. The house sparkled. It hadn't been this clean since his mother died. He thought back to the pristine mobile home. This must be what Rosa did to work off steam. Sam picked up a book from the floor. His mother's Bible. Well, he had caught Rosa praying more than once.

He'd been unable to understand a God

who would rob a family of the woman they so obviously needed, and they, *he,* had needed Anna.

Rosa had lost her entire family.

Sam started feeling a bit guilty. Maybe Rosa knew something he didn't or maybe she was a bigger person than he was.

He headed for the kitchen. Even the inside of the refrigerator sparkled, Sam noted, as he pulled out two sodas. Heading back to the living room, he paused by the bookcase to retrieve a photograph album and headed up the stairs.

From the first bedroom, he could hear his father's snores. He paused at the second bedroom, and although it felt strange, he knocked. Rosa didn't answer, but she hadn't locked the door.

"I brought you a soda." His voice echoed into the silence of the room. She'd been at work in here, too. A candle burned a cinnamon scent into the air. Flowered sheets replaced his old, reliable white ones.

Rosa didn't move but he could hear her breathing, and the sound told of wariness. She lay on the bed, uncovered, with her back to him. His mother's cotton robe fell in folds around her body.

He'd only known her four *long* days but he was starting to get used to having her around, worrying about her, working with her.

Sam didn't know what triggered his need to help Rosa. He hoped it had more to do with his belief that she was innocent than the fact that he couldn't get her out of his mind. A whisper inside his head warned him to run from this woman because each moment he spent with her cemented an attachment he couldn't deny. Yet, he couldn't run. She was the key witness to a string of crimes that might date back to the Walter Peabody execution.

Finding the truth left her vulnerable to unfavorable odds. Hiding the truth allowed corruption to pollute a system meant to protect.

A system he believed in.

Sam placed Rosa's soda on the table by the bed and sat on the same trunk as last night. "My brother and I loved coming here as children. There's a tree house in the back. Dad helped us build it when I was about seven. He had no more than pounded the last nail in, and I took a tumble down the ladder. Broke my leg in two places."

Her breathing calmed, and sensing her relaxation, Go Away curled into her side.

"Dad probably told you about Dar, my brother. He's two years older than me. We found tons of arrowheads and pieces of pottery in the woods. Dad put them into frames. They're at my house in Gila City. I've been offered major bucks for them, but I don't want to sell. I sometimes think those were the best days of my life. Dar used to —"

She still lay on her side, but now one eye peered at him suspiciously. "I want to go to sleep."

"No, you want to lie here and stew in fear, guilt and denial."

"What do you know?" She pushed herself up, sending the cat scurrying from the pillow.

"Fear, guilt and denial make bitter friends and lifelong enemies."

"What?" She squinted.

He flipped open the photograph album. "My mother started this on the day I was born. She'd already filled two with baby pictures of Dar. Did your mother keep photograph albums?"

"Yes."

"Where are they?"

"The pictures?"

"Yes."

"I don't know. Maybe the cops have them . . ." Her voice trailed off.

Sam continued, "Mom was a full-blooded

Navajo. You probably saw the pictures downstairs. Dad was doing construction in Chinle. She was one of the maids at his motel. He was staying there for two weeks. That's all it took. He married her, brought her back here, and they spent thirty-eight years together."

Rosa rolled over and pushed herself up and stared at him. Her eyes were unreadable. They reminded him of his mother's.

He could get lost in Rosa's eyes.

"Nice try," Rosa commented.

"What?" For a moment he thought she'd read his mind.

"You're trying to make me see you as a real person, instead of a cop."

"Cops are real people."

"I went to college, too. I'll bet we took some of the same psych classes, Mr. Psych Major."

"Let's not talk about the murder, let's talk about your family. It can't hurt."

"It can't hurt?" Her arms crossed against her chest. "How can it not hurt? My family is gone. Because of me."

"Why are you blaming yourself? You went into hiding to save them."

"Lot of good it did."

"I can help you put away the people who did this."

"I hope so. I certainly hope so."

For a few minutes, they sat in companionable silence.

Then, he said, "Tell me about when you first met Eric. You were, what, thirteen?"

"Twelve. His sister introduced us. Mary and I were in the same class since kindergarten. When we were in fifth grade, Sister Clara put our desks next to each other and we became best friends. Eric was a year behind us in school. I guess I started noticing him in fifth grade, and then that summer, before seventh grade, we started hanging out."

"Seventh grade, that's pretty young."

"We just did the mall, the roller-skating rink. You know, nothing serious."

"And then your family moved when you were in the middle of seventh grade after your brother died."

"Yes."

"And you didn't try to contact Eric after that?"

"No."

The gut feeling urged Sam to return to childhood questions; the cop feeling in him couldn't resist pressing her about his ex-partner. "When did you meet Cliff Handley?"

Withdrawal became a palpable presence.

Rosa leaned forward, meeting his gaze straight-on. Her eyes didn't blink. The smell of his dad's Ivory soap wafted over the candle scent. Rosa's half smile wasn't humorous. "How about, instead of me telling when I met Cliff Handley, you tell me how you could be a partner with this man and not know him at all."

This time, since she wasn't handcuffed, she locked the door. As if on cue, a phone shrilled, and she heard Sam clump down the stairs to pick it up.

So far she'd found two ways to annoy the cop. The first was her cat, but Rosa had the sneaking suspicion that Sam wasn't as opposed to cats as he let on.

The second was to let him know that he wasn't on top of things as much as he thought, but even that felt like a hollow victory.

She returned to bed, wishing she had Anna's Bible, wishing it were two years ago and she'd never agreed to Jimmy's and Eric's scheme to weed out Tony's connection to the drug cartel, wishing this whole mess was over, had never started because if Sam continued to believe her, continued to stick his nose where no one else dared, he could also get killed.

Her last thought before closing her eyes was that his believing in her was a controversial comfort.

A sharp rap on the door woke her up. Glancing at the red numbers glowing from his clock, she groaned at the early hour.

"Rosa," Sam hollered, "get dressed. We're moving."

"What? Why?"

The knob turned, and the door creaked as Sam tried to open it. "We have to go. We've got plenty to do."

Rosa blinked away dizziness and stretched out a hand to steady herself against the dresser. A photograph, one of Sam in a football uniform, fell over.

"Rosa! Come on!"

"Where are we going?"

"There's a suitcase under the bed. You've got exactly one minute to get your stuff together. Then, we're out of here."

"But —"

"Fifty-two seconds."

It was a lime-green suitcase, one that matched the green shag carpeting of Sam's bedroom. It was strangely reminiscent of the suitcase Rosa had hidden under her bed back in —

No, there had been an explosion.

Rosa put on the clothes he'd bought her yesterday at Kmart, and then packed three pairs of sweats and all of Sam's mother's sweaters. The only shoes available were a pair of old, pink slippers and the boots she'd thought about escaping in yesterday. In the corners of the suitcase, she wadded a cotton nightgown and a few pairs of men's socks. Snatching soap and shampoo from the bathroom, she could hear a one-sided conversation coming from Elmer's bedroom. Sam was telling his dad to hurry.

Rosa and Go Away were the first ones to the door. Sam handed her a black leather jacket. "You're not taking the cat."

"When did the cat get here?" Elmer's pale face offset uncombed tufts of sporadic hair.

Sam warned her. "Rosa, be reasonable. I'm not even sure where we'll finally wind up tonight."

Rosa hugged Go Away tighter and set the suitcase down.

Sam opened his mouth, but before he could speak, Elmer reached over and patted Go Away. "The cat can stay at Jerry's. He won't mind."

Sam's mouth closed. Rosa almost felt sorry for him. The man needed a pet. That's probably why he was making such a fuss about Rosa; he needed something, someone,

241

to take of.

"Who's Jerry?" she asked. "And why is Elmer coming with us?"

"Jerry's my brother," Elmer explained. "And Sam here has some idiotic idea that there's safety in numbers. He doesn't want me out here alone."

"With only sporadic telephone service and no 911 privileges," Sam added.

"I can take care of myself," Elmer insisted.

"I'm going to need some help with Rosa," Sam said. "Dad, *you'll* be a big help."

"Liar."

Elmer sat in the back. His knees had to be pressing against the back of her seat, Rosa knew, because Sam's Ford 250 was not an extended cab. Rosa offered, but Sam would not even consider letting her get in the back.

"What, you think I'm going to jump out while it's still dark, while there's snow on the ground, and when I'm finally thinking about letting you help me?"

"Maybe" was all Sam offered.

Rosa shivered and tried not to think about how early it was, how tired she still was and how scared she was.

There were no stars, nothing she could see to assist Sam in deciding whether to turn right, left, or drive straight ahead.

In the backseat, Elmer shifted uncomfortably. "Sam, the lights."

"I'm not going to use the lights."

Elmer leaned forward. "You've got to."

"Dad, if I use the lights, we might be seen. Should anyone, later, trace Rosa to our place, I want you involved as little as possible. It's bad enough the Dundees saw her."

"I don't like this," Rosa said.

"Funny," Sam snapped. "I thought you were used to living on the edge."

"You never get used to living on the edge."

"Oh?" Sam's fingers tightened on the steering wheel. "Why don't you tell me —"

"I thought you didn't want to talk until you got to the main road," Rosa reminded him.

"You sound just like an old married couple," Elmer piped up from the backseat.

Rosa felt a hot blush cover her face and was glad the darkness kept Sam from noticing.

And Elmer's gibe worked. Silence reigned as Sam cautiously traversed the dark, slippery terrain. As if sensing Rosa's anxiety, Go Away snuggled into her lap, still shivering from the cold. He licked at one paw, clearly annoyed that he'd gotten wet and only making himself wetter.

Once they reached the main road, and

Sam visibly relaxed, Rosa couldn't resist returning to his question. "So, you thought I had gotten used to living on the edge, always looking over my shoulder. Well, I didn't look over my shoulder enough, because if I had I could have avoided you."

"Rosa, you were speeding, a little bit."

"A little bit? And you *had* to stop me? You couldn't go stop a bank robbery or a mugging or . . ."

"I stopped you because you *were* speeding."

"Everyone speeds."

Sam glanced down at the speedometer. "No, not everyone."

From the backseat came a chuckle. No doubt the last twenty-four hours had been more entertainment for Elmer than the last few years.

Rosa almost chuckled, too. When had she last laughed freely, enjoyed banter, felt safe? She shifted in the seat until she felt comfortable, and then said, "Tell me more about Eric."

To her surprise, Sam obeyed.

"No attempts have been made on his life. Billy Atkins, that's Ruth's brother-in-law who works at the prison, says he's a model prisoner. Eric's gained weight and is starting to look a lot like Tony. Prison changes people. You do know that, Rosa? He *is* a Santellis."

He wanted her to trust him, yet he was blind! He kept coming back to Eric's surname as if that was the only determinant in what made him. People saw what they wanted.

"Why do they want to kill you, Rosa?"

She shook her head. "You never stop."

"No, and if you are half as smart as I think you are, you'll decide to trust me completely before anyone else gets killed."

They left the mountain road that heralded the way to Elmer's cabin. The deserted, icy road shimmered in front of them like a scene from an old *Twilight Zone.* Snow had a tendency to encourage intelligent people to stay indoors. What did that say about them?

I am not afraid.

What was that scripture in Psalms that had helped so much yesterday:

When I am afraid, I will trust in You. In God, whose word I praise, in God I trust; I will not be afraid.

What can mortal man do to me?

"You have to turn on the headlights now, Sam," Elmer advised.

Sam complied and turned onto the main highway.

Rosa stretched, dislodging Go Away, who climbed over the seat to join Elmer in the back.

"Feel free to catch some sleep," Sam advised. "We'll be on the road for a few hours. We'll stay at Jerry's long enough to change your looks."

"Jerry's a dean at one of the community colleges," Elmer explained.

College deans must make pretty good money, Rosa thought a few hours later. They'd left the grayness of winter and crossed some invisible barrier that welcomed sunshine.

Jerry Packard lived in a picturesque neighborhood nestled near the Camelback Mountain. Blue skies, green grass, a clear driveway and orange trees, made their early-morning drive out of Tonto Ridge seem a mirage.

Elmer filled her in concerning Jerry's history: widowed, three daughters and one son, a bookworm, no pets. Both Sam and Elmer exchanged looks and then looked down at Go Away.

"Don't worry," Rosa promised, "I'll figure out how to make some sort of litter box and lock him in a bedroom."

After Jerry escorted them into his home,

without so much as even one distasteful look in Go Away's direction, Rosa thought she'd never seen two men so much alike, and Sam was their descendant. Looking at him, it was hard to imagine that he'd ever be short and squatty. A sudden desire to see family photos made Rosa stop in her tracks. Unfortunately, the pictures on Jerry's walls were all of Jerry's family.

Rosa ate a piece of toast and downed a glass of milk while the men discussed changing her appearance. Since they didn't ask her for suggestions, she didn't offer any. It might be interesting to see what they'd come up with.

After a moment, Sam and Jerry headed for the attic. Jerry just knew that his three daughters had trunks up there. Inside, he said, would be clothes they didn't want to throw away, but didn't want to take with them, so, of course, Daddy had room to store them.

The two men returned with three trunks.

Unlike two years ago, and then again six months ago, this time she let others re-arrange her looks. After looking through the first trunk, and holding up a brown, leather-fringed jacket, Elmer thought the Native American look would work. Jerry said Native Americans no longer had a look. Sam mentioned that Lucy Straus, her last disguise, had been Native American. His "been there, done that" argument worked.

Elmer liked the next trunk, too. Obviously, two of Jerry's daughters were polar opposites because this trunk contained Western clothes. A snap shirt with breast piping. A belt with the name Gina hand-tooled on the back. Pocket jeans with a bit of a flare at the leg. Dingo boots. Rosa put her hair in a ponytail and donned the slightly dented, dirty white hat.

"Good," said Jerry.

"Good," said Elmer.

"It'll do," said Sam.

"Not a chance," Rosa yelped after she attempted to walk across the room. The pants didn't allow her to breathe, and the cowboy boots pinched her feet just enough to make each step a challenge.

The men opened the last trunk. A few minutes later Rosa sported clothes that would have made a gypsy proud.

Looking in the mirror, in the guest room, she shook her head. "No one dresses like this. I think this will draw attention to me instead of away from me."

"You look fine," Elmer said.

"You look like half the kids on campus," Jerry agreed.

"You look ridiculous," Sam muttered. "But it works. Now do something with your hair." He disappeared, and after a moment his voice could be heard talking on the phone.

Jerry and Elmer hovered and offered advice while Rosa added her new belongings to the green suitcase.

Who knew where they'd be tonight?

She might possibly be in jail, again.

Fat lotta good the suitcase would do then. She paused, wondering if she should even bother. As if sensing her indecision, Go Away climbed in the suitcase, settled down on one of Anna's old shirts and looked imploringly at Rosa.

"No, you can't go," she said, gently pushing the feline onto the bed.

Go Away, of course, climbed right back in.

Poor Go Away. Ever since Sam arrested Rosa, Go Away had been getting little to no quality time.

Elmer pulled the unwilling cat from the suitcase and cradled him. "Don't worry, Go Away and I will get along just fine."

"Ready?" Sam appeared in the door frame.

"Not yet." Rosa took a breath. Funny, now, when she was finally doing something that might actually mean redemption for all involved, she didn't feel ready. Maybe she'd never feel ready, *be ready*. Maybe this was more than she could handle.

All she felt was out of breath and terrified.

"Rosa," Sam urged.

She snapped the suitcase shut. Jerry found an old pair of tennis shoes that a daughter, who knew which one, probably not the gypsy, had left some years before, and then Sam was nudging her toward the door.

"We have things to do" was all he'd say.

You'd think they were going on a two-week vacation. Both Jerry and Elmer walked them out, with Jerry offering last-minute advice on how to baby the Cadillac. Elmer parked Sam's truck out of sight in the backyard.

Jerry had an old, brown Bronco that didn't get used enough. He'd drive it to work and back.

Elmer said he'd be too worried to go anywhere.

Worried. Yes, Rosa understood the concept. She started to tell him that worry would not add a day to his life or make their quest any easier, but the words would make her a hypocrite.

She was worried.

More than worried.

She was taking more chances than she had taken since grabbing that stupid bag and running.

Staring over at Sam, Rosa realized he was worried, too: worried that his onetime partner might be Gila City's new, most notorious criminal, worried that he might be putting his loved ones in danger's path, worried that someone would see him in Broken Bones when he should be in Tamir, worried that he might be putting his trust in the wrong person.

Oh, Father, all this worry when we should turn our cares over to you. Father, give me strength today. Give Sam strength today. Help us, Lord, to do right today. Thank you for bringing us this far.

She didn't get to utter "Amen". Elmer rapped on the window before she could get the words out. After rolling down the glass, she took the book from his hands.

"Anna's bible," she said. "I didn't even see you take it from the cabin."

"It was on a table in the living room where you'd been reading it. I want you to take it. You might need it."

She nodded.

Looking over at Sam, and noting the expression on his face as he stared at his mother's Bible, she figured he might need it more.

Rosa waved until the two older men faded from sight. Then, she bowed her head again. God had been so good to her. She snuck a look at Sam. Yup, God was answering her prayers again and again. She needed to thank Him. This time she managed an uninterrupted "Amen" before raising her head and looking over at Sam. He was staring at her with a look of disbelief.

"What?" she asked.

"Were you praying?"

"Yes."

"Why?"

"Well, if you're doing what you claim to be doing, then God is answering my prayers. He needed to be thanked and I need encouragement. Notice how I said 'if you're doing.' It's really hard to believe this whole mess might be coming to an end. For the last two years, God's the only one who knew the truth, the whole truth, and nothing but the truth."

He shook his head and gripped the steering wheel. Rosa got the idea he could do with a little talk with his heavenly Father. She checked out the interior of Jerry's Cadillac. The vehicle gave the word *clean* a whole new level of definition. According to the registration, the car was over four years old. According to the smell and condition of the leather seats, the Caddy might well have been driven off the sales lot last week.

"Okay, Rosa," Sam finally spoke. "It's back to you and me."

After two years of doing everything on her own, she was beginning to appreciate "you and me." Actually, she was beginning to like it. "So," she said, clearing her throat, "are you finally going to tell me what we're doing? Where we're going?"

"In about fifteen minutes we're meeting Mitch, the guy from Internal Affairs, and a few others."

With Sam Packard, Cliff's one-time partner, backing her up, providing his own eyewitness accounts, surely justice could be served. The authorities would listen to him when they would doubt her.

She'd finally found the credible witness.

"Where are we meeting?"

"A restaurant downtown."

As if sensing her discomfort, Sam said, "You can trust Mitch. I would, with my life."

"Once you claimed the same thing about Cliff."

"True, but we can't do this alone. Mitch is the man who can turn this into more than just a witch hunt. He can bring Cliff down."

"And after the meeting?"

"It depends on what happens at the meeting. They might insist on putting you in a safe house —"

"No, I'm staying with you!" Now she wished she had a steering wheel to grip. She'd learned to rely on this man much too quickly.

"I'm hoping for that, too, but we have to do whatever is best for the case. If all goes right, I'll convince Mitch to let us go to Tucson. We'll see if we can find Mary Graham."

"You didn't tell me Mary was in Tucson."

"I'm not sure she is. Ruth came up with a possible address, but it could be a dead end." He pulled into a restaurant's parking lot.

As if on cue, Rosa's stomach growled.

"I'm just not feeding you enough," Sam noted.

She made a face. "Well, luckily, we're going to a restaurant. Is that smart?"

"Rosa, I know Mitch. He'll take everything nice and easy. We just want to know everything that happened that night in Terrance Jackle's apartment."

"Everything?" Rosa whispered.

"Everything," Sam said.

"Everything," Rosa repeated. "Well, I can

tell you that since I had a front row seat to murder."

THIRTEEN

The restaurant wasn't open. Rosa followed behind Sam and watched as he first knocked on the back door and then greeted a man in a food-stained apron.

"Mitch is in back, in the banquet room," the man said.

The back of the restaurant smelled like simmering soup, coleslaw, and meat. A timer sounded. The restaurant guy stopped, took a tray of rolls out of an oven.

The place was empty of customers and eerily quiet. Rosa didn't think she'd ever been in a restaurant before when there wasn't noise, more noise, and then some more noise: dishes clanking, waiters hurrying, people visiting. Even elevator music was missing.

Sam opened the door to a private meeting room. Three men and a woman waited inside. They stood. Sam took her arm possessively and said, "This is Rosa Cagnalia.

You're going to be amazed at what she has to say."

Sam didn't know how amazed.

"I'm Mitch Williams with Internal Affairs," the youngest-looking gentleman said. He was dressed in brown Dockers, a white shirt and a striped tie. He didn't offer his hand.

Another gentleman was dressed much the same, except he also had on a jacket to hide the few extra pounds he carried. "Rafael Gonzales," he introduced himself. Rosa took the hand he offered. He was twice the size of Mitch, clearly Hispanic, and spoke without the trace of an accent.

"My supervisor," Mitch explained.

"We're very interested in what you have to say." Rafael sat down and pulled a tape recorder toward him and fiddled with the knobs.

The final man stood. He was dressed in a T-shirt and jeans. Dark hair fell forward into his eyes. "I'm Lucas Hathaway." He held out his hand. Rosa took it. He was Jimmy's captain. He wouldn't know about her but remembering all the times Jimmy quoted the man, Rosa knew she was in the room with a man Jimmy idolized. She'd seen Lucas's picture in the paper back when Eric was on trial. He'd attended the court session every single day.

He claimed he wanted justice for Jimmy.

He hadn't gotten it.

"Let's sit down." Sam pulled out chairs for Ruth and Rosa. The other three men were across the table.

The door opened and the restaurant manager wheeled in pitchers of water and iced tea. Fruit and pastries were arranged artfully on a plate, as if this were an everyday, professional meeting. The man disappeared for a moment and reappeared with a pot of coffee. Glasses, cups, plates, silverware, were already on the table.

Sam poured water for Ruth, Rosa and himself. The other men all took coffee. No one moved to touch the food.

Mr. Gonzales turned on the tape recorder. "This is January 21. Present are . . ."

He droned on for a few minutes.

Then, Ruth began. "We've got a wiretap on Cliff's phone. Judging by his calls, so far, he hasn't a clue we've got Rosa. Also, if he knows the Santellis boys are in jail, he's doing nothing about it. Of course, they've got high-priced help, and probably don't need or want his help. What he has done, though, is give us a couple of names."

Mitch continued, "Jeff Martin and Daniel Booker. We've taken them into custody.

We're pretty sure they're the two officers who helped kidnap you. Near as we can tell, Booker's been one of Cliff's lackeys for years. Martin is fairly new. He came on board after Jimmy's death. He has a sick kid and needs money. We think his conscience will win, and he'll eventually give us the information we want. Cliff hasn't realized they're MIA yet."

Rafael, clearly the most relaxed person in the room, said, "Rosa, we need to know what happened that night. What happened to Jimmy, what happened to you, what happened to the money?"

She nodded. She liked that it would be taped. She liked that there were so many officials from different departments. The odds were that even if one was on the take, maybe the others would prevail in the end.

"I'd like to start with a prayer," she said. Never in her life had she imagined herself in a position to ask a roomful of strangers to engage in prayer. It was politically incorrect, basically uncomfortable and totally needed. She'd prayed for the moment for so long, and now that it was finally here, it only seemed right to begin by publicly thanking the Lord.

"I'm not sure —" Mitch began.

Beside her, Sam squirmed. All week, he'd

stared at her when she prayed at meals. Silent, respectful, but not engaged. Was he really that removed from his faith? She didn't think so.

With sudden insight, she realized he was struggling with himself. In many ways, because of her, he figured he should say the prayer.

"I'll say it," Rafael stated.

Mitch stuttered, "This is highly irregular —"

"Sometimes political correctness goes too far. More of these type of meetings should start with prayer. We'd get a lot more done," Rafael said and bowed his head.

Rafael's every mannerism spoke of a spiritual nature. He had the look of a man who knew where he was going and what he was doing.

Would she ever have that?

Mitch's mouth opened in surprise. Glancing around the room, Rosa watched as Ruth and Lucas both bowed their heads. Sam reached over and took Rosa's hand. They both bowed their heads, and Rafael began.

"Lord, we begin something today that is distasteful. Today we look into the life of a man we all want to respect. And, Lord, we might find out he deserves no respect. Guide us, Lord, as we listen to Rosa. Give

her the words she needs to help us understand. Give us the questions to ask. Thank
you, Father, for trusting us with your
servant Rosa. Amen."

If anything, Rafael looked more at peace.
Lucas and Ruth pretty much remained the
same, and Mitch looked somewhat stunned.

Sam felt like an outsider because he knew
prayers weren't always answered.

But what if God didn't listen? What if, as
with Sam's mother, God's answer *again* was
no?

He didn't have time to deal with his fears,
or maybe what he feared most was hope.
Rosa sat up straighter, pulled the tape
recorder closer and began.

Sam had listened to witnesses spill their
guts before. Most spoke in fast, jerky lan-
guage. As if they'd feel clean only after they
confessed. Rosa spoke slowly in a voice that
almost scared Sam.

"We were in Terrance Jackle's living room.
He had a second-story, one bedroom, just
two blocks from the hospital. Very little furniture."

To anyone else in the room, it would appear that Rosa was a woman of steady
nerves, great control. But, sitting next to
her, Sam could see something no one else

could. Just like Eric, back at Florence Prison, she couldn't keep her hands from shaking.

It made her human.

It made him want to stop the tape, take those hands in his and comfort her.

But he couldn't do that. He was a police officer, and she was a key witness in a crime that had brought Gila City to its knees and would again.

"Now there was a nice fellow," Rosa continued, "in and out of jail on drug-related charges. Somehow he always managed to be out more than in. Why is that, Sam?"

"The system's not perfect."

"No, and that night certainly showed why. His place was always a party — which is why I guess he didn't have much furniture. It kept getting broken.

"There were two guys in the bedroom, snorting coke. I don't remember their names, but they were always there. One of them always brought his girlfriend. I think her name was Lindsey. Penny, Tony's mistress, was in the bathroom. Jimmy and Eric were over at the table chomping on chips. The three guys on the sofa seemed nervous, a little more than usual.

"I was sitting in a chair across from the

sofa, wishing my life was as easy as the sit-com episode no one but me was watching, wishing my soda was cold, wishing the smell of cigarette smoke would go away and wishing I were anywhere besides here. We'd been to Terrance's place before, many times, and never had I felt tension like this night. Usually everyone just sat around saying, *Whoa, man, how's it hanging?* Not this night. Something big was going down, but, then, that's why we were there. Eric thought a major player would be stopping by. We were so hopeful. And then the door opened. I wasn't surprised when Tony Santellis walked in. Sardi was close behind. They're always together. I didn't know who the other man was until Jimmy said, 'Dad.' "

Sam's water glass tumbled. Cold liquid slid across the table. Lucas Hathaway grabbed the tape player. Rafael sopped at the mess with napkins. Ruth ran to get some towels.

He thought he'd come to terms with Cliff's involvement in the drug trade. But he hadn't. Now, hearing Rosa involve Cliff in an actual time, place, situation . . . and of all times, places, situations, *the* one involving his own son!

Cliff had been at Jackle's apartment! He'd witnessed the death of his son! No wonder

263

the man was a walking time bomb.

Sam could tell everyone wanted Rosa to continue. Looking at her, he realized she wasn't even aware that the water from his glass was dripping onto her skirt — a colorful gypsy skirt that belonged on stage, not on a woman breaking the heart of the man who loved her.

Loved her?

No, he didn't believe love happened that quickly. He'd only known her six days. Of course, he'd known *of* her for more than two years.

She was silent, lost in some other place and time, thinking about that night, reliving that night.

Carefully, Sam took his own napkin and mopped up the water dripping off the edge of the table. Carefully, he pushed the glass away. He needed to calm down. Yeah, right, as if that was going to happen. Rosa probably had no idea how connected Sam had once been with the Handleys, both Cliff and Susan, plus their children Jimmy and Katie. She probably thought he'd spilled his drink because of shock. No, shock wasn't a strong enough word. Sure, sometimes cops went to the other side. Money, or lack of, was a big issue in the department.

Cliff had coached both Jimmy's and

Katie's Little League teams. He'd taken Jimmy through Boy Scouts and Katie through swim team. If Cliff were home, there'd always be a grill loaded with hamburgers and hot dogs; a backyard hosting a baseball game; a wife doling out sodas; a dad who knew all the kids by name.

A favorite neighborhood dad would be the perfect go-between for a neighborhood dealer. Cliff could relay to Tony which kids to approach, which kids to avoid, when to lie low.

He studied the woman sitting next to him. Rosa remained silent. No doubt she needed to gather her thoughts.

He certainly did.

He'd admired Cliff so much. Most of Sam's days off had been spent in Cliff's backyard with his sometime girlfriend, Michelle, by his side. Marriage and babies had been on his mind then. Funny that he'd be thinking about Michelle now. He didn't even know where she was. They'd broken up right after Sam's mother died.

She claimed Sam had changed.

Watching the brave woman sitting next to him, Sam realized that it wasn't that he'd changed, it was that he'd never really loved Michelle, he'd just felt comfortable with her.

Like he'd been comfortable with Cliff.

Complete acceptance of the truth closed in on Sam. How could he have missed it? No wonder Rosa hadn't confided in him at first.

She was right. Until the last couple of days, he wouldn't have bought her story. He'd been hoping for, counting on, a nice confession from her fingering Tony as the hit man and blaming Tony for the drug problem in Gila City. He wanted Cliff to be a hit-and-miss connection. He wanted Cliff's involvement with a Santellis to be about Jimmy's death.

He'd been hoping in vain.

"Sam, if you need to be excused, we all understand. You can listen to the tape, later, without such a crowd to contend with." It was soft-spoken Rafael who brought them back to task.

"No, I'm fine."

If Rosa could make it through telling the story, he could make it through listening to the story.

"Ma'am, are you ready to continue?" Rafael asked.

It took her only a moment to start again — each word shattering his memories of a man who at one time had been a hero.

"The door opened. Tony Santellis walked in. Sardi, too. They're always together. Cliff

266

was last. Eric and I froze, but Jimmy said 'Dad' just loud enough for Cliff to hear him. It happened so fast, but yet I can remember like it was in slow motion. Eric sensed something. I know he did. He turned toward Jimmy."

Her voice softened, almost reverently. "And Cliff raised his revolver and shot Jimmy."

Fourteen

Stunned silence filled the room, but only momentarily. Then, both Mitch and Lucas jumped to their feet, took out cell phones and retreated to separate corners. Rafael scribbled frantically on a yellow tablet.

Ruth stood up, went over and whispered something in Rafael's ear. He picked up his notebook, beckoned the other men, and they all left the room. Rosa stared at the table. She didn't want to look at Sam because she could hear him, hear the big, tough cop.

Sam Packard was doing something she'd not allowed herself to do in two years: cry.

She envied him. "Do you still believe me?" she whispered. "Cliff killed his own son. The money meant more to him than blood."

She finally looked up, at him, and the stark pain in his red-rimmed eyes told her more than words. He honestly realized that Cliff Handley — multidecorated cop, war hero *and ex-partner* — was more a criminal than a cop.

More a criminal? Make that *all* a criminal.

"I believe you." He said it while trying to discreetly wipe tears from his eyes.

God had answered her prayers. He'd sent her a helpmate.

It is not good for the man to be alone. I will make a helper suitable for him.

It was one of the few verses she'd always known. She remembered from her school days: The story of the beginning.

Today could very well be a beginning.

Sam took her hands in his. He held on, tightly, and she could feel lingering traces of his tears. The connection of a simple touch comforted her as much as it seemed to comfort him.

Maybe this was the beginning of something more than justice.

She started to ask him to pray with her, but a knock sounded, and the others came back in.

"Sorry," Rafael said. "But we need to keep going."

Everyone sat where they'd been before. No one mentioned Sam's red eyes. The tape went back on, and Rosa resumed as if she'd never been interrupted.

"Jimmy said 'Dad.' Everything happened so fast. Eric sensed something. He turned toward Jimmy. The gun went off. Jimmy fell. I ran over. Eric went to his knees. I'm not sure what he was thinking. It was too late. There was so much blood. And Jimmy's eyes were open, staring at nothing."

Rosa turned and stared at Sam. "Jimmy died instantly. People keep forgetting that, and Cliff was aiming his gun at Eric. I gotta give Tony credit; he knocked it out of Cliff's hand. No matter what, Tony took care of family. He wasn't going to let Cliff kill Eric. Tony was yelling, Cliff was yelling, people were heading for the door. Eric yelled in my ear 'Go.' I did, God help me. I headed for the door. I knew nothing would ever be the same, ever.

"It was the first time I felt scared." Rosa shook her head. "I didn't know what scared was. We'd been there an hour. I'll never forget that apartment. Where everybody was, what happened. The money was in a garbage bag on the coffee table. Jason Hughes had been keeping an eye on it. Only after all the shots were fired, no one was watching it."

"Jason Hughes is dead," Sam said.

"I know. They're making sure no one is

left alive. After all, if I talk, it would be too easy for one of the others to make a deal. Tony's taken care of his own, but everyone else is, was, free game. Anyway, Jason was sitting there, mouth open, too high to move. I grabbed the bag as I ran out the door. Don't ask me why."

"How much?" Lucas asked.

"Over seven hundred thousand dollars."

Mitch shook his head. "That's a nice chunk of change. Where is it?"

"I have it, most of it, and I've kept track of what I've spent investigating Cliff."

"That won't keep you from jail," Mitch said.

Rafael held up his hand to speak, but Sam jumped in first. "She's not going to jail."

"You can't promise her that," Mitch said carefully.

"He's right," Lucas agreed.

"Gentlemen," Rafael said patiently, "whatever deal we decide to offer Miss Cagnalia needs to wait until after we hear *all* she has to say."

"You don't need to offer me a deal. I'll pay for my crimes." Rosa's voice was even, her look unwavering. "And, believe me, I never wanted that blood money. Most of the money I spent wasn't for me. The last time was buying that stupid car. I'd already

271

started replacing the money when Sam arrested me."

It was the first time he'd seen her look anything but assured, in control. Even when he'd pulled her out of the deserted mine, she'd been more mad than scared.

"You didn't need a top-of-the-line Mustang," Mitch said.

"She bought it used," Sam argued.

"No, Mitch is right." Rosa said. "I didn't need a sports car."

"Then why did you buy it?" Rafael asked, matter-of-factly.

"To help a guy out at work. He was about to lose his house and needed the money. But I could have helped in a different way."

"No one's going to think less of you, Rosa, for buying a decent vehicle. Keep talking." This was Rafael again.

She looked somewhat resolved as she took them back to the scene in the apartment. "Sardi stopped me at the door, and I heard Eric yell to let me go. Sardi did. Eric was the quiet brother, you know. I think Sardi let go out of surprise more than anything else. I doubt if Eric had ever issued an order before.

"I ran to my car, but I knew they'd be after me, and I knew Tony knew my car, so I drove straight for the hospital, parked it and stole a friend's car. I knew where she kept her purse, and I knew when her shift ended. I knew exactly how much time I had. Looking back, I'm amazed at how rational I was during that whole night, that whole next week. I didn't even feel bad about stealing her car until later. I remember being so careful to stay within the speed limit.

"I stopped by my apartment and grabbed my cat and address book. Nothing else. I had no time. Funny, I'd managed to hold on to my purse from the minute things went wrong. I took Barton next door. I think my old neighbor still has him. I stopped at a nearby teller and withdrew all the money I could. Then, I drove all night, stopping at tellers, until I made it to Flagstaff, ditched the car, used the teller one last time — so it would look like I went from Phoenix to Flagstaff and they'd be looking for me meandering north — and hitchhiked back to Prescott. I'd never hitchhiked before, especially at night. It's funny to think, but it wasn't until I stuck out my thumb, that I realized I couldn't change my mind, couldn't go back. You see, it wasn't just the simple matter of getting Eric to stand between me and Tony."

"You think Eric could have done that?"

"Yes," Rosa said without hesitation. "He

did it. Why do you think he's in jail? He took the fall, and Tony's supposed to leave me alone."

Rosa looked back at her audience. Continuing in the same no-nonsense voice, she said, "Unfortunately, what Eric couldn't do was stand between me and Cliff."

"I'm sorry, Rosa. I can't even imagine the terror you must have been feeling." Sam tried to take her hand again, but she moved away.

Rosa closed her eyes and kept talking. "I got lucky. A trucker picked me up. He gave me a lecture on the dangers of hitchhiking. I cried the whole way, and he stopped and bought me a candy bar and a soda. He was a nice man. The trucker, I never got his name, thought my boyfriend had kicked me out. I told him my mother lived in Prescott. All I could think is I had to try to hide my trail."

"Why Prescott?"

She opened her eyes. "One of the girls I went to nursing school with lived there. I knocked on her door, told her I was in trouble and stayed two days, which was long enough to figure out just what the news was reporting about Jimmy's murder. Eric was arrested, and they were looking for me. My picture was everywhere. My parents were on the news begging for information about me. I, almost broke, almost called them, but, you see, Cliff was on the news, too, talking about his son, the son he murdered.

"I didn't leave my friend's house even once during that time, and luckily, she believed me when I told her I had been working undercover for the police. I doubt she'll ever invite me to stay again, though. By the time I took off, she was as afraid as I was."

Lucas frowned. "But you weren't undercover. If you had been, there'd have been records, Jimmy would have told me."

"I wasn't official or anything like that, neither was Eric. Think about it. No way did Eric want his name associated with being a snitch. Not with his family, his brothers. We banded together out of some misguided hope, need, to do something about a problem we thought was out of control. Jimmy wanted paperwork and official approval, but Eric would never work against his family."

"Do you know how Eric and Jimmy hooked up?" Lucas now had a notebook out.

"Jimmy was undercover in the neighborhood. He joined a softball league Eric belonged to. I don't know how they figured out they were on the same side of the law, but they did. Then, Eric hurt his arm playing baseball, and they wound up in my emergency room. Eric knew how I felt about drugs because of what they had done to my family, to Frank. He convinced Jimmy they needed me. My part seemed so simple. All they wanted for me to do was to tell them the names of any patients coming to emergency with drug-related problems."

"Not a bad idea," Lucas begrudged.

"It seemed easy enough, harmless even. They were especially interested in first timers. They wanted to talk to the people who were scared. They were trying to find out who was directly above Tony, his supplier, and who Tony was supplying, the neighborhood dealer."

"Did you have any successes finding connections in the emergency room?"

"Believe it or not, Jason Hughes was our first guinea pig. He overdosed early in his drug habit career but was too stupid to stop. I pretended to be Eric's girlfriend, and Jason was impressed that an emergency room nurse would have a connection to the Santellises."

"Good plan, and one that would never have been approved by our legal system," Mitch said. "You completely ignored any laws surrounding a person's privacy. You were a vigilante. Such ploys usually end in grief. Like this one did. You do know that?"

Rosa stood. "So, if the cops won't, or can't, do their jobs because of legal red tape, what choice is there?"

"The law —"

"— doesn't work. The law says guilty until proven innocent, and I know lawyers who think innocence is just the matter of a price tag. That doesn't inspire me to think much of the system."

"Not all lawyers think like that."

"And not all cops are honest."

"I don't want to argue," Mitch barked. "I just want to get to the bottom of this. I want justice served."

"Me, too," said Rosa. "And justice will only be served by putting Cliff Handley in jail. For almost two years I've been gathering evidence against Cliff Handley."

"And just what are you trying to prove?" Rafael asked carefully. Sam thought Rosa had been doing a pretty good job of telling them. Apparently, Rafael thought there was more.

"She's saying," Mitch said slowly, pursing his lips in a way that let Rosa know he didn't quite believe her, "that Cliff wasn't just involved in the drug trade. He was in charge of it."

"Yes, that's what I'm saying," Rosa met Mitch's look dead-on, and Sam was suddenly proud of her.

Mitch shook his head. "What's amazing is I'm beginning to believe you. Why did Cliff come out that night? You have any idea?"

"You know, he's going to have to answer that one. I'd guess money," Rosa said simply. "That and he was beginning to think himself invincible, above the law. Plus, he was getting older, ready to retire. I could hypothesize for an hour. I've thought about his motivations that much. I think he felt like nobody knew who he was. He'd always hid his trail well. Not even his wife knew. I've known all along that a simple accusation wouldn't be enough to convince you guys. I needed proof. I've been trying to pinpoint very specific criminal behavior and then find witnesses, credible witnesses. I never dreamed I'd add kidnapping to his list of sins. You have Sam here as an eyewitness to that."

Mitch didn't look convinced or happy, yet asked, "Who are your other witnesses?"

"Wanda Peabody. She'll testify that Cliff forced both her husband *and daughter* into the drug trade. I have a statement from her. I made three copies of it, and they're in safety deposit boxes across Arizona along with the other witness accounts and Cliff's money."

"Where did you hide the keys?" Sam asked. "Don't tell me your mobile home?"

"No." Rosa looked uncomfortable, and Sam knew she didn't want to tell them where the keys were, didn't want to trust them, *him.*

"My friend in Prescott has one, I have one, and Wanda has one. From the start I was a bit worried about counting Wanda as a credible witness but I never doubted that she sided with me completely. She knows how evil Cliff is. And, I have to say, with all the other things that have happened this week, I'm thinking she's looking more credible every day."

Rosa took a deep breath. "Credible witnesses are hard to come by. I mean, I count myself as a witness who can and will testify against Cliff, but my picture is still on display in most of the post offices between Gila City and Phoenix. The only other person I have willing to testify against Handley is an ex-employee of Yano's used car lot who witnessed a bit more than he should have. He quit and didn't tell anyone. He will probably need a little bit of a nudge — he's terrified — but I think the right person could convince him to testify. He's most worried about how many other people are willing to testify and how sure I am that Cliff and Tony will be put away forever."

"You? Wanda? And some guy you don't want to name?" Mitch sounded incredulous. "That's all you came up with in two years?"

"I'm sure there are more people out there who know Cliff Handley for what he really is, but finding them and then getting them to come forward isn't all that easy — especially when half my goal is staying out of sight and not being recognized."

"Just exactly what did this employee of Yano's see that has him so terrified?"

"He saw Tony and Walter Peabody together the night the two border patrol officers died."

"So?" Mitch looked confused.

"It was at the exact moment the border patrol officers died, so Walt couldn't have killed them."

Rafael scribbled for a minute on his notepad, and then said, "We need his name, Rosa."

"Good luck getting him to talk," Rosa said wryly as she gave it.

"We need more," Mitch said snidely. His fingers tapped a beat on the table. It wasn't a joyful noise.

Of all the men in the room, he was the one Rosa considered a loose cannon. Sam sure trusted him, though. And, maybe, out of all the men in the room, he was acting most like a cop: dubious.

Sam cleared his throat. "There might be someone else. Rosa's next door neighbor at the trailer park. His name is Seth Grainger. The day her trailer blew, he came outside with two beers. It didn't occur to me then that the second beer might have been for whoever was messing with Rosa's trailer. It occurs to me now, and Ruth has looked into Seth. There's no doubt he knows Cliff. It's a long shot, but. . . ."

"And as a matter of fact, we have one more idea." Rosa's appetite finally returned. She poured herself a cup of coffee and took a cherry pastry. "Sam and I want to track down Mary Graham, Tony's sister. I think we might be able to get her to talk."

"There is no Sam and you," Mitch said. "You are still a felon. You'll —"

"This afternoon, you'll be tucked away in a safe house. We can't take the chance something will happen to you," Rafael said kindly. He put down his pen. He no longer appeared serene.

"Mary *probably* won't talk to me," Rosa stated, "But she *definitely* won't talk to any of you."

"We'll bring her in," Mitch said.

Rosa opened her mouth, but it was Lucas who spoke. "You can lead a horse to water, but you can't make it drink. Mary's a Santellis. We've brought her in before. Many times. She's never been forthcoming with information."

"I think Lucas's right. But if anyone can get her to talk, it's probably Rosa. The timing's never been better." Ruth inched her chair closer to the table.

If Mitch looked dubious, Ruth looked exhilarated. She announced, "I took the time to research her."

"Why?" Lucas asked.

"It only made sense. I was investigating Tony, Eric, everybody else in the family."

"And what did you find?" Sam asked.

"Mary's husband, Eddie, went to jail a few months ago, for dealing."

"No surprise," said Mitch.

"No surprise," Ruth agreed. "The surprise is what happened afterward. Mary took their son and dropped off the face of the earth."

"Just like you, Rosa," Mitch noted. "Only you stole some money."

"I'm sure she felt she had no other choice, like I felt I had no choice."

Mitch leaned forward, looking and acting much like Sam had that day he and Ruth had interrogated her. Were they back to this? Good cop, bad cop? He certainly knew his role. "There's always another choice. Turning yourself in to the authorities. Telling the truth. Letting the system do what it's supposed —"

"Yeah." Rosa sat back and nodded. "A system in which Cliff Handley had a corner office."

Ruth interrupted, "The word is, concerning Mary, that just before Eddie went to prison, the little boy got into Daddy's stash and almost died. Afterward, Eddie wanted to go to jail, seemed he found it a safer place than home."

She opened her mouth to continue, but before she could say more there was a knock on the door, and the restaurant owner walked in carrying a portable phone. "It's for you," he said, handing the phone to Mitch.

"I specifically said no calls." Agitated, Mitch stood, grabbed the phone, waited until the restaurant guy backed out of the room and growled into the receiver, "I specifically said no calls."

He had everyone's full attention. From the start, he'd been the tense one. The member of the team who fidgeted, pursed his lips whenever something struck him wrong, and who'd downed most of the coffee. High-strung didn't begin to describe him.

Whoever was on the other end wasn't giving him much of an opportunity to speak. He paced. His mouth opened to a silent *O*. Finally, he said, "You're kidding."

Glancing around the room, Rosa figured no one believed the person on the other end was kidding.

"Sure it does!" Mitch finally snapped. "It changes everything."

Turning off the phone, Mitch looked at the faces around the table. He settled his gaze on Rosa. "Tell me," he said. "Are there any witnesses left, besides you, who can testify that Cliff shot his own son?"

"Tony and Sardi Santellis."

"Nope," he shook his head, "Not anymore. They were released just twenty minutes ago and gunned down on the prison steps. They're both dead."

FIFTEEN

This time it was Lucas and Ruth who flew to the corners of the room with their cell phones. Rafael scribbled frantically on his yellow tablet.

Mitch pursed his lips. "We've got Jeff and Daniel in custody so they're not suspects. No way could Cliff have done this. We haven't let him out of sight since Wednesday. Even his phone is tapped. If he sneezes, we're so close we could pass a tissue. Who else is involved, Rosa?"

"Rosa," Sam said gently. "What else can you tell us?"

"Nothing. Some bloodhound I am. My research didn't even pick up Jeff's and Daniel's involvement."

"If Cliff ordered Tony's and Sardi's death, then there has to be someone else involved, someone with the connections to execute a hit in plain sight." Mitch still paced. The energy he emitted was in such contrast to the rest of the men. He stopped and looked at Rosa.

"I've already made arrangements," Rafael spoke up.

"No," Rosa said. "I'm not taking a back-seat now. I deserve to see this through to the end."

"You're not trained —" Mitch started.

"For an amateur, I've certainly accomplished quite a bit," Rosa interrupted.

Mitch didn't say the words, but Rosa could see the phrase "beginner's luck" on his face. He shook his head. "Nice try. You need to be under armed guard, constant surveillance."

"And while I'm twiddling my thumbs, what will you be doing?"

"Watching Cliff, tapping his phone, bringing in his cronies —"

"Talking to Mary Graham?" Rosa asked.

"Yes."

"You already know she won't talk to you."

"She'll talk," Mitch huffed.

"*Maybe* she'll talk to you," Rosa said, "but if I go, there's no maybe involved. She'd positively talk to me."

It was the assurance that Rosa could, *would,* get Mary to talk — especially now that Tony and Sardi were dead — that convinced Rafael to let her and Sam have one more day, twenty-four hours, to strengthen the case against Cliff Handley.

Ruth had the address. Seemed Eric was doing a bit of talking and Billy was doing a bit of listening.

Rosa almost felt sorry for Sam. Each of the men in the room let him know that if something happened to her, if something tripped up this case, then he'd be the fall guy. His career would either be over or in the toilet.

Virtually the same thing.

They all knew that with only Rosa as a witness, there was no hope of pinning Jimmy's death on Cliff. Who would believe a father capable of killing his own son? What kind of cop would do that!

So, they would settle. They'd go for the kidnapping and drug charges.

Rosa knew those two offenses wouldn't put Cliff away long enough to make the people she'd involved willing to testify. In truth, those two crimes weren't enough to convince her to take the stand.

Well, Cliff was a smart man. The fact that he'd spent more than twenty years on the take testified to that.

"I'm glad that's over," Sam said as he started the car. Almost immediately, he made a face when the radio kicked on to a local country music station. He started to change the channel, but Rosa stopped him.

"I like Trisha Yearwood."

"Country songs are depressing. Everyone cheats, dies or gets hit by a train."

"Hmm, so you've listened to a fair share of country music?"

He shook his head, more in disgust than in answer.

"You know," Rosa said, reaching over and turning off the radio, "Country music is very realistic. Think about it. We're chasing a man who cheated the government, a man who is responsible for the deaths of many people and a man who deserves to get hit by a train."

She said the last few words slowly, not liking their sound, not liking the way the words made her feel.

Why should she feel guilty for wishing Cliff Handley dead?

What kind of forgiveness did her heavenly Father expect her to show?

All of the sudden, memories threatened to erupt into tears. She looked at Sam. Even after all of this, he probably didn't wish his ex-partner dead.

That made him a better person than she was. That made him the one most like Cliff.

"I tried, you know?" Rosa's stomach

roiled. For two years her life had been a nightmare, her life had spiraled out of control, and her family suffered the consequences of her choices. During that time, she'd pushed feminine emotions into the abyss of her mind and focused all her emotions on destroying Cliff Handley.

In many ways, she'd almost destroyed herself along the way.

Then she'd started attending Cliff's old church in order to know the man better, and instead she'd gotten to know the Man better.

"Rosa," Sam said patiently. "Tried what?" Dark circles owled his eyes. He'd spent so much time and energy clutching the steering wheel, at least since Rosa had been noticing, that she suspected Grand Canyon-like grooves were being formed.

"Tried to forgive Cliff Handley, and I'm still trying."

He loosened his grip on the steering wheel. "Well, maybe we both can work on forgiveness later. I've got a couple of questions for God, too, and we could sure use His help now. Do you have the address Ruth gave us?"

"Yes. It's here somewhere in this stack of papers she gave me."

Sam nodded and took a moment to call

Ruth to fill her in on their progress.

When he hung up, Rosa looked at him. They hadn't gone that far, hadn't really done anything. Progress took all of two sentences and really wasn't much of anything.

"I wanted to touch base. I trust Ruth," he said simply.

There it was. That little five letter word: trust. It could make or break a relationship. She'd been so buoyed since the meeting. People believed her! She'd even told them where the safety deposit box keys were. Now the sinking feeling that had been her companion for the last two years returned. It was so hard to let go. She'd been chasing after Cliff, alone, for so long.

"I understand."

And maybe she did.

"Ruth did have a few things to say," Sam said. "The sheriff's not releasing the news of Sardi's and Tony's murder and, so far, according to Cliff's tapped phone, he doesn't appear to have a clue about the Santellises deaths or your reappearance."

"Good." Rosa stared down at the address that meant nothing to her. Poor Mary. In the last year, Mary had seen her father into a nursing home, the Alzheimer's finally exceeding the care a private nurse could offer. She'd seen her son overdose, her husband go to jail and soon she'd deal with the death of two of her brothers.

With only Kenny at the wheel, the Santellis family just might fade into black.

Rosa turned her attention to the papers in her lap. Ruth admitted to researching Mary and had the printouts to prove it. Maybe somewhere in this mess there were more clues as to the depth of Cliff's and the Santellises' crimes.

After shuffling through a few, Rosa said, "These are my papers plus a few more. The ones on top are about Mary. You know, now that Tony is dead, I think there's more of a chance Mary will talk to me. She was so scared of him." Rosa fingered the paper in her hand while staring at the businesses zooming by as Sam left Phoenix behind.

"We weren't allowed to be friends. My parents told me to stay away from Mary and her family. Her father was a wiseguy. Of course, I thought, back then, that the term wiseguy simply meant her father was really smart."

Sam chuckled.

"We both liked horses, and books. I'd go to her house on Saturdays —"

"Your parents didn't know?"

"Not a clue. In some ways, my dad was partially to blame. He coached Tony in Little League — that's where Tony and Frank became friends. Frank and I could hear him talking to our mom when they thought we were asleep. It tore Dad up to know what Tony *could* be compared to what he *would* be. We were fascinated by this whole other world we didn't know, were forbidden to know. My brother and I would head out on Saturday morning and not come back home until late Saturday afternoon. Until he got so deep into drugs, Frank would go to the skateboard parks. He was good. Before I became friends with Mary, I'd go to the mall with friends. Mary was more fun. We'd make jewelry. Her mom taught us how to crochet. And, if Eric and Kenny were around, we'd play board games. For a long time, I couldn't really see what my dad meant, how the Santellises were anything but a typical family."

"You don't talk about Kenny much."

"He was the baby. Tony and Sardi didn't have much use for him, and they pretty much thought Eric a waste of time."

"You know, Rosa, you'll be the one to tell Mary that two of her brothers are dead."

"I know."

Sam nodded. His expression more or less indicated that they all had enough to deal with.

It was all finally happening. Everything she'd worked for. Only it wasn't working out quite the way she wanted.

She hadn't wanted Tony dead, or Sardi for that matter. *Had she?*

Two years ago, she'd have said *yes.*

A year ago, reeling from the news of her parents' deaths, she'd have said yes. But then she'd thought Tony to blame. Now she was more inclined to think Cliff.

But today, after laying down her burdens to the authorities who could actually make a difference, who could actually arrange for justice, death almost seemed the easy way out.

Thinking about the two men who would never again touch a loved one, never again order a hamburger, never would have an opportunity to sit across from a man of God and hear the good news, she suddenly understood why it was best to let God enact His judgment.

Unbidden, a scripture came. Proverbs, the eleventh chapter:

The truly righteous man attains life, but he who pursues evil goes to his death.

Too many people had died over this whole mess.

Sardi had been Tony's shadow since childhood, a paler shade of deceit. Up until their arrest a few days ago, they'd lived next door to each other. Their kids were close in age. Somewhere in the Bible it said not to follow the crowd in doing wrong. Sardi hadn't needed a crowd because being a lackey for Tony was a full-time job. A job he'd been born to.

Tony had been his father's son through and through.

And, Eric had been born to the job, too, but had resisted. Glancing at the new information Ruth had included, Rosa knew that Mary was starting to resist, too, for the sake of her young son.

While the scenery changed from urban sprawl to Indian gaming land to the landscape John Wayne Westerns were made of, Rosa read Ruth's research and reentered the world of Mary Graham and Walter Peabody.

She almost felt jarred when Sam pulled off the interstate at the Sun Lakes exit.

"I'm hungry," he said.

One thing for sure, she figured a few minutes later, Sam Packard was the quintessential cop, even out of uniform. He circled the parking lot twice until he found the perfect spot, one that would allow him to exit without backing out. Once they entered the restaurant, he checked out the restrooms, the dining room, and even the back before choosing a table.

She didn't blame him. After all, a chance encounter with the Santellises in a grocery story parking lot had introduced him to her. Who knew what a chance encounter with a Santellis in a fast-food restaurant might do? Kenny would find out about his brothers soon enough. And Cliff had to be figuring out that his house built on sand was crumbling.

After ordering for both of them, Sam chose a table that enabled him to see everyone who entered and exited. Once satisfied that the ghosts of the Santellis brothers weren't lurking behind the Frosty maker, he made a quick call to Ruth.

Rosa was privy to raised eyebrows and lots of "Uh-huhs."

"Well?" Rosa asked after he finally disconnected.

"The media is aware that you are alive and well and not in New Mexico. Kenny Santellis has disappeared. Cliff is acting strange, but so far hasn't made any phone calls or left his house."

He finished his hamburger in three bites, grabbed a couple of fries and glanced around to ascertain all was well before finally saying, "Eat. We need to get moving."

Well, she'd eaten on the run before — with him as a matter of fact. She bowed her head and said a quick prayer. He bowed his head, too, then put a few more fries in his mouth without seeming to notice that food was supposed to have flavor and be enjoyed.

As for Rosa, she knew that hot French fries beat cold French fries every time so she took a minute to enjoy before finally saying, "I've gone over much of Ruth's research. She did a good job of fleshing out some of the details I couldn't find."

"Tell me the most important stuff."

"Let's start with the Peabody case."

"We seem to always come back to him."

"Actually, not him. Her."

"Wanda?"

"No, Penny."

"Penny?"

"Walter's daughter."

He stopped eating. "I remember. She was a runaway. I saw her picture on the wall at Wanda's trailer."

Rosa almost choked on a fry. "You didn't know about Walter's daughter?"

"I joined the force after the bust. I went to his execution, and I did some of the last-minute paperwork, I even spoke with his widow, but his daughter must have had little or nothing to do with the murders. I don't remember her name listed on any of the reports, and if it was, I don't remember the information inspiring me to think it was important. Why is she important?"

"Two reasons. The first I know from Eric. When Penny was fifteen, she got caught dealing at Gila City High. I'm not sure if she was dealing with Walter's permission or not, but that really doesn't matter. She was busted — or should I say *not* busted because she was caught by Cliff. Before this point, I still think he hovered on the side of honesty. This is where I'm unclear. I can't prove anything, and I can't find Penny to ask her more questions. Believe me, both Wanda and I have tried."

"Why didn't you bring Penny up back at the restaurant? We could be on the lookout for her."

"I promised Wanda I'd keep Penny's name out of it if I could. Plus, I didn't read until a few minutes ago that Ruth had already figured out Penny's involvement." Rosa took a sip of her drink. "Ruth did a good job. She ran Penny's social security number.

Last time Penny had a job was eight months ago."

"You think she's dead?" Sam asked.

"No, she has money. She doesn't really need to work. Tony takes care of her. Sometimes, I think she tries to escape the life."

"Penny." Sam put down his hamburger and said slowly, "Penny. You said her name earlier. You said she was in the bathroom at Terrance Jackle's apartment. But, she wasn't on my list of those present. I don't remember checking up on her."

Rosa shook her head. He still denied the obvious, but then if she were in his shoes, maybe she would still be in denial, too. "Who gave the names of those present?"

"C-Cliff."

"Anybody collaborate?"

"Your friend Eric."

"Eric would leave Penny off."

"Why?"

"It goes back to family. The same reason why Sardi let me leave the apartment. He responded without thinking to Eric's request. Family. Eric hates what his brothers do with every fiber of his being, but he still loves them. He didn't mention Penny because of Tony. Tony takes care of his own, and Eric helped him out this time."

"Tony didn't take care of his friend Terrance Jackle."

"No, but then Terrance wasn't Tony's girl-friend."

"Girlfriend? But Tony's married."

It was an inane statement: Tony's married. Yet, listening to Sam actually assume that the marriage vow might mean something to a man like Tony Santellis was touching.

It meant that the marriage vow meant something to a man like Sam Packard.

"Yes, girlfriend," Rosa asserted, "and believe it or not, she is a nice woman."

"You've spoken with her?"

"Many times. When I was working with Eric and Jimmy, I probably ran into her about once a month. After Jimmy's death, I tracked her down. She used to hang out at a seedy bar off Grand Avenue. I hid in the backseat of her car one night and made her talk to me."

"Made her?"

"It wasn't hard. She hates Cliff."

"I can't believe you didn't tell me this earlier! What did Penny Peabody tell you?"

"Two things. One, she didn't see who shot Jimmy, and two, she met Tony when she was just thirteen while he was working at the car lot. Soon she was pushing at the high school. One day Cliff cornered her. She was all of fifteen and thought she'd be in prison the rest of her life. Instead he convinced her to set up a meeting with Tony — a meeting beneficial to everyone. Thus began Tony's and Cliff's partnership."

"Did you ask her about the Backseat Double Homicide?" Sam asked, leaning forward. "The case that sent her father to death row?"

"No, later, especially after I met the guy who worked with Yano, I wished I had, but it didn't occur to me at the time. Then, later, I couldn't find her again."

She was silent, watching him. Sam no longer looked at Rosa. Truly, he no longer spoke to her. He was remembering a time in his life when he'd thought it all made sense. "Those two border patrol officers were found, hands and feet bound, in the back of their squad car." He shuddered. It looked as if he was trying to shake off a memory. "I saw their pictures, met their families. Walter's fingerprints were all over the vehicle. It was Cliff's case. You know, even all these years later, I remember Walter. Something about his eyes always bothered me."

"His eyes?"

"And your eyes bother me." His hand reached across the table and cupped her cheek, a minute caress, and then his fingers stilled.

Rosa couldn't, didn't want to, move. His hand was warm, and she found herself leaning toward him, toward the warmth.

"Even before I knew who you really were, back when you were insisting your name was Lucy, your eyes reminded me of Walter's."

Sam removed his hand. For a second, Rosa wanted to snatch it back. For the last few years, her whole life had revolved around the Santellises, and drugs, and murder, and hiding, and in all that time, she couldn't remember being touched by anyone.

She'd been afraid to allow anyone, except Jesus, to get close enough.

"I saw Walter Peabody buckled into the electric chair," Sam said. "I saw him look at those of us in the audience. Before they put on the black death mask, I watched his eyes. He did not wear the expression of a guilty man, and neither do you."

She wiped the crumbs from her French fries into the bag. "Well, I'm glad I don't wear the expression of a guilty *man,* but I think the analogy would work better if you hadn't been partnered with Cliff for such a long time. I mean, you practically lived with the man and you didn't recognize the guilt in *his* eyes."

"There's a big difference." Sam gathered all their trash and put it on a tray. "I never had to look at Cliff's eyes while he was strapped into an electric chair."

Sixteen

They stopped for gas in Casa Grande, about halfway to Tucson, Arizona. Why hadn't Mary gone farther? Tucson wasn't far enough. But, then, Gila City hadn't been far enough, either. What was Mary up to? Suddenly, Rosa couldn't wait to find out.

"You know," she finally spoke. "I've made twenty million mistakes in my lifetime. One of the biggest was thinking that if I left my family in the dark about what I was up to, they'd be all right.

"They weren't, and now they're dead." Her voice cracked. "Cliff Handley did it. I know he did."

"You sure it wasn't Tony?" Sam asked.

"No, he more or less told me it wasn't him while he walked me to that hole he dropped me in. And, yes, again, here's a murder Cliff orchestrated but there's no witness."

Sam gripped the steering wheel with both hands. His knuckles turned white. He stared straight ahead and said nothing. Good thing, too, because Rosa didn't know if she could take words of sympathy or any touches of compassion. She continued. Her words so softly spoken that had this been part of the taped confession back in Phoenix nothing would have made it on the tape.

"I had all that money I could have given them, but I didn't know how. I should have found a way, sent them to Australia, Timbuktu, Houston!" She choked. "But, they'd have insisted on staying. Dad wouldn't miss work. And Mom, well, she loved her friends and volunteered at the hospital two mornings a week. No way would they be willing to leave." Rosa felt her throat closing until the very act of swallowing echoed through the car like a loud, painful hiccup. "They'd have insisted I go to the cops. That's the main reason I didn't contact them, tell them. But I always thought there'd be time."

"Rosa." Sam took one hand off the wheel and started to reach for her, but she flinched and stumbled on.

"I should have paid someone to kidnap them. After all, I know plenty of thugs." She recognized the hysteria in her voice and willed herself to calm down. *Breathe.* "Would you like me to tell you in more detail how they died? I listened to the account on the radio, you know, because I couldn't bear to see the pictures. Our media has a way with the graphic horrors of society. Or would you rather I tell you what their deaths have done to me?"

"We'll put Cliff away. I promise."

She nodded.

His cell phone rang. No classical music jingle for Sam Packard. No, his was just a boring hum that reminded Rosa of her dad's electric razor. Sam started a greeting but stopped before finishing. Obviously, the person on the other end didn't want to waste time on platitudes. He held up a hand, signaling Rosa to hold her questions. An almost impossible task, she had to sit on her hands, especially when he said, "You're kidding. I knew I shouldn't have taken her to my dad's place."

Finally, after about five minutes of non-stop diatribe from the other end, he said, "We just left Casa Grande." Then, he did some more listening. He also nodded a few times for all the good it did. The person speaking couldn't see him. Rosa wanted to snatch the phone from him and hear for herself. About the time she thought she'd die of curiosity, Sam said "Goodbye, Ruth," hit the power button, and expelled a gust of air. "Well, Cliff knows."

"Knows?"

"That you're alive. That he's no longer safe."

She suddenly understood the gust of air and imitated it. She'd let her guard down a bit and had forgotten to expect the worst. Oh, she'd expected Cliff to find out Tony and Sardi had been killed. She'd expected him to find out about her, too, but not yet. "How?" she squeaked.

"Of all things . . ." He shook his head again, only now she understood why. "You remember the Dundees?"

"Yes."

"The newlywed charade you and Dad were so proud of backfired. You see, while it was so sweet of them to drop off a gift basket, it wasn't nearly so sweet of them to e-mail quite a few of our mutual friends and tell them about my surprise nuptials."

"What?"

"The tiniest detail. One I didn't foresee. I guess someone finally called Cliff to laugh about my not taking enough time off for a honeymoon with my new wife, *Lucy.* Why didn't you think of a different name?"

"It happened so fast."

"Ruth says Cliff peeled out of his driveway as if he was being chased.

"Will he be arrested now?" Rosa managed

to croak.

"Yes." He shook his head. "I don't know what Cliff is thinking."

"He's not thinking."

She would have said more, but Sam didn't seem much in the mood for small talk as they sped toward Tucson. Rosa finished reading all of Ruth's paperwork and wrote in the margins. When all of this was over, she was taking Ruth to dinner, a fancy dinner, a dinner of thanksgiving. Of course, that dinner might have to wait until Rosa got out of prison. Rosa figured Ruth would be willing to wait.

Would Sam be willing to wait?

Wait for what? For the woman who had worked so hard to put his partner behind bars.

Cliff's wife, Susan, had stopped waiting for her husband two years ago. Rosa stared at the date Ruth had written down. Susan had filed for divorce the same month Rosa's parents died.

"Sam, have you spoken with Susan Handley lately?"

"I tried to see her last Thursday. She'd moved."

"I think we're making a mistake."

"About what?"

"We're heading for Tucson and Mary Graham hoping for a credible witness. It's iffy at best. Susan filed for divorce just after my parents died, about the same time Dustin Atkins died. That's pretty coincidental, wouldn't you say? I think she's the one we need to pursue."

He started to respond with a "Not really," but then he thought of her neighbors saying she'd not stuck around long enough to meet them.

"Did Ruth provide an address?"

Rosa read one.

"No, that's where I went to yesterday." He grabbed his cell phone and hit Redial. In a matter of minutes, Ruth provided Susan's new address.

While Rosa listened, Sam called Rafael. Rosa could tell Rafael wasn't happy with the change of plans, but he agreed to let Sam proceed. At the next exit, Sam turned around and started back the way they'd come.

"Susan owns a dress shop in Gilbert," he told Rosa. "It should still be open."

She looked at her watch. She'd always remember this as the Saturday that never ended. She'd awakened at a ridiculous hour in Tonto Ridge, she'd breakfasted in Phoenix, she'd lunched in Casa Grande, she'd seen the Tucson skyline, and now it looked as though the supper bell would ring in Gilbert.

Gilbert, at one time, had been a sleepy offshoot of Phoenix. Then developers and the wealthy descended and now it was a full-fledged town. Susan Handley had opened a dress shop right on Gilbert Road. It wasn't hard to find. SUSAN'S was its name. Either she didn't really fear for her life, or she didn't have the heart to run far and effectively. When Rosa and Sam arrived, it was well past the time of late-afternoon shopping, and only a handful of teenagers loitered on the sidewalk.

"Duck down," Sam said, parking right in front of the store.

Rosa obeyed. Huddled on the floorboard of Jerry's Caddy, she closed her eyes and prayed while listening for any sound that might indicate Sam was in trouble.

None came.

"Okay, you can get out."

If mannequins in the store's windows were an indication, it also catered to women who had more plastic in their wallets than cash and good sense. In all honesty, Sam couldn't recall ever being in a ladies' dress shop. Cliff's mother owned one, but Sam had always waited in the car if Cliff needed to run in for something.

Susan's walls were the color of blood, and the whole place smelled like flowers, too many flowers. The airconditioning unit was on overload, maybe because sweaters were half-price. Rosa, even in the middle of a bust that might mean jail time for her, managed to look interested in a green pantsuit displayed just to her left. Sometimes, Sam just didn't understand women. Susan Handley moved toward them, her face taking on the anticipatory smile of a hunter moving in for a kill. She no longer looked like the soccer mom who helped hand out hot dogs at backyard cookouts. Her hair was a different color and curled right at her shoulders. However, she still wore more jewelry than any woman Sam knew.

Except for the wedding ring that used to bind her to Cliff. It was missing.

"May I help —" She saw Sam and the anticipatory smile turned into a grimace. "Please tell me you're here looking for a dress for your new bride."

"Hello, Susan."

Susan made a strangling sound. Rosa wouldn't describe it as human, but she understood the woman's pain. There were three shoppers browsing the racks. They all looked.

"You're not going to faint, are you?" Sam asked.

"No."

"We need to talk."

"I have nothing to say to you."

"Is Katie here?"

Susan didn't answer. She suddenly looked old, lost and incapable of making decisions.

"Susan," Sam said gently. "Cliff's about to be arrested, and he's not acting rationally."

"I'm sorry, ladies," Susan announced loudly while clapping her hands. "SUSAN'S is closing for the day."

"It's almost six o'clock! You're going to close anyway in a few minutes. Why the rush?" a customer protested.

From behind a dressing room curtain came a muffled expletive and a "You've got to be kidding" groan.

Susan cleared the place in twenty minutes. She locked the door and led Sam and Rosa into a back office.

Katie Handley jumped up and rushed to give Sam a hug. After that, she turned to greet Rosa.

"You must be Lucy, Sam's wife. I was about to buy a congratulations card and mail it! I'm so glad to meet you."

Sam took Rosa by the elbow and sat her in one of the chairs in front of Katie's desk. "Rosa, are you all right?"

"She looks like Jimmy," Rosa whispered.

"Rosa?" Susan whispered.

"Rosa?" Katie lost her smile.

Before Sam could say another word, his phone sounded. The two Handley women stood at a distance and glared at Rosa while Sam took the call. It was Rafael. For a man who never raised his voice, Rafael certainly proved why yelling wasn't necessary. He didn't waste words and he left no room for discussion. In just four sentences, Rafael informed Sam that Cliff had disappeared, that Wanda Peabody was missing, and that Tony's and Sardi's murders had been broadcast over an illicit Internet site. Then, Rafael ordered Sam to take Rosa and the Handley women to the safe house they'd arranged this morning. The Handleys would stay there and Rafael would make other arrangements for Rosa.

Now!

As he depressed the power button, Sam noticed Rosa staring at the pictures displayed on a filing cabinet behind Katie's desk.

Family pictures.

Cliff wasn't in a single one.

Jimmy was.

Comprehension came swiftly. Here sat Rosa with her past threatening to erupt and in front of two women who blamed her for something she wasn't guilty of. Gently, Sam said, "Susan, listen to me, Rosa didn't have anything to do with Jimmy's death. And she couldn't help him after he was shot."

"That's not true," Susan spat.

"It is true," Sam said. "And I'll prove it to you once we're in the car and heading out of here. We can't stay. It's not safe."

"Is Cliff coming here?" Susan asked, suddenly looking frightened.

"We don't know where Cliff is."

Rosa stood, so fast she bumped the desk. Books and paperwork fell to the floor. "What do you mean you don't know where Handley is?"

"The cops lost him."

"The Gila City cops? The ones who couldn't keep up with the Santellis brothers after they shot at me. These are the ones who've now lost Cliff Handley. Maybe they wanted to lose him! Maybe the whole police force, the whole town, is corrupt."

"That's not true, and you know it. Be sensible. No cop in his right mind is going to side with Cliff now," Sam insisted.

"You mean they know," Susan said in

wonderment.

"About what," Sam said quickly before Susan could rethink her words.

"About what, Mom?"

"Does Katie have to be involved in this?" Susan asked. "Can't we send her somewhere, somewhere safe?"

"I'm taking all of you somewhere safe," Sam said.

"Mom, what's going on? This is about Dad. This is why we moved to Gilbert. It wasn't just a silly argument, was it?"

"Ladies," Sam urged. "We need to leave, *now*."

"I saw the date," Rosa said. "The date you filed for divorce. January 12, two years ago."

"So?" Susan's response was halfhearted. Sam didn't know if he wanted Rosa to back off, or if he wanted the truth. Katie certainly wanted the truth.

"What are you hiding from me, Mother. What did Daddy do?"

What did Daddy do?

Maybe the question should have been what *didn't* Daddy do.

"Susan?" Sam nudged.

With an apologetic look aimed at her daughter, Susan said, "It's all going to come out. Better you hear it from me. He ordered the Cagnalias' execution, from the phone in our living room. I overheard the whole conversation."

Yes, Susan Handley would be a very credible witness.

He escorted them from the shop to the car and took his place behind the wheel, glad to have something to do with his hands.

So, Susan Handley had overheard Cliff issue the order to kill the Cagnalias. No wonder she'd taken her daughter and fled. Still, she probably figured killing Rosa's parents was more for revenge than a career move.

Judging by the look on the ladies' faces, it was going to be a long drive to the safe house in Phoenix. Susan and Katie were in back. Neither were willing to sit by Rosa. Both were terrified.

Rosa simply looked shellshocked.

"Susan, you heard Cliff order their deaths? When? Where? Why didn't you tell anyone?" Sam hated the traffic on the freeway. He hated what Cliff had done to the three women in his care. He hated that he felt almost willing to bully Susan to find out what she knew.

Susan didn't answer.

"Come on, talk," he insisted. "We have to find Cliff before he hurts anyone else."

"Can't you turn *her* over to local authorities here, Sam, and then take us to Gila City." Katie wanted to know.

"Rosa's in just as much, if not more, danger than you. She is not, I repeat, the enemy. And the only way to fix things is to work together."

"A safe house? Why not jail?" Katie wanted to know. "Why is she with you?"

"Tell her, Rosa," Sam urged. "This *is* Jimmy's sister. And, Susan *is* Jimmy's mother. They deserve to know."

And so Rosa told them about working undercover with Jimmy. As Sam listened to her summarize her involvement, he realized that she would make an excellent public relations officer. She knew just what to say. She started with the personal. She knew Jimmy's favorite movie, food and the name of his girlfriend. She knew his favorite childhood memory with his sister. By the time Rosa started with the night in Terrance Jackle's apartment, she had won them over, convinced them she had been Jimmy's friend, and both the Handley women were leaning forward.

They got to the safe house, really an apartment, before Rosa had time to mention who had shot Jimmy. Good thing. Sam had been wondering how to interrupt. Now was not the time for Susan and Katie to find out that information. Not without grief counselors nearby. Not without some sort of warning.

Of course, in truth, there was no way to prepare them for the ultimate price Jimmy had paid for Cliff's sins.

Rafael and Mitch both were at the apartment waiting. Rafael pulled Susan into a hug and led her and Katie to a table in a corner of the living room. Sam relaxed some, and was again reminded why Rosa had been so hesitant to trust. Cliff and his family knew everyone.

Two undercover cops lounged outside. Another, who looked ridiculously young, sat in the kitchen area, drinking a soda and watching the scene in the living room with interest.

A few minutes of eavesdropping on Rafael and Susan's conversation brought little closure to what he and Rosa had been worrying about. No one knew where Cliff was. No one knew where Kenny Santellis was. Wanda Peabody hadn't been heard from.

Sam sat on the couch next to Rosa. "Are you ready for all this? What you've been aiming for is about to happen. Think about it." He glanced over at Susan Handley who was deep in conversation with Rafael while Mitch paced the room. "You've got yet another credible witness."

"*We've* got," Rosa said. "And I'm still feeling vulnerable. After all, one witness is missing. Another witness is not committed, and then it is rather scary to think that the rest of us are gathered in one place. I think we should scatter."

"We're safe," he assured her. Across the room, Katie Handley broke down in tears. Rafael patted her back and handed her a tissue.

Rosa closed her eyes. "I'm amazed by how much she looks like Jimmy."

"When they were little, Cliff always joked that it would be Katie who went into law enforcement. She's the one who always wanted to hear his stories. Jimmy could have cared less."

"What changed?"

Sam reached over and took her hand and squeezed. "It makes so much sense now. Jimmy got disgusted by how many of his friends got involved in drugs. He wanted to make a difference."

Rosa nodded. "He did make a difference. Jimmy was a good cop, nothing like his father. I can tell you that."

"You're right." Susan Handley had left the

table where she'd been spilling her guts to Rafael. Her hair was no longer beauty parlor perfect. Her makeup could best be described as melting. Sam didn't know who needed him more: Rosa or Susan. He stayed by Rosa.

It felt right.

It felt like where he was supposed to be *forever.*

"You're right," Susan repeated. "Jimmy was a good cop, nothing like his father. You wanted to know why I didn't tell anybody about Cliff's actions against your parents."

Rosa tensed, and for a moment, Sam thought he might have to hold her back. From what, he wasn't sure. He knew her enough now to know she wouldn't go after Susan. He knew she wanted to know the whys of it all. He also knew she'd taken about as much as she could during these last few days.

Pride swelled when she relaxed against him and simply said, "Yes."

"Because no one would have believed me." She aimed her scowl at Sam. "Right, Sam?"

All he could do was nod and feel an emptiness as Rosa withdrew.

Emptiness had been absent from his life since pulling Rosa out of that hole. Really, since watching her crouch next to her car and pray.

Emptiness had taken hold of his life when his mother died, when he turned his back on God, and had neglected to pray.

"But I believe you now," Sam said. "And I'll do everything I can to make right what Cliff made wrong." He turned to Rosa. "Rosa, when this is over, I'm not going away. Ever."

It was the wrong time and place to let her know that he was more than half in love with her, but Sam was half-afraid if he waited for the right moment, there wouldn't be one. And, he wanted, needed, for her to know that he saw her the way a man *should* see a woman. That somewhere in the middle of all this, he'd fallen in love with her.

In just six days.

Impossible. Improbable. Undeniable.

Judging by her response, or lack of, she wasn't surprised. But, then, maybe she didn't realize how much he was trying to tell her in so few words.

To his relief, while she didn't return to his side, she also didn't let go of his hand. It felt right, and at the moment, to keep her safe, he'd hold on to the hand forever. He was just working up the courage to tell her so when Susan started in again.

"At first, I thought I'd heard wrong. Then, your parents died, and I was living with this man who —" she slowed, choking on her words "— could kill people. Still, I thought he'd gone over the edge with his revenge. I didn't know about the others. I didn't know how long he'd been involved. He changed after Jimmy died."

"No," Rosa said. "He didn't change at all."

SEVENTEEN

Mitch hollered, "Sam, Susan, I need you over here for a minute!"

They followed orders and joined Mitch, Rafael and Katie at the kitchen table. Rosa joined the cop in the kitchen. She opened the refrigerator and took out a soda. She grabbed one for Sam, too, and walked it over. Even in the middle of all this, she could think of him? Take care of him?

Impossible.

"So, what do you think, Sam?"

Tearing his eyes away from Rosa, Sam looked at Rafael. It didn't take a genius to realize that Rafael not only knew Sam wasn't paying attention to him but also knew just exactly what, *who,* Sam was paying attention to.

"About?"

"About Susan's offer to act as bait," Mitch snapped.

"Absolutely not. Cliff is unbalanced."

"Exactly what I said." Mitch stopped pacing and glared. "The man shot his own son, he wouldn't hesitate to shoot an ex-wife."

The words hung in the air, and Mitch took a step back. Nervous tension seemed to seep from his body like a deflating balloon.

He muttered a strangled, "I . . ."

Susan stood, and Sam thought he'd never seen a woman increase in stature in just a matter of moments. She fixed Mitch with a glance that would have downed a lesser man. As it was, he looked helpless. Not a natural look for Mitch.

His shell-shocked look matched Katie's exactly.

Susan turned to face Rosa. Sam turned with her, following her gaze toward the kitchen. Rosa had one hand on the microwave door and one hand covering her mouth.

Susan barely got the words out. "Cliff shot Jimmy?"

Rosa removed her hand. "Yes, I was there when it happened."

Susan crumpled to the floor. The keening sound that came from her didn't sound natural, but Rosa understood. She'd cried many a night, for Jimmy, for her parents, but never as Susan cried. Never like a mother who'd just lost her child, again.

A voice is heard in Ramah, weeping and great mourning. Rachel weeping for her children and refusing to be comforted because they are no more.

The men couldn't seem to move. Sometimes, against men, tears were the most powerful weapon. Susan's tears dampened the carpet. Katie, who'd been silent since she'd entered the safe house, trembled.

Cliff was responsible for all this. "Get her to the hospital," Rosa told Rafael. "She's in shock."

Mitch, guilt taking the edgy look from his face, took Katie by the arm. At just a nod from Rafael they headed toward the door. It didn't appear that Susan was even aware of what was going on, but when her daughter moved, Susan tried to sit up. Her tears changed into gasps.

Rafael took out his phone and in just a few words arranged for a grief counselor to meet them at the hospital. He then called Lucas, issued an order and lifted Susan to her feet. Joining Mitch, he helped escort the women out of the apartment. Sam, white-faced and serious, all cop again, paced the room.

Rosa needed him, but he needed time.

The microwave dinged, but Rosa was no longer hungry. She sat at the kitchen table and prayed, for Susan, for Katie, and for all this to end.

A few minutes later, Rafael returned and started things moving once again. The young cop, who looked as if he'd rather be anywhere but here, was ordered to stay with Rosa. The more they found out about Cliff, the more they realized the depth of his deceptions and his willingness to eliminate those who got in his way.

They were moving to yet another location, one so many people didn't know about. The three of them, Sam, Rafael and the young cop spent a ridiculous amount of time circling Rosa, making sure she was out of sight, making her duck down once she got in the car. Then, Rafael took off, and the young cop followed Sam and Rosa in a plain brown sedan much like the one Sam had driven when he pulled her out of the hole in the desert. Ironically, their destination took them back toward Broken Bones and the empty desert that surrounded it.

"Where do you think Cliff is?" Rosa tried not to shiver. She didn't need to be afraid.

Sam was right next to her.

"If I were him, I'd be on my way to Mexico."

"But you don't think that's what he'll do?"

"No, I think he's lost all ability to rationalize."

She nodded and stared out the window. Before long his phone rang. He uttered a terse hello and then almost dropped the phone. The car swerved as he grabbed for it. "Don't you dare do anything rash," he ordered the person on the other end. He followed that with a threat, "If you hurt her . . ." Then he lapsed into silence. Finally there came a series of "Wait! Wait! Wait!" before Sam threw the phone as hard as he could at the windshield.

Rosa covered her face in case it bounced and then dived for the phone because Sam was going to need it.

Sam gave a half laugh, half grunt. "Cliff Handley's at Walt's old gas station. He's holding Ruth hostage and claims he's already shot Wanda."

"Oh, no," Rosa whispered. "This is my fault. What does he want?"

"You," Sam said cautiously and slowed the car down to a crawl. He looked at Rosa. "He wants you."

"Let's go," Rosa said. "What better time

to take him on than when you're there to watch my back."

"Not a chance." He took his cell phone from her hand and called Rafael. In a few hurried, terse statements, Sam filled Rafael in on Cliff's phone call.

Sam listened for a few minutes and then hung up. "They're heading for Gila City. Rafael is calling both the sheriff and a SWAT team."

Sam glanced behind him and pulled over to the side of the road.

"Oh, no, you don't." Rosa grabbed the door handle and held on. "You are not leaving me here. You are letting me come to the gas station with you. It's the only way to make sure Wanda and Ruth have a chance. It's the only way I get closure!"

"No, absolutely not."

"What did Rafael say?"

"Rafael wants you safe. I want you safe."

"I only feel safe when you're watching me."

"I'm going to be too busy to watch over you. They're bringing in a negotiator, but I know Cliff and that will be a waste of time. I need to be the negotiator. I can convince him to turn himself in without anyone getting hurt." Sam stepped out of the car. He motioned for the cop trailing them to pull alongside.

Rosa panicked. No way was she allowing herself to be left behind. Not when she'd come this far. "You're not in a position to negotiate. You're too involved."

"Which is exactly why I'm the one who should do it. I can speak for you, I can speak for Susan, and I can speak for myself. Cliff knows me."

"But," Rosa said gently, "the Cliff you want to reason with is not the Cliff you knew. I'm the one who needs to be there. He hates me. Hate is a strong motivator. He doesn't hate you, he doesn't hate Wanda, he doesn't hate Ruth. I can get a reaction out of him."

"He hates everyone, especially himself," Sam said. "I can take care of this. You go to the safe house. Let the authorities watch over you. When everything is over, I'll call you, immediately, I promise."

"No." If she had to, she'd walk the rest of the way to Gila City. She would not be left behind! "I worked for this more than two years. I deserve closure. And, I know for a fact he'll kill Ruth. She means nothing to him. I mean something. I know where the money is."

"I'm not taking you. And I'll gladly risk your anger if leaving you behind keeps you alive." Officer Friendly, who wasn't so friendly, returned.

"Sam," Rosa said. "What if I were the cop and you the victim? What if Cliff had murdered your family, friends, and taken away everything you'd ever held dear? Would you be happy waiting in some safe house with a guard you didn't even know?"

The cop in question got out of the car and started toward them. Sam insisted, "He'll protect you with his life."

"Not like you would. Please, I'll stay in the car. I promise. I promise."

I promise, she said. He understood her want, need. She did, in so many ways, deserve the closure she'd mentioned. She, more than anyone else, had put together the case against Cliff Handley. He started to apologize, to tell her no one more time, and then he heard the sound he'd yet to hear from her. The sound of tears.

She hadn't cried when Cliff tried to choke her.

She hadn't cried when he'd pulled her broken and bleeding from the deserted mine.

She hadn't cried when he stitched her shoulder.

Tears. The one feminine trait that brought

him to his knees.

If he left her behind, he'd only worry. "I'm going to regret this to my dying day," Sam muttered before walking over to explain to the young cop.

"No, you won't." Rosa sniffled.

She'd ridden shotgun with him now for days. Except for Cliff, he'd never felt so comfortable with a partner. She wasn't as grumpy as Cliff, or as chatty as Ruth. Looking over, Sam noticed her lips moving. She was praying again. Praying, no doubt, for Eric. Praying for Wanda and Ruth. Praying for Susan and Katie. Praying for him. Praying for them all. Maybe she'd even find it in her heart to pray for Cliff.

She had this prayer thing down pat.

For the first time in a long time, he wished he did.

"Why don't you pray out loud." The moment the words left his mouth, he wanted them back. Admitting he needed to be in touch with God meant that he was willing to trust . . .

Trust?

He'd spent all this time working on getting Rosa to trust him . . . Could it be that at the same time, God was working on getting Sam to trust Him?

Sam stopped wrestling with his thoughts

and started listening to Rosa pray.

It felt good.

A minute later, heading in the direction of Walter's gas station, Sam figured the ulcer he was developing had Rosa's and God's names all over it.

What was he thinking? Taking a civilian to a hostage situation. Since coming into contact with Rosa Cagnalia, he'd not only lost sight of the golden rules of law enforcement, but he'd rewritten at least eight of them. Not that his revisions would ever be adopted by any sane police officer. No, Sam Packard figured suspension without pay was the least of his worries.

Shaking his head at his own vulnerability, Sam grumbled a few complaints — grumbling made him feel better — and then he got on the phone with Mitch and gleaned as much information about the locale as he could. Rosa listened intently. By her occasional nod, he guessed she already knew some of the story.

After Walt Peabody went to jail, another man purchased the gas station and kept it going for about six months. Sam remembered Dustin surmising that too many customers expected more than fuel when they pulled in. For an honest man, it would have been disconcerting. After that owner folded, the gas station had gone up for sale.

Yano's used car lot was still in business. Good thing, because without the Used Cars sign, there'd be no light at all. The gas station was a ghost of what it had once been. The fence that at one time surrounded it had long ago fallen victim to vagrants. The pumps were gone and part of the awning had fallen down. Three cars were parked in the street. Two were in Walt's parking lot. Police cruisers blocked traffic coming and going. Sam parked in the street and got out. The officer assigned to guard Rosa parked behind him, finally starting to get the gist of just how serious the situation was about to become.

"Sir, I don't think —"

"Stay here. Make sure she doesn't leave the car."

He drew his gun and Rosa obediently stayed put.

Walking toward the gas station, Sam was taken back in time. There'd been two service bays and two pumps out front, and Walt had provided full service instead of flavored coffee or bagels. There'd been a Coke machine outside and a few boxes of gum on top of the cash register that Wanda usually manned.

Rafael was on his phone. Lucas and Mitch

were talking with some uniformed officers. The perimeter of the station was heavily guarded. Sam knew at least eight officers circled the building. That's how many he'd have recruited.

"Is the negotiator here yet?" he asked, joining Rafael's group.

"Negative." Mitch was back to being all business. If his earlier slip of the tongue with Cliff's ex-wife had ruffled him, no one could tell now.

Sam took the binoculars Lucas offered and perused the station. For the most part, it was too dark to see anything. Lucas pointed and Sam focused on a body lying just inside the door where Walt's customers had entered to pay. It was slender enough to be Wanda, but the blackness effectively covered whether the body was male, female, young, old, dead or alive.

"Have we positively identified the woman as Wanda?"

"Negative." Mitch aimed his own binoculars at the body. "If we move beyond the pump ledge, Cliff shoots at us."

"Is he aiming to kill?"

"Oh, yeah."

A lump clogged in Sam's throat. "Have we heard anything from Ruth?"

"She's alive." He looked down, as if getting his bearings, then stated. "We've heard her scream."

Rafael ended his call. "It's going to be another fifteen minutes before reinforcements arrive. I don't want to wait. If Wanda Peabody is still alive, we need to get to her now."

"Has Cliff said anything?" Sam asked.

"He wants a helicopter, $750,000 and Rosa."

"Surely he doesn't believe that will happen."

"I think he does," Mitch said sadly. "Because the last time he yelled his request, he put another bullet in the woman lying on the ground."

EIGHTEEN

It was cold in the car and dark. The most Rosa could make out were the outlines of men who seemed unwilling to engage in much movement. Considering that it was Cliff holed up inside the gas station, Rosa figured she was looking at fairly intelligent men. Intelligence certainly was a gift of God, but in Rosa's opinion it was not enough. Not when she had the faith to pray. Bowing her head, she petitioned God on behalf of all the men risking their lives. She placed her fear in God's hand. Only God could get her through this night.

She'd already had a front seat to Jimmy's murder, she didn't want to watch the sequel tonight. Yet, she'd insisted on attending. If she were to admit the truth, it wasn't the thought of Cliff Handley finally coming to justice or even her distress that Ruth was now suffering at Cliff's hands that made her want to return to Gila City. No, it was the thought of not knowing what was happening to Sam Packard that she couldn't bear. In all honesty, she probably started having feelings for the man when he rescued her cat. And, she loved him all the more for now putting his life on the line to rescue Ruth.

Sam had never enjoyed the cumbersome bulletproof vests so necessary to his profession. Putting one on in anticipation of a meeting with his ex-partner, revered mentor and onetime friend, felt especially oppressive.

The crisp midnight air whistled at the back of Sam's neck. Sweat beaded. The five pounds of polymeric material shouldn't add heat, not in this kind of weather. Sam figured his nerves were haywire.

A familiar feeling since Rosa had rammed into his life.

An itch started at his hairline, then jumped to his lower back before finally settling on his left ankle. Scratching wouldn't relieve the annoyance.

Rafael seemed to have run out of orders and instead switched to giving advice. "Keep calm, Sam. Even if Cliff loses it, you can't."

Sam nodded and checked his gun.

Rafael continued, ' "The only way to

bring Cliff in alive, is to treat him like the man you once knew."

Yeah, right, Sam thought as he tried his radio, made sure it worked, then hooked it to his belt.

Rafael droned on, his voice a monotonous hum that actually made a difference. "Tell him stories about Ruth. Make him see her more as a person than a hostage. Make him like her."

When Rafael was finally satisfied that Sam was a virtual Goliath, Sam started toward the gas pump dock and destiny.

"Cliff! It's me, Sam."

Silence resonated.

"Cliff, you gotta know that what you've asked for is impossible. Please, let Ruth go. She has nothing to do with this. She wasn't even on the force when you were. Let me take her place."

"You got *Lucy* with you, Sam?" Cliff spat.

What was it Rosa had said right before he'd agreed to let her tag along?

The Cliff you want to reason with is not the Cliff you know. He could almost hear her voice, see her smile, smell the scent that was Rosa, feel her love. And tagging along with his thoughts of love, unbidden, came thoughts of the God that Cliff Handley didn't know and how that absence allowed evil to dwell.

Sam had partnered with Cliff for years and hadn't recognized him for what he really was.

Sam had partnered with Rosa for only a week and knew what she really was: everything Sam Packard wanted, needed. Rosa was good, kind, caring. She made Sam want to be a better man — a man who knew what love really was and who knew God.

"Cliff, none of this is Rosa's fault. She's already made a statement to the police and so have others. Eliminating her will not make all this go away. Let Ruth go. I'll take her place." Sam inched around a pole, exposing himself, and almost cringing at the thought of a gunshot he expected but did not hear.

"It's too late!" Cliff yelled. "I know it's over. I'm willing to go down, but I'm taking Rosa Cagnalia with me."

"We're not giving you Rosa, but if we can get you the $750,000 will you let Ruth go?"

"No."

Before Sam could make another offer, Ruth screamed. Sam rushed forward into the sound of the gunshot he'd expected earlier.

There were more screams. In front of him, behind him, from him. He hit the ground, feeling clumsy because of the vest. His chin connected with the cement and blood washed over his tongue. Behind him, he could hear shouts, doors slamming, and of all things, someone coughing.

It took him a few minutes before he felt safe — no, not safe, but willing — enough to push himself up. Once he made it to one knee, he heard more shouting.

"Grab her!"

"Idiot, you were supposed to be watching her!"

"Oh, no!"

He turned and what he saw didn't surprise him. Rosa was barreling across the pavement toward him. She wasn't looking left, right, or even toward the gas station. She was looking at him.

Even with the commotion he could hear Ruth's cry of warning. He could hear the click of Cliff's handgun. And, Sam Packard, who'd always laughed when he'd heard cops talk about being superheroes and having superhero strength, lunged the impossible distance to shield Rosa.

And prayed the whole way.

Prayed with the same earnestness that he'd prayed when his mother was lying so sick in bed.

The gun's report sounded, as Sam knew

it would, and he felt something hit his back even as he slammed into Rosa and knocked her to the ground.

He bit his tongue again, but he was glad for the pain because it seemed to effectively block whatever he should be feeling from getting shot in the back.

For a woman who claimed to have not cried in two years, Rosa was making up for lost time. He could feel her tears on his cheeks. She cupped his face in her hands and her fingers trailed the mixture of blood and tears.

God had answered his prayers. She was alive.

"I bit my tongue," he blustered.

She cried even harder.

Rafael and the others charged past them. Twisting, Sam loosened Rosa's grip and turned to watch. Two cops went to the body lying in the gas station's doorway. Once they pulled her toward the nearest cruiser, he could see the wild gray hair that so defined Wanda Peabody. "She's alive," one of the cops called.

Good, Sam thought, she's proclaimed Walt's innocence for almost twenty years. She deserved to see justice done.

Ruth's crying blended with the noise Rosa made, and Sam thought that weeping had never sounded so good. It meant that Ruth was still alive, not only still alive, but kicking. A third woman stepped from the darkness of the bay closest to the street. She held a gun.

Rosa choked off her crying, but her sniffling almost kept Sam from understanding her question. "Penny, is that you?"

NINETEEN

She'd turned into a girl. It had only taken four weeks. Amidst interrogations from the Gila City police, the feds, and internal affairs, Rosa managed to find the time to dye her hair back to its natural color, join LA Fitness, and drag him — not kicking and screaming, because he had a cracked disc — to church.

Small towns had a lot to offer. The Fifth Street Church had welcomed him with open arms. They'd told him stories he hadn't known about his mother. They'd brought dinner to his apartment when they knew Rosa wasn't around.

They reminded him of the joy he could take by believing in hope — believing and trusting in God.

He'd gone forward and repented of his sins, asked forgiveness, and words couldn't describe the peace he'd felt afterwards.

Well, in some circles police officers were

known as peace officers!

He loved it; he loved her.

What he didn't love was time spent off work because he could barely bend. The report called it blunt force trauma. Cliff, luckily, had used only common ammunition, or it could have been much worse.

Still, the time off allowed him to spend every day with Rosa, getting to know her without the shadow of his ex-partner along.

It would be a long time before the whole story about Cliff came to light. Penny Peabody knew more than she was telling, knew more than she was capable of telling. Since the night of Cliff's death, she'd been under psychiatric care. That state was especially interested in the fact that ballistics showed that the same gun that had killed Cliff had also been responsible for Tony's and Sardi's death.

Penny felt little remorse for killing Cliff. He was responsible for the death of her father and her fiancé. She'd been living in the back room of Walt's gas station and had been a little too visible after Tony's and Sardi's death. Ruth, of all people, took a call about a prowler. Cliff had no one else to follow, so he'd been following Ruth. He'd been hoping to snag Sam or Rosa. He hadn't expected to deal with both Wanda and Penny.

Wanda would live but was still in the hospital.

Rosa visited her every day.

As for Rosa, Sam intended to marry her just as soon as she, as everything, calmed down. Sooner, if she'd agree to it. They had a few things to work out. Rosa wasn't quite ready to settle down in Gila City. Cliff's hometown was reeling from the news that a favorite son was actually a black sheep. They'd accept her with open arms soon enough, though.

"So, what do you think?" Rosa asked. She put one hand on her hip and pretended to walk down a runway. Go Away tripped along behind trying to dislodge the hat Ruth's daughter, Megan, had placed on his head.

Sam rolled his eyes. This was ridiculous. He'd thought spending the day at Jerry's would be relaxing, easy, fun. Instead, he was privy to a ludicrous fashion show that no one in law enforcement should be subjected to.

Both Elmer and Jerry were enjoying it tremendously.

Ruth and Megan were active participants.

"Might be a bit snug under the arms," Ruth noted.

Rosa raised her arms. "You think?"

"I think." Ruth nodded. "But then I'm shorter than you."

"Sam?"

He raised both hands helplessly. "Don't ask me."

"But I want to look perfect when I'm walking beside you."

"You'll look perfect," he managed to say. "If you ever walk beside me dressed like that."

"What about shoes?" Rosa asked Ruth.

"I buy high-gloss oxfords online. It's cheaper."

Sam groaned.

"I also buy my Chukka boots online," Ruth added.

Sam groaned again. "Rosa, please. Don't make me give you advice about police uniforms. I think you're moving much too fast. The full pardon is still aeons of paperwork away, and it was only three weeks ago that you didn't trust the police and now you want to *be* one of them."

She smiled at him. "Yes, but you changed my mind. I trust the police now."

"Please," Sam moaned. "You really don't want my advice about police jackets and belts and stuff. You really don't want —"

"And here," Rosa said, "I was thinking

about asking your advice about a wedding dress. Hmm."

Sam started to go to one knee but stopped the minute the pain kicked in. "You're kidding."

"Nope."

"I'm outta here," Ruth said and guided Megan out the door and into the Arizona sunshine. Jerry and Elmer followed.

Sam held his back and moaned.

Rosa grinned. "And here I was dreaming about you proposing while down on one knee. Maybe I should wait until you're all better."

"I am all better." He meant it. He had a job he was proud of, a woman he loved, and was discovering more every day about the God he'd almost turned his back on. Before he uttered another word, he took a moment to pray, then raised his head and said, "It doesn't get any better than this."

Dear Reader,

Oh, the joys of being a writer! Rosa and Sam introduced themselves to me five years ago and wanted their stories told. Sometimes an idea for a book just won't go away. Dutifully, I sat down and started writing, but life interfered. Marriage, a new home, baby, job and book contracts required Rosa and Sam to wait many years before their happily-ever-after could be told.

When I finally dived into their story, I realized how much I appreciate God's presence when the world is seemingly spinning out of control. I fell in love with the idea of "Listen to my cry for help, my King and my God, for to You I pray. In the morning, O Lord, You hear my voice; in the morning I lay my requests before You and wait in expectation." It made me aware of how I need to lay my requests before God every morning in order to feel the comfort He offers, the Promised Land He offers, the happily ever after He offers

Special thanks go to Richard Solita, a retired police officer and the author of *Twenty Years of Vaudeville and a Pension: What Really Happens Behind the Badge, Based on True Stories of Chicago's Finest,* who read my manuscript and tried to save me from any serious mistakes concerning a policeman's life. And I also thank my readers! I hope you enjoyed Rosa and Sam's story.

Have a blessed day.

Pamela Tracy

QUESTIONS FOR DISCUSSION

1. Fear is often what motivates the telling of a lie. Fear motivated Abraham to lie about Sarah being his wife. Fear motivated Peter to deny the Savior. When Rosa is arrested, she lies about her name and background. Is there any justification for Rosa's actions — her lies?

2. Is there any one of us who has not lied? What does the Bible say about lying? What could Rosa have done instead? What would you have done?

3. At first, Rosa did not feel she could tell Sam the truth because of his history with Cliff Handley. List some of the events in the story that finally led Rosa to divulge the truth to Sam.

4. How did Sam respond at first? Have you ever had a friend betray you by not being

the person you thought she was? What happens after a friend's betrayal? How difficult is it to still be a friend?

5. Can you think of an event or events in your life that helped you unburden to someone besides the Lord? How did you feel after sharing your story?

6. What traits did Sam have that made him a hero? What traits did Rosa have that made her a heroine? Do you share any of these traits? Which ones? How do you use them to God's glory? Which traits would you most like to develop in your own life? Think about someone in your life who is an example to you because he or she has many of these traits.

7. Sam drifted away from the church after his mother died, but truthfully, he started drifting during his partnership with Cliff. Sometimes it's the subtle nudgings that change our course and not just a blatant happening. Can you think of someone in your life whose influence caused you to stumble? How can you change your course and make your influence cause the other person to see the example of Jesus?

8. Cliff Handley at one time was a good, honest cop. What prompted him to fall so deeply into sin? Was it the quest for power or the quest for money?

9. Eric Santellis sat in jail for a crime he did not commit — partly because of his last name. After he is released from prison, what can he do to help his reputation? Should he fight to establish his "good" name or should he change his name?

10. At the end of the story, it is implied that Rosa was considering the possibility of becoming a police officer. Before running from the law and changing her name, she was an E.R. nurse. Both professions are "helping" professions. Why is she considering the change? What advice would you give her?

ABOUT THE AUTHOR

Pamela Tracy lives in Arizona with a newly acquired husband *(Yes, Pamela is somewhat a newlywed. You can be a newlywed for seven years. We're only on year four)* and a confused cat *(Hey, I had her all to myself for fifteen years. Where'd this guy come from? But maybe it's okay. He's pretty good about feeding me and petting me)* and a toddler *(Newlymom is almost as fun as newlywed!)*. Pamela was raised in Omaha, Nebraska, and started writing at age twelve *(A very bad teen romance featuring David Cassidy from* The Partridge Family*)*. Later, she honed her writing skills while earning a B.A. in journalism at Texas Tech University in Lubbock, Texas *(And wrote a very bad science fiction novel that didn't feature David Cassidy)*.

Readers can write to her at www.pamela kayetracy.com, or c/o Steeple Hill Books,

233 Broadway, Suite 1001, New York, NY 10279.